"DO YOU KNOW WHAT'S HAPPENING TO US, EVE?" ADAM WHISPERED.

His hands were caressing her with hungry abandon, and she could feel her stubborn resistance flowing away. "Eve, oh, Eve." He pulled her to him, overcoming her with his eager mouth. "Let me come to you tonight."

Yes, yes, she nearly cried out. She felt herself melting in his arms . . . and then suddenly her head cleared. This was all happening too fast. She was falling in love with a man she hardly knew, a dangerous man who could break her heart and leave her bereft.

Abruptly she pulled away from him. "Please, Adam, we have to stop." She stalked from the room without another word.

CANDLELIGHT SUPREMES

UNDER THE SIGN OF SCORPIO

Pat West

A CANDLELIGHT SUPREME

Published by
Dell Publishing Co., Inc.
1 Dag Hammarskjold Plaza
New York, New York 10017

Dell ® TM 681510, Dell Publishing Co., Inc.

Candlelight Supreme is a trademark
of Dell Publishing Co., Inc.

Candlelight Ecstasy Romance®, 1,203,540, is a registered
trademark of Dell Publishing Co., Inc.

ISBN: 0-440-18463-0

Printed in the United States of America

August 1986

10 9 8 7 6 5 4 3 2 1

WFH

For Jeanne Szigeti,
who never forgot House
of Scorpio

To Our Readers:

We are pleased and excited by your overwhelmingly positive response to our Candlelight Supremes. Unlike all the other series, the Supremes are filled with more passion, adventure, and intrigue, and are obviously the stories you like best.

In months to come we will continue to publish books by many of your favorite authors as well as the very finest work from new authors of romantic fiction. As always, we are striving to present unique, absorbing love stories —the very best love has to offer.

Breathtaking and unforgettable, Supremes follow in the great romantic tradition you've come to expect *only* from Candlelight Romances.

Your suggestions and comments are always welcome. Please let us hear from you.

Sincerely,

The Editors
Candlelight Romances
1 Dag Hammarskjold Plaza
New York, New York 10017

UNDER THE SIGN OF SCORPIO

CHAPTER ONE

The secretary hung up her phone. "He'll be right with you, Ms. Darcy."

Eve thanked her with a smile. The woman did not smile back. Pin-neat but harried she returned to her typing. People were friendlier in Chicago, Eve thought. Still, five months in New York City had trained her to its style. Maybe the deputy commissioner was a tough boss. That wouldn't bother her; she'd handled that.

The Windy City's top astrologer, Eve had served as consultant to the police in the famed "Star Slayings," helped them find the killer whose trademark was an astrological symbol scrawled at the scenes of his crimes, the mark of Aries, the Ram. For a grueling two months Eve had tolerated the skepticism of police assigned to work with her; some resented the fact that she was a twenty-eight-year-old woman engaged in "witchcraft," others the fact that she was un-available. But she hadn't thrown in the towel. She wasn't the towel-throwing type.

One reason was her strong, stubborn birth-sign, Taurus; the other was a deep sense of responsibility she'd inherited from her father, who had held on to the farm throughout every hardship and disaster.

Eve reviewed the situation in Chicago. Her personal life had colored everything there. The love affair with Paul had undermined her badly, scattered her concentration, made her work even harder. But even with that handicap she'd won out. So New York should be a comparative piece of cake. She had nothing else to think about now except the "Astro Killer."

She glanced at the neat arrangement of newspapers on the table in front of her; all the headlines were a grim reminder.

In one respect this case was different. Eve had a personal interest.

The victims had been women astrologers.

She looked up, catching the secretary's anxious eye. The woman was looking at the headlines too.

The murmur of male voices from the inner sanctum rose to an indignant growl.

No doubt Eve Darcy was the topic of debate.

"How about a seance, while we're at it?"

Deputy Commissioner Carlin's grin irked Inspector Kane. They both knew his protests weren't worth a dime; the order had already been sent down from up above. But John Carlin and Adam Kane were friends, so Carlin had granted Kane the courtesy of airing his objections. They had enormous respect for each other, but that did

12

not prevent frequent collisions. "What are you so hot about, Adam?"

"We don't need this soothsayer, John. I'll have this thing sewed up if you leave me alone."

"It's out of my hands," Carlin said. "There've been three killings and we're running out of time."

"There won't be a fourth," Kane asserted. "We've got some time. Asbury was September twenty-fourth; Baker, October twenty-fourth; Cartwright, November twenty-third. We've got twenty-six days until December twenty-third, and I'm going to break it open this week. With this loony's alphabet in mind, I've got the *D's* covered like a snow blanket—this Darcy woman and the other one. You saw my battle plan."

Carlin nodded.

"And we're not fooling around with the dates. I'm beefing up the patrols a week before, just in case," Kane went on. "What do we need this gypsy for?"

"The mayor and the commissioner say we do. Why go over it again? The Darcy woman helped crack the Chicago case."

"The *papers* say she did," Kane retorted. "Her kind of junk sells copies. You know that. All I need right now to foul us up is some weird biddy communing with the spirits."

"You've got it wrong, Adam. I'm sorry, but you haven't given me a solid reason to go against the brass. You're just going to have to bite the bullet." Carlin consulted his watch. "Our appointment was ten minutes ago."

Scowling, Kane watched Carlin press a button on his desk. His antsy-looking secretary opened the door. If that woman smiled, her face would crack, Kane thought. He got to his feet.

He nearly went down like a bowling pin. The woman at the door couldn't be the stargazer.

She was stunning.

Kane felt like the city's prize fool. Carlin must have known all along because his smile was mocking when he said, "Ms. Darcy, thank you for coming."

She looked so damned down to earth. Carlin turned to Kane with a twinkle. "Eve Darcy . . . Inspector Adam Kane, who's in charge of the case."

Kane couldn't believe it; it was too corny to be true. Adam and Eve. The glint of sardonic humor in her sleepy-lidded gray eyes told him she'd gotten it too.

"How do you do, Inspector." Her voice was husky and calm, matching her full-blooded attractiveness. She was not the designer-jean type, Kane was glad to see. She was soft and curvy, and her dress revealed her body without flaunting it. Her shoulder-length hair was soft and fine, too, so shiny it glittered in the dull fluorescent light tinged with November grayness from the windows. On such a serious face the sleepy eyes and full mouth were titillating in contrast. Her faint tan made the gray eyes startling.

Kane glanced at her left hand: no ring. He was surprised at himself for checking—he hadn't done that in years. He was so surprised that he

14

could only mumble in reply. Eve Darcy offered him her hand and he shook it. Her handshake was all business, but her hand was as soft as her body looked. She probably trades on her sexiness to sell that astrological boloney, he thought. Knocks guys over.

She wasn't going to knock him over, though. He conveniently forgot that he'd felt like a bowling pin after a strike.

Eve glanced into the inspector's dark, intense eyes. He looked about as friendly as an eagle whose nest had been invaded. He seemed to dislike her already. She'd bet her license he was a Scorpio. That sign, according to her own deep conviction, was dynamite for Taurus. In this case it was quite amusing—a Taurus like her and a Scorpio like Kane could destroy each other through sheer stubbornness.

Nevertheless she had to admit he was appealing. She liked big men, and he was as hefty looking as a light heavyweight. His pale-brown hair was short, something else she liked, and the craggy features and grim mouth were very masculine.

His air of intelligence was almost daunting. Or could have been to someone else; Eve wasn't exactly stupid herself, and she hadn't come here to be intimidated.

Her earthy intuition picked up the crackle of resistance in the air between them. Apprehension crawled along her skin.

Deputy Commissioner Carlin was the last person she'd expected—Libran, smooth, with well-cut white hair, a twinkly manner. Under the smoothness, though, she detected honesty and strength. She liked him. "Some coffee?" he asked. "It's freezing today."

It occurred to Eve that his secretary hadn't made such an offer. She shook her head, smiling.

"Let's get to it, then. To save time, why don't you run us down on what you know so far." Carlin leaned back in his chair.

"On September twenty-fourth Linda Asbury, twenty-six, was waiting for a subway to Queens when she fell to her death in front of an oncoming train," Eve recited. "On October twenty-fourth Karen Baker, twenty-seven, was struck by a bus on Staten Island. Sara Cartwright, twenty-four, was hit by a bus in The Bronx on November twenty-third. All were attractive, all astrologers. The first incident was a tragedy, the second a 'coincidence.' But with the third, witnesses came forward, stating they believed they'd seen someone push all three victims. The assailant could have been a man or woman. Dressed in dark 'unisex' clothes."

"Very succinct," Carlin commented.

"That's what I *know*. I speculate that the usual letter will follow *A, B,* and *C,*" Eve added drily. "With a last name like Darcy, you could say I have a vested interest."

Carlin's dry smile matched her tone. "I like your style, Ms. Darcy. You can see from this," he handed her Kane's report, "that we agree. We figure the next move will come around December twenty-third or so."

"I wouldn't say 'around,' Commissioner. I'd make it the twenty-third on the nose."

Eve's statement was like a string that pulled up Carlin's brows. "How so?"

"September twenty-fourth was the first day of the astrological month Libra, October twenty-fourth began Scorpio, November twenty-third, Sagittarius. December twenty-third will be the first day of Capricorn. It follows the pattern."

Kane made an exasperated sound, but Carlin was interested. "Any other speculations?"

"Well, astrology's a small world even in big cities," she offered. "I haven't gotten wind of any feuds serious enough for murder. I'd bet on a disgruntled client. That's what the Star Slayer was. Unfortunately this killer's not obliging enough to leave his symbol. I've evaluated my clients and I don't even have a probable. But I suppose that's been checked out," she concluded politely. Carlin looked at Kane.

"Every whichaway." Kane had such a deep voice it was almost basso. Eve couldn't help reacting to it. "We interviewed hundreds of nu—clients"—his slip rocked her even temper—"even the ones who went to card readers and psychics. We checked out those who were even slightly dissatisfied with their . . . what are they called?"

"Charts, readings," she supplied curtly.

"Thanks. Even some who thought of bringing legal action because their horses didn't come in or their stocks fell." Kane's chuckle heated up Eve's slow burn. "To a man, or woman, each was the type who wouldn't hurt a fly."

17

Carlin frowned. "What about evaluating client charts? I understand that helped you in Chicago. We can give you all the computer help you need."

"That's just what I was hoping," Eve said. "It's conceivable for a client to blame the astrologer for 'bad news' . . . which is actually just a difficult trend the astrologer *reveals,* doesn't *invent.*" She smiled. "It's happened to me a few times in Chicago. But then there's a confidentiality question, about releasing a client's personal data. . . ."

"We already have releases prepared for clients to sign," Carlin assured her. "Believe me, after the mysterious deaths of three astrologers, they're eager for clients to cooperate."

"I *do* believe you." Eve glanced at Kane, sensing his annoyance. Maybe he was mad because she and Carlin were getting along like a house afire. Kane obviously had been opposed to her hiring. It wasn't going to be the piece of cake she'd assumed, working with someone who was so obnoxious. And so attractive. The last admission went against her grain. But she'd handle both problems. She'd handled other tough cops; she'd been immunized by Paul.

"All right, then, let me cover the other basics." Carlin covered them fast and with great clarity. Eve's notebook and pen were at the ready, and she took down the new material in rapid shorthand.

When he was through she looked up.

"Well, then," he said, "I take it you'll work with us, Ms. Darcy." She nodded. "Good. Your

18

fee won't be astronomical, if you'll forgive the expression. . . ."

"That's not my main motivation," she said, returning his grin. "I want to stop this person. And I'm not too crazy about joining the honor roll under the *D's.*"

Carlin laughed.

Kane didn't. "There aren't going to be any D's." That deep, heavy voice was still doing things to Eve's nerves, and she avoided the Inspector's eye.

The Commissioner got up and held out his hand. "We're in business, then. I assume you've got some people lined up to help you with the charts."

"Yes. Three, who've tentatively agreed to help, subject to your approval." Eve had met them at an astrology conference just recently and had been impressed by them at once. "I'll call them right now, if I may."

"Adam will show you where to hang your hat, where everything is, who everyone is."

When they walked into the outer office, Carlin's secretary was intent on proofreading something she'd typed. "Angela."

Carlin's voice startled her. Her head jerked up. Eve was more than ever impressed by her tension, immaculate appearance and spit-and-polish desk. Eve decided she was a Virgo with a nervous stomach.

"Ms. Darcy, you'll be seeing a lot of my secretary, Angela Myers. This is Ms. Eve Darcy, a very fine astrologer. She'll be giving us a hand in the Astro case. And I'm sure you'll do everything you can to help, won't you, Angie?"

Angela Myers bobbed her smooth graying head and gave Eve a tight little smile. "Of course. How do you do, Ms. Darcy?"

"Please." Eve smiled. "Just Eve."

"Very well." Myers did not thaw, or return the invitation. Eve felt sorry for her; she was as stiff as starch, and Eve wondered what was troubling her. Myers and Kane were some friendly pair.

But there was no time to linger on that, because Carlin was saying to Kane, "I guess that wraps it up here for the moment, Adam. I'll turn Ms. Darcy over to you."

Eve thought she heard a warning note in the commissioner's casual remark; he seemed to be saying, *Ease up.* She repressed a chuckle.

"Sure," Kane said casually. "Let's go. This way. Bye-bye, Angel."

Out of the corner of her eye Eve saw Angela Myers grow stiffer. It was certainly an inappropriate nickname for someone with those baleful eyes, that thinness that was almost painful. And Eve's pity deepened. It seemed cruel of Kane to call her that when she obviously disliked it.

Damn it, she thought, *I've got to stop reacting to this man so emotionally. There's no place for it here. Not when I'm just getting healed . . . not when my life, and other women's lives, are on the line.*

". . . computers?"

Eve tuned in. Kane was asking her something. Fortunately the racket in the hall was a good excuse for not having heard him. "I beg your pardon?"

"I was asking how much experience you've had with computers," he said more loudly.

"Quite a bit. I use one in my work, of course." She was sharply aware of his massive arm; it brushed hers now and then as they walked down the busy corridor.

"Good." He stopped at the end of the hall in front of an unoccupied office. "Would you like to check this out first, and call your coven . . . or take the tour now?"

She was furious over the equation of her team with a gathering of witches. But she wasn't going to bite the bait. "Let's take the tour, Inspector. I wouldn't want to waste your time."

The tour was thorough and took most of the afternoon. Eve gritted her teeth, ignoring the antipathy under Kane's politeness. Now and then she caught a bright gleam in his hard black eyes. She couldn't tell whether he was amused or angry, but she really couldn't care less. She was going to avoid him as much as possible.

To her relief he was called away during the tour and a handsome Lieutenant Hansen took his place. Eve's relief was short lived: it wasn't ten minutes before Hansen asked her to have dinner with him. She calmly declined.

Eve noticed that a sharp-eyed young woman sergeant had overheard the exchange, and grinned at Eve. A few minutes later, when Hansen was running down some other staff for Eve to meet, the sergeant approached her.

"Hi. I'm Marnie Osborne. You're the astrologer?"

Eve nodded, introducing herself.

"How about some coffee?" Osborne offered.

"I'd *love* it."

She followed the sergeant into a corner of the computer room, where a coffeemaker and cups were set out. "Black, please. If I *smell* cream and sugar, I gain weight."

"*I* should have your problem." Sergeant Osborne sounded envious. She was as lean as a whippet. "You've got the whole building in an uproar. The guys' eyes are out on sticks." She handed Eve the coffee, with a dry smile.

Eve flushed, laughing. The woman was awfully personal; her blue eyes had an avid look that made Eve a bit uncomfortable, but she had to admit Osborne was funny. And her accent sounded familiar.

"Are you from the Midwest, Sergeant?"

"Bullseye, Ms. Darcy. Ohio." The sergeant grinned. Her sharp eyes were a strange mismatch for the freckle-dusted face, the short blond hair curling around her ears like little puppy-tails. "I think it's great you're on the Astro case. I read everything about your work in Chicago . . . but of course we all did, even Killer Kane." She shut up abruptly, reddening. "Oh, boy, I shouldn't say that about the inspector. He's a good cop."

"That's all right." "Killer" was certainly an unhappy nickname under the circumstances; Eve wondered if he were trigger happy. But that was

22

absurd. She was getting paranoid. "I'm sure he is. But I don't think he has much use for astrology."

"None at all . . . *or* for women in police work. He and Hansen think a woman's place is in the cave."

Eve let out a hearty laugh. Osborne had such a comical expression, even if her humor was bitter. Eve wondered, though, why Hansen had been mentioned out of nowhere. Then Eve recalled how intently Osborne had observed them when Hansen asked her to dinner.

"I've got an awfully big mouth," Osborne admitted.

She did indeed. And Eve hated gossip. Still, a preview of her co-workers' foibles could be helpful. Eve added up Osborne's dancing eyes, slender hands and body, and her humorous malice. "A witty *Gemini* mouth?" she hazarded. "And Hansen's a Sagittarius." Certainly if he were the sign Eve took him for, a Gemini would find him very attractive.

"You're good." Osborne's untidy brows shot up. "That's what we are. Look, I'd better get going. I just wanted to welcome you aboard. You may not get anybody else's, except the DC's, working with people like Killer Kane and Nutsy Myers."

"Why 'Killer' and 'Nutsy?' "

"Well, Killer because of Cain." Osborne spelled it out. "And I shouldn't call Angela that. It's Hansen's idea, not very nice."

"What's Hansen's?" Eve couldn't help asking.

Osborne flushed. " 'Handsome.' He's got ev-

eryone calling me 'Mouth.' " Now there was no
mistaking it, Eve thought. The sergeant's gaiety
was desperate.

"Oh, dear," she murmured.

"The inspector's really not a bad guy," Osborne rushed on, as if eager to change the subject.
"His wife died a couple of years ago in childbirth,
and the baby died too."

"I see." He'd been hurt, then, worse than she
had herself. Some of her resentment lessened.

Osborne's eyes widened. "Uh-oh, here comes
the lieutenant. It's a good thing you turned him
down. He's very married. His wife's so jealous
they can't have a female *parakeet*. A *Scorpio*."
Now Eve suspected why Hansen's name had
popped up in Osborne's conversation. She might
be infatuated with him herself, perhaps "warned
away" a lot of women.

"What's the matter, Mouth?" Hansen demanded. "If you've run out of work I've got
plenty." He must have caught the drift of Osborne's remarks; he seemed inordinately angry,
though.

"Just going, Lieutenant. I was getting Ms.
Darcy some coffee." Osborne walked away.

Hansen seemed embarrassed over his anger
and smiled at Eve.

"So, Lieutenant, are they ready now?" she
asked.

He took her to meet the rest of the staff in the
Astro case.

It was nearly six o'clock by the time she was
ready to leave. She'd lined up her team for the

24

next day, made copious notes, and felt very optimistic. The department's sharpest, most experienced men were on the case; they'd *have* to get him.

Eve looked around her temporary office, proud of how much she'd already done. Fortunately there was plenty of room, so she'd had desks and chairs brought in for the team, a couple of typewriters, and a cabinet for their records and supplies. She inventoried the latter and found them sufficient. They'd get their minicomputer tomorrow.

She decided she'd bring in a small coffeemaker of her own so that they wouldn't have to depend on the other offices. She could already imagine the effect that her team would have on the mostly male staff. Two of them were single and quite beautiful; the married third member was also most attractive.

Eve had been vividly reminded of her own femininity in this world of men and random uniformed women. Adam Kane, she thought, was the malest male of them all. But she didn't want to linger on that.

Her curiosity was still teased by Osborne's hints about Angela Myers.

That reminded Eve she'd left her coat in the closet outside Carlin's office. It was time she picked it up and went home. It had been a day and a half, starting at six A.M. so she could catch up with other work before she came here. Tomorrow would be tighter.

Eve gathered up her belongings, and made her

way to the DC's office. She was relieved that Myers had gone for the day; the woman made her uncomfortable. Her shining desk looked like an illustration in an office-beautiful magazine.

The DC's door was open. Eve heard voices.

One was Kane's. "I've rescheduled the whole damned thing. And my guys are really burned, John. I can't believe you're acting on the word of one fool woman."

Eve felt anger spill over her.

"But you gave me an order," Kane grumbled, "and I've carried it out."

There was a low murmur from Carlin. Eve hoped they wouldn't hear her; she was in no mood to talk to the bearish Kane. But when she opened the closet the knob clicked. Damn.

"Someone there?" Carlin called out.

Eve snatched her coat off the hanger and called back, "Eve Darcy, Commissioner."

"Oh. Come in a moment, would you?"

She surrendered to the inevitable and went in. Both men were on their feet, Carlin smooth and genial, Kane impassive. She smiled at the DC, nodded coolly to the inspector.

"I won't keep you, Ms. Darcy," Carlin said. "I just wanted to compliment you for settling in so fast. They tell me you got quite a lot accomplished already. Everything go all right?"

She translated that as *Did you get the proper cooperation?* and answered, "Just fine, thanks. You got my message, I imagine." She'd left one with Angela Myers advising that she and her team would be there at nine the next morning.

"I did, thank you. I don't know if you heard our little . . . discussion just now." Carlin shot an ironic glance at Kane. "But we've changed our target date to December twenty-third, in line with your theory."

"That's very gratifying," she said warmly, avoiding Kane's eye. "I'll say good-night, then."

"Good night, Ms. Darcy," Carlin responded. There was a mutter from Kane. She nodded to them and walked out, hurrying toward the elevator bank.

There was a large crowd waiting, among them a couple of people she'd met that day, and she greeted them with a smile. All of the elevators seemed slow to come, and suddenly she had an attack of nerves.

The Astro killer was out there somewhere, waiting. In her preoccupation with the trees of busyness and detail she'd forgotten the horror-forest. That was her style, practical to the last gasp. She shivered in her long, heavy coat. *Last gasp* was hardly a happy phrase under the circumstances.

To add to her discomfort she noticed that Adam Kane had joined the waiting group. She acknowledged him with a brief nod, then walked over to the windows to look out. It was already very dark.

When the elevator came, Eve found herself getting in next to Kane. In spite of her resolves his magnetism pulled at her body. His very size and strength made her feel less vulnerable, momentarily secure. It was awful; she couldn't let a feel-

27

ing like that mix in with this case. Finally the elevator reached the lobby floor, releasing them into the chilly air.

She could sense he was just behind her. Then she was outside, assaulted by the strong wind sweeping the great tiled plaza round the Roman magnificence of "Number One." Much as she wanted to get home, she was almost sorry to leave the building: its proud architecture proclaimed, *I am the law; I am authority, protection.*

"Ms. Darcy." She turned.

Kane was there, his coat collar turned up against the cold. The brim of his hat shadowed his dark, glittering eyes. "Where are you parked?"

Naturally he knew all about her, down to her driver's license. And of course his report had specified a guard on her house, just like Chicago.

"Two blocks away."

"I'll walk you," Kane said curtly.

She made no protest. It occurred to her that she'd parked in a rather dark spot. As if he'd read her mind, he added, "From now on use one of our spaces."

She felt like an idiot; it nettled her. But he was right. Involved in the investigation she was an even greater target.

Kane was walking so close to her that he must have felt her shiver.

"Cold night," he remarked. "But I guess after Chicago it's not much to you."

Actually the wind velocity in Chicago was a myth; it was less than New York's. But this was the first time he'd come close to friendliness, so she went along. "Next to the winds from the Lake this is a breeze."

She looked up and caught his smile. That was also a first. All he'd done before was smirk. His smile was a white dazzle in the half-light and it shone from his eyes, making him seem almost human. There were lines of weariness and strain on his face, and she thought, *He's carrying a big load.*

When they reached her small car, he held the door open for her to get in, and glanced in the back.

"Ms. Darcy," he began slowly, "I owe you an apology for that crack today about the 'coven.' That was pretty raw." She was amused at his expression. The apology came out like an extracted tooth.

"It certainly was. But I accept." He looked strangely vulnerable, not snarly and fierce at the moment. "Can I drop you somewhere, Inspector?"

He hesitated. "Well . . . yes, thanks. My car . . . It's not far. You could drop me at the entrance to the bridge."

The oddity of that mystified her. She wondered if it were a stakeout, if it had to do with the case, but she made no comment as they got in and drove off.

"This makes our job a lot easier, Ms. Darcy, the fact that you drive. The Astro seems to be fond of public transportation. But you never know," he added grimly. "You read in my report that we've got men on your house. I take it you're going straight home."

"Yes."

"Good. From now on we'd like to have an idea of where you are. I guess you know the drill, after Chicago."

She did indeed: she'd had to report her movements to the police like a child to its mother. "Yes."

They were approaching his mysterious dropoff point. She slowed to let him out.

"Thanks, Ms. Darcy." He touched his hat brim and she saw the dark glitter of his eyes reflect the light; they looked like hard coal. "See you tomorrow. Be careful. You're important to Carlin."

He shut the door and was gone.

As she drove onto the bridge, Eve was fuming.

She was important to *Carlin*. Kane must be a Scorpio, and he might have a Scorpionic Mercury, too, to make him so brutally sarcastic.

The sign which Mercury occupied influenced thinking and expression.

She caught a sidelong view of the jeweled splendor of downtown Manhattan. Determined to put Kane from her mind she concentrated on New York's unique beauty and excitement.

Baghdad on the Hudson . . . her second chance.

With part of her mind conscientiously on her driving, she let the other part drift westward to remember.

Straight off a farm in the "Lincoln country" of

Illinois, Eve had entered the University of Chicago. The school and the huge city had not gone to her head, as her parents feared. She'd maintained her high standards in the face of all rebellious change and opposition. For a decade she'd remained the old Eve, until she'd met Detective Paul Bracken on the Star Slayer case.

By that time she'd built a solid reputation in her profession, to which she'd come obliquely and much to her parents' surprise. Eve had begun school with an interest in political science, thinking of herself as a pragmatic, practical human being. Her roommate had been just the opposite, a fervent astrology buff. Eve good-naturedly teased her friend about that obsession, thinking it was a lot of balderdash. But then one day she'd idly picked up one of her roommate's books and became interested in spite of herself. She read more and more on the subject, her concentration so intense that she began to neglect other subjects. Eve discovered to her astonishment that the discipline of astrology was more complex than she had ever dreamed. It made her chosen specialty seem very dry. Political science embraced only one aspect of life, astrology all of them. It was far richer, more satisfying, than any other study.

Eve's parents were dismayed when she announced her intention of becoming an astrologer. But her desire grew even stronger after she took her first course in astrology, and met a brilliant teacher who told her she had a genius for it. The teacher had studied for two years in London at a prestigious institute. Determined to follow his path, Eve dropped out of school, went to work, and began to save money to pay for her education. Her parents certainly couldn't afford to finance her.

During that time her father was killed in an accident on the farm. Her embittered mother, who could neither face living on the scene of her husband's death nor continue running the farm itself, sold the property to a large corporation that was offering high prices for land. Eve's mother told her sadly, "You can go to London now, without worrying about the money. I want to feel that *some* happiness will come out of our tragedy."

Eve spent a happy two years in London, qualifying as an astrologer whose credentials were acknowledged by the reputable American associations. She came back to Chicago, where her mother was living, and went into practice. The reputation she gained led to her consultant job with the police in the "Star Slayings." And Paul.

Till then she hadn't given much thought to romance. She had the usual dates, vaguely assumed that someday the perfect man would appear. Eve was far from cold, but none of the men she'd met moved her in that special way, so that she couldn't imagine living *without* him, as her mother said of her father.

Then the wrong one came along instead, in the form of Paul Bracken. He'd moved her, all right; she loved him to distraction, blind to his neurotic selfishness, excusing his distaste for marriage until she couldn't stand it anymore.

The unhappy aftereffects lingered on. When she'd been hired by the Chicago police, the affair began too soon, swiftly ended, and it had taken every ounce of her will to pull herself together, cope with the job at hand.

Then her mother had died. She reeled from the double blow. But she'd survived and planned to keep on surviving.

Eve turned off at her exit and drove toward her apartment on Sidney Terrace. She loved Brooklyn Heights with its tree-shaded streets, walks paved in bluestone lined by rows of old brick and brownstone houses. Some of the houses dated back to the days when the area was New York's most desirable suburb. Sidney Terrace gave Eve a commanding view of the harbor, the splendid downtown skyline of Manhattan.

Eve's building on Sidney Terrace was a tiny two-story house that looked like something out of a fairy tale, with its pointed roof and white façade, arched windows shaped like a church's. Like a "sign from fate," Eve had found the apartment through a friend. The lucky break had been all Eve needed to pull her away from Chicago with its bitter memories.

Parking, Eve blessed the neighborhood association again for the new streetlights. And added thanks to Kane: an unmarked car with two men in it was parked nearby. Her shadows. She walked easier with them behind her.

Eve hurried up the carpeted stairs to her top-floor apartment, starving and eager to unwind. As soon as she opened her door, the Astro killer seemed as remote as a creature of fantasy, only this peace and beauty real.

Her living room was furnished with family pieces as well as new furniture. It was a beautiful room of polished brass and serene earth colors of russet, greens, and sand.

And yet when she began unloading her briefcase and glimpsed the headline of the afternoon paper, she knew she'd been kidding herself. The Astro killer was alive and well in New York.

Nevertheless Eve Darcy was tired, grubby, and ready to eat. After a shower she padded barefoot into her kitchen. She warmed the morning's coffee, drank it while she cooked dinner. Eve was a devout gourmet-for-herself and never skimped like other single women. She liked the full treatment of china and settings, even solitary candlelight.

Though it was more fun with others, she admitted. She looked forward to having the "team" over for dinner.

Serving herself steak and salad Eve wondered what it would be like to cook for Adam Kane.

That was a foolish thought. She pushed it aside, turning on some soft music and choosing a pleasant love story to read while she ate.

She was surprised to find that the book distracted her from her meal, and she soon set it aside.

She decided it might have something to do with Adam Kane. Obnoxious as he was, he was

34

the first man to have attracted her in a long, long time.

But that would never do. The man positively disliked her. And he, in turn, had infuriating ways. All she needed was a personal complication in the midst of this deadly-serious assignment.

Which reminded her of the plans to go over, the notes to be read. She finished eating, took care of the dishes, and made another pot of coffee to perk her up. Alert again, she delved into the fascinating aspects of the Astro murders. When she surfaced it was eleven o'clock.

Stretching she got up and wandered to the window to enjoy the glittering view of the skyline. Then she opened the window and leaned out. The dark car was still there. "Thanks, fellas," she murmured, and lowered the window against the icy air.

Safe as she felt with the watchers there, it took her a long time to go to sleep. She kept going over the day, thinking of the people she'd be working with—Osborne, with her bitter humor and desperate eyes; Hansen, with his unpleasant secret life; Angela Myers, so tense and hostile.

And Adam Kane, to whom she'd be reporting. She had to smile at the absurd coincidence of their first names, in the light of their adversary positions. But his nickname wasn't funny.

Not when that other person was still out there, that faceless creature who was a killer for real. The killer of A, B, C . . . and D?

It wasn't so peaceful now to be alone. It would be heavenly to have someone's consoling arms around her . . . the right man's arms. Adam Kane's arms looked very strong.

But she'd better not start thinking that way. It was enough that her life was under siege, without becoming hostage to her runaway emotions.

CHAPTER TWO

Morning scattered the ghosts from Eve's dreams. She woke early, galvanized by her Scorpionic Mars. Even the continuing gray of the sky, glimpsed from her bedroom windows, couldn't oppress her. She was raring to go.

She smoothed the creamy quilt with its bright star-burst design over her postered bed and set the green pillows in place. Then she took an apple-red wool dress from the closet. It would brighten the day in the steel-colored environs of Number One.

Not long after, with a good breakfast inside, Eve was walking out her front door. She was eager to get a head start before the team arrived at headquarters.

Her shadows were still parked a short distance away, and she thought she saw another car following when she drove off. Even in broad daylight it was good to know they were there.

This morning Eve parked right outside Number One in the area Kane had recommended. He was right: there was no point in playing Russian roulette with her neck. She'd be coming out after dark.

She got to the office with forty-five minutes to spare and spent most of them checking out the computer, looking over equipment and supplies.

"Good morning!"

Eve was setting up the coffee corner when she heard the soft voice at the door. She turned to greet the newcomer. "Iris. I knew you'd be the first."

It was only eight forty-five, but Iris March, in her own words, was always "pathologically early." A willing and conscientious Pisces, Iris said Pisceans were so unsure of practical matters, the only way they could be on time was to be early.

"You look wonderful," Eve said.

Iris smiled. It was more a grimace than a smile, as if she were trying not to cry, another trait of those ruled by Neptune. "Thank you kindly." Iris wore an easy-fitting dress of bright-green wool that enhanced her green eyes and extreme slenderness. Her small head, with its short, dark-brown hair, looked impish over her cowl collar.

She had a faraway manner that didn't fool Eve. Iris's intuitive brain never quit; she picked up subtleties beyond the obvious. She was the team member Eve liked best, her idea woman.

Absently Iris hung her gray cape, surveying Eve with her other-world eyes. "You look marvelous, Eve. That's your color. Like Eve's apple. Except you should be named Lilith instead."

According to the Talmud, Lilith was "the

38

mother of demons," preceding Eve in Adam's life.

Here we go again with this Adam and Eve number, Eve thought.

"Coffee?" she invited.

"I'll get it." Iris poured her coffee absentmindedly, tipping Eve that she was already at work, more intent on her thoughts than external matters. "You know, I've been thinking about Lilith, as a matter of fact. The 'dark moon.' Wasn't it prominent in the Star Slayer's chart?"

"You're sensational. Way ahead of me. That's on my checklist in the preliminary plan."

"Where's my spot?" Iris asked good-naturedly. A Pisces didn't care where she worked as long as it was out of the traffic. Eve had picked a sequestered corner for her. "I can't wait to get into this work," Iris said. "Can I see the plan?"

Eve handed it to her. "Where's Clare? I thought you two were going to drive in together."

"She had to pick up something. She'll be here on the stroke of nine." Iris went back to her reading.

Eve laughed. Clare Bentley was a meticulous Virgo, expert with charts, files, graphs, and computers. A stickler.

The ninth stroke of St. Andrew's neighboring chime echoed away as Clare walked in. Eve and Iris looked at each other, smiling.

"We don't need St. Andrew's," Iris kidded. "We've got Clare." The Virgo team member was immaculate. Her matching lavender sweater and skirt glorified her blue-gray eyes and straight,

39

short blond hair. "If I'm late you'll know I'm dead."

They looked at each other. That wasn't so funny right now, not to women astrologers. "Sorry about that," Clare murmured. "It's no joke to a D." She glanced at Eve.

"Forget it." Eve's reply was steady. "They're guarding me like royalty." She smiled at the chagrined Clare. "When Betty gets here, we can start our war council."

Clare hung her navy-blue coat very straight on a hanger. "She'll be fantastic, Eve. She's got as much in her head as a computer."

"Exactly why I asked her. She'll be our historian." Eve handed Clare the preliminary plan.

"She'll be the housekeeper too. This place'll look like a home by tomorrow," Clare said, and started reading.

A few minutes later a full-bodied woman with long red hair and deepset, sexy brown eyes rushed in. An enormous tote bag was slung over her shoulder; her gloved hands cradled a flower-pot sprouting a sick-looking philodendron. "Sorry I'm late," Betty Rivers gasped.

"Any curtains in there?" Clare demanded.

"Get off my back, nitpicker!" Betty teased her friend. "Hi, everybody. I'm hoping a change of scene will cure this invalid." She set the plant tenderly on top of a file cabinet under a light before she took off her brown greatcoat and hung it slapdash. Under the coat she wore a matching suit with a bright gold blouse.

Eve waited for her to get settled, thinking that

Betty was a textbook maternal Cancer. She watched Betty taking coffee mugs out of the giant tote. "I couldn't resist these," she said. "I thought they'd make us a little more *hamish*." Betty passed the mugs out. Each one had a taupe astrological glyph, or symbol, on an ivory ground —the *H*-like glyph of Pisces, for Iris; the Taurean circle surmounted by an arc, for Eve; and the big Virgo *M,* with its backward final stroke, for Clare.

"Thanks! These are lovely." Eve filled hers with fresh coffee. "Okay. Shall we get started?"

By ten they were well under way. With the assignment of tasks accomplished, Eve suggested a tour. "The main thing's the computer division, of course. Your baby," she said to Clare and Betty.

All of them used computers in their home offices which were patched in to the astrological association's master computer, but the mathematically minded Virgo Clare and the Cancer record-keeper Betty were more attuned to them than Eve and Iris, who depended heavily on intuition.

The tour went just as Eve had expected. When they walked into the computer section her good-looking assistants caused quite a flurry. Eve was delighted with the way her team handled themselves: Clare was so regal she could be positively intimidating, and the solidly married Betty and the fragile, lovely Iris just floated along without noticing. Iris hardly seemed to be physically pres-

41

ent, but Eve knew that her intuitive mind was absorbing data like a sponge.

Eve wondered where Kane was, and Hansen, for that matter. Then she wished she hadn't considered Hansen; as if her thought had summoned him, he blustered into the computer section, all PR and wide smile. And Eve wondered how much of a coincidence it was that Sergeant Osborne showed right up on Hansen's heels.

Her amusement deepened when she noticed her team's reaction to the Don Juan, Lieutenant Hansen: Sagittarius was not very compatible with Cancers and Virgos, to begin with. It could be positively abrasive to a Piscean. After checking out Betty's wedding ring and receiving a frozen glance from Clare, Hansen zeroed in on Iris. She was usually about as solid as a puff of smoke, and was just as evasive now. Iris's withdrawal went right over Hansen's head; he was too insensitive to catch it.

Eve thought, *He must be a very poorly aspected Sagittarius;* generally they were as sharp as the arrow in the Centaur's bow. But as Iris kept evading, Hansen went on bumbling after her. It was all Eve could do not to laugh out loud.

Poor Marnie Osborne wasn't smiling, though. The smitten Gemini looked pained. She tried to cover herself with jokes. Just before the end of the computer tour Eve saw Osborne take Iris aside and say something to her in a low voice. Iris just smiled vaguely as if she really didn't know what Osborne was talking about.

"Were you being warned?" Eve asked Iris amiably as they were heading back to their office, with Clare and Betty walking ahead.

"Yes. How in the world did you *know?*" Iris demanded, grinning. "Oh, I forgot. Your Moon is in Pisces. Of course, you pick up things. Yes, that idiot's married, the sergeant told me. I told her even if he weren't, I wouldn't get near a fire sign, and he's got to be one."

"Right on. Sagittarius."

"I should have known he was fire," Iris declared. "I felt like an emery board was being rubbed on my skin."

Eve laughed.

Back in the office the team took a coffee break but still talked work. Eve got out the reports she'd prepared the night before, together with Adam Kane's. "You might want to get into these now," she said. "The Star Slayer and the Astro cases. They should give you a lot of ideas."

The women started glancing over them.

"I keep coming back to jealousy," Iris commented. "One of the strongest motivations there is. All the victims were pretty, and young. I see the police have been investigating rocky marriages, other personal aspects. Maybe we should go more deeply into synastry, chart comparison. That's quite a task, of course."

"It certainly is," Clare said gloomily.

"I think you've got something, though, Iris," Eve interjected. "The department has the resources and the experience in this area. But we can interpret subtleties they can't. Clare, maybe you and Betty can follow one avenue, and Iris and I another. Let yourself dream, Iris," she added, only half joking. "I know you're inspired by being around water. But don't go walking around the lake in Central Park, or on the beach at Coney Island. Not right now."

Iris met Eve's eyes. "I read you."

Betty commented with abrupt Cancerian moodiness, "Did you know my maiden name began with a *D?* It was Dobson."

Eve felt a slight chill. "How long have you been married? I mean, how long has your married name been listed in the directories?"

"Not that long. And some of them haven't caught up."

"I think I'd better notify Kane," Eve said. She dialed the DC's office. Neither Carlin nor Kane was in. Eve left the message with Myers, who efficiently repeated it back.

"All of a sudden this is a different case altogether," Betty said dolefully.

"Maybe not," Eve consoled her. "You're known almost everywhere as Rivers. I'm probably making too much of it myself. I just want to keep on top of everything." She realized that might not be very reassuring. To distract Betty she asked them generally, "How are the client charts coming? Any possibles?" No one had any. "How about Lilith?"

They'd also come up blank on that.

"That reminds me," Clare said, "I want to check out something else in Computers." She hurried out.

Eve and the other two got back to work, but

Eve noticed that Betty was having a hard time concentrating. So was Eve, as she worked on the chart of one of her own clients, evaluating it in relation to the Astro case. It couldn't have had less to do with the murders.

The subject was a highly evolved, very healthy Sagittarius. Eve was distracted by the thought of the obnoxious Hansen. He was a totally different type of Sagittarius—unevolved, fickle rather than independent, rough tongued instead of simply frank, hardly intellectual. And married to a Scorpio, of all the incompatible signs.

The phone-ring scattered her thoughts.

"Sergeant Benson, Ms. Darcy. Inspector Kane asked me to call." Eve had an immediate reaction, to her dismay. "He wanted me to tell you he'll be dropping in on you about four-thirty."

Eve thanked the sergeant and hung up, dreading four-thirty. Adam Kane was so damned hostile to their discipline. And at the same time she was rather vulnerable to his attractiveness. A bad combination. And she hadn't had the greatest track record for staying detached in Chicago.

But she was going to this time, no matter what. She plunged into work again. It was tedious and exacting, double work now that they had chart comparisons as well, but she was glad. Pretty soon she'd forgotten Adam Kane and everything else in the intensity of her pursuit. She scarcely noticed when Clare returned.

"Everything all right, ladies?"

Eve looked up at the sound of a male voice. They shouldn't have left the door ajar. Anything could get in, she thought irritably, in this case Hansen. He stood with his hand on the door frame, giving them all his big phony smile.

"Fine, Lieutenant," Eve said. The others barely acknowledged him.

Hansen wandered in, although Eve's voice had had no invitation in it. "Have everything you need?"

Everything but peace and quiet, she longed to say.

"The inspector wanted me to keep tabs, see that you don't run into problems." Hansen's bright-blue gaze flicked over the charts on Eve's desk.

She doubted that Kane had told Hansen to look after them. Kane hadn't even wanted them hired, for Pete's sake! Still, she was disturbed by her own unreasoning hostility. Hansen *was* on the case. All the same it looked like a ploy, an excuse for Hansen to get to know Iris and Clare.

Eve made herself smile. "That's very kind of the inspector. But we're doing fine, thanks."

The words were hardly out of her mouth when Osborne appeared in the hall. She had the good grace not to come in, but she motioned toward Hansen.

"I think you're being paged, Lieutenant," Eve noted.

Hansen turned and saw Marnie Osborne. His good-natured twinkle faded like water-doused sparklers. A mean look came into his eyes. Eve had never seen such a quick, unpleasant transformation.

Hansen strode to the door and snapped, "What is it, Mouth?"

Osborne murmured something.

"Ten-four," Hansen growled. "Is that *all,* Sergeant?"

The question was a curt dismissal. To Eve he seemed needlessly cruel, in the light of Osborne's pathetic infatuation. He had to be aware of it; no one could be that insensitive.

Osborne nodded and, after an avid survey of the team's office, went off.

Hansen went back to his gallantry. "Well, if any of you ladies need help, you know where to call me."

Eve waited until he'd walked down the hall. After what seemed a polite interval she shut the door.

"That'll be the day," Betty remarked, "when I need that man's help."

Eve and Iris laughed. Clare, looking preoccupied, got up and paced a little, staring out the window.

"Problem?" Eve asked her.

"Lilith." She turned around and added, "Nothing to bother you with, at this stage. I'm just trying to work out a faster, better method of correlating the star data with the other info."

"Don't tell me. Hansen came in just as you were about to find it," Eve remarked dryly.

"You've got it."

"Could you work it out better at home? Look here, everybody, we really didn't work that out before, and now's the time to get it settled. Whenever you feel you can do your problem solving better elsewhere, please be sure to tell me. We're not exactly nine-to-fivers," Eve remarked.

"I'm fine here," Clare said, and the others murmured agreement.

They went back to their respective tasks. Eve noticed gloomily that the "Unlikely" file tray was getting bigger and the "Likely" contained very few folders. A discouraging ratio. But then, they'd just gotten started; there was a mountain of checking ahead. And somewhere in all that data they just might find the Astro Killer. Eve clung to that conviction, starting her next study.

She was so lost in thought that the tap on the door startled her. When she called out, "Come in," she was amazed to see Adam Kane. She glanced at her watch. It couldn't be four-thirty.

"Hello, Ms. Darcy. Ladies." Kane had a social smile.

"Inspector." He certainly looked friendlier than yesterday, but Eve couldn't trust him, not after what Osborne had told her about his opposition to the team. "I'd like you to meet my associates." She introduced them, waiting for the usual male reaction to their good looks.

There wasn't any. Kane was merely courteous and pleasant. "I'd like to talk with you a moment, Mrs. Rivers. Thanks for the memo," he said aside to Eve. Then he spoke to Betty again. "There may not be any cause for alarm about your maiden name, but I always like to take too many precautions rather than too few. Just rou-

48

tine." His tone and smile were dismissive, but they didn't fool Eve. "Could we talk?"

Betty nodded. "Of course." He held the door open for her.

Clare and Iris stared after them, very quiet, and no one seemed able to get back to work. Eve shifted restlessly. She couldn't concentrate on her daily report for the DC.

In a very short time they were back. Eve glanced at Betty; she looked upset and rather uncertain. *Damn Kane,* Eve thought. *I'm being threatened, too, but we're both safer here than at home, for that matter.* Eve hoped Kane hadn't discouraged Betty completely. She was a dynamite astrologer.

"I was glad to hear Mrs. Rivers's husband is going to meet her here every night," Kane remarked to Eve.

She felt new annoyance. Did he think she was a perfect fool? "I made it a point to warn everyone about security," she answered sharply. "Ms. March and Ms. Bentley will be driving in together from now on, and parking right next to me, in the spot you recommended."

"Very good, Ms. Darcy." He sounded like a teacher commending a bright student, and that lit Eve's fuse again. This man could certainly do a job on her equilibrium, and she was famous for her calm.

"Speaking of husbands," Betty said with a kind of false brightness, "I'd better get downstairs. He'll be waiting."

"Why don't we all just wrap it up for today?"

Eve suggested. Kane had done a job on all of them, she thought sourly, and now she might lose Betty. She couldn't wait for him to leave so she could get back to work.

But he lingered after the others were gone.

"Was there something else, Inspector?"

"I just wondered how things are going." He sat down on the edge of her desk and she was dismayed to find that the nearness of his big body rattled her.

"I was just about to start my daily report to the DC," she hinted. She was not going to let him get to her, not while she had breath in her body. It occurred to her that the reason she found him attractive was very simple: her Mars was in Scorpio, his sun sign. That's all there was to it. And she'd just guard against it.

"I won't keep you. But you seem to have gotten off to a good start." He glanced around the well-organized office.

"Yes, we have. But so far all we have are more zilches than likelies."

He grinned. "I'm not surprised. It took us months to catch the Son of Sam, and then a detective in Brooklyn did that, anyway. It was four months before we nabbed the Subway Slasher. We hardly expected you to solve the case this morning."

I'll bet, she retorted silently. *You don't expect astrologers to come up with* anything.

"May I ask what you told Betty Rivers?"

"Sure. I just cautioned her, told her she'd be under observation," he answered casually.

"She looked frightened after your conference, Inspector."

"Aren't you, Ms. Darcy?"

"Yes. But I think we'll be able to get a line on the killer."

The corner of his mouth lifted. "I see."

His tone was so amused and indulgent that Eve found herself getting angry all over again.

"You don't like this detail, do you, Inspector?" she demanded. If she'd hoped this sudden offensive would surprise him she was disappointed.

"No." His eyes leveled with hers. "I think astrology is superstitious nonsense. And I don't like women working with the police. In the first place it's dangerous—especially for you and Mrs. Rivers. In the second place you-your team"—the elision was so quick Eve wasn't sure it *was* one—"is very distracting to the operation."

"We're not responsible for Hansen, if that's what you mean," she said coldly. She regretted the indiscretion as soon as it was out of her mouth. She rarely slipped up like that.

Kane raised his sandy brows. "Hansen? He's got nothing to do with your end of the case."

She knew it. Hansen *hadn't* had any business hanging around the team.

She couldn't seem to control her tongue. Almost before she knew it, she countered, "Oh? Maybe you'd better tell him, Inspector. I don't think he knows that."

Kane looked miffed. "Hansen's not at issue. I'm talking about the way you people clutter up an investigation." His voice was cold and hard as metal.

Eve reddened. It was bad enough to have misread his objection as personal, but "clutter up" was the last straw.

"I'm following orders, Ms. Darcy. You must have known I was against this"—he waved at the desks—"from day one. I don't believe in this stuff."

In spite of herself Eve took the bait. "It's not a matter of 'belief,' Inspector. Astrology's not a religion. It's a discipline like any other. A system of classification, a school of psychology, if you will. It's based on the physical movements of physical bodies and their effect on other physical bodies."

Kane just looked at her. It was an admiring look now, but still tinged with the amusement that riled her. "I've found that many Scorpios share your opinion," Eve continued. "I take it that you were born in November, the early part."

Now he looked neither amused nor admiring. Simply astonished.

"How in . . . how did you know that?"

"An educated guess. You wouldn't be interested in the technical evidence." She relented. There was no point to this war; it couldn't be anything but counterproductive. "Look here, Inspector. We're stuck with each other, at least for the duration. Don't you think it'll be easier on everybody if we keep these discussions to a minimum?"

He was nettled. She'd finally gotten to *him*, it seemed.

"You've got it, Ms. Darcy. See you tomorrow." He got up and walked out, closing the door softly.

Eve rubbed her tired eyes. She wondered just what she'd accomplished, angering Kane like that. Probably all she'd done was to turn him into a dangerous adversary. That could make the job even harder.

What bothered her was her strong desire to needle Kane. With a man like Hansen she just wanted to keep a distance. But with Kane—he'd gotten under her skin. Deeply.

But there was more at stake here than her personal feelings. She had to remember that her life, and other women's, were on the line. And if anyone could ferret out the Astro killer, it was a team of astrologers. Her own very special team. No personal pique must stand in the way of that. All their reputations depended on it too.

She'd just have to take every day as it came.

And hope that Betty wasn't going to be frightened off.

Enough of that. She turned with renewed energy to the report for Carlin.

The next morning Eve was gratified when she received a scribbled note from Carlin: *Fine report. If not too burdensome, keep 'em coming.*

Even the weather was in accord with her brighter mood: the grayness had fled from the sky and the office was filled with the pale glow of the winter sun.

Today Eve and Iris were engaged in a different

53

investigation, the astrology of the victims. Clare and Betty were deep in computer checkouts of clients, all of whom had gladly signed releases.

Eve's Piscean Moon had presented her an inspiration in the middle of the night: the clients' might not be the only charts needing study. The psychology of their counselors was very important too. Eve had delegated to the gentle Iris the task of talking with two of the victims' relatives, asking permission to study the victims' charts. The third victim, Cartwright, had apparently been alone in the world. The others' relatives had been eager to help the investigation.

By noon Iris and Eve had completed their studies. In the charts of each astrologer there was an indication of violent and sudden death.

Eve and Iris looked at each other in silence. This opened up a whole new avenue of work and speculation.

Iris glanced over at Betty and Clare, who were intent on the small computer. Eve knew that Iris was thinking of Betty and the danger she was in. Their Cancerian partner had been in one of her moods all morning. Eve conjectured that Betty's husband was not too happy over her involvement in the project, especially now that the matter of her being a possible D had surfaced.

Lunch time would be the best opportunity to discuss things freely with Iris, Eve decided. "Hey, eager beavers!" she called out to Betty and Clare. "Noon."

"Okay," Clare said absently, with one last

whack at the buttons, and Betty took a note from the final data on the screen.

When they'd left, Eve said, "Now. How are we going to handle this? Betty's skittish already. This problem may be right in her chart, and she's got to know it. Perhaps she's blocking it out. Let's check up on her and the other astrologer, DeLuise. I checked my own progressed chart last week."

"And . . . ?" Iris looked anxious.

"I've got some pretty sticky aspects in Mars next month," Eve admitted.

"Oh, swell." Iris's sarcasm was shaky.

Eve shrugged it off. "I'm careful, believe me. Let's take a look at Betty's and DeLuise's charts."

While Iris worked at the computer, Eve thought about the new aspect of the case. Were they going far enough, checking only these two astrologers? What if the killer suddenly decided to jump around the alphabet? But that didn't fit the pattern. Anyway, if she started thinking like that she'd go mad—and get Iris and Clare hysterical besides.

"It's coming," Iris called out. Eve went to the computer and watched the data flash on the screen. The computer was printing out Betty's progressed horoscope.

"Uh-oh," Iris broke out. "Mars in Scorpio, Pluto in close square conjunction. Bad news."

"Saturn's not too jolly either. Is it possible Betty hasn't checked her progressed horoscope?" Eve demanded.

Iris folded the printout. "Entirely. Being safely among the R's, she probably hasn't bothered. You know how astrologers are."

"I sure do. Like the barefooted shoemaker's children," Eve conceded. "Too busy with other people's charts to do our own."

"Well, we might as well check DeLuise too." Ms. DeLuise had been born in the same year as Betty, within days of Betty's birthday. And both had been born in New York City. "Same aspect," Iris murmured.

"What do you bet DeLuise lives on Staten Island and rides the ferry?" Eve speculated.

Iris referred back to the printout. "You win. Cliffwood Avenue, Staten Island."

"I hope she doesn't decide to walk along any cliffs," Eve commented darkly. "Is her practice at home?"

Iris looked. "Yes, fortunately. Cuts down trips to the city on the ferry. And she has a car."

"Fine. I'm sure the police have already warned her about public transportation, and she may have done her own chart." Eve frowned. "Maybe I should give her a call. Maybe *not;* we're supposed to be consultants, not cops. I'll make up a memo for Carlin and Kane."

"Shall I phone it to Myers for you?"

"I think this is a little too long for the phone. I'll do it and take it upstairs myself. I can use the exercise; I'm not a gorgeous feather like you." Eve smiled at Iris and let out an exaggerated sigh over Iris's narrow figure.

When Eve walked into the DC's outer office

with her completed report, Angela Myers was on the phone in low-voiced conversation. Eve didn't want to intrude, so she wandered into the reception area to wait.

But Myers's sharp voice rose and carried. "I told you, Mother, a hundred times. I have no influence over him at all. No one listens to me. I'm just their servant. Leave me alone about it." Myers banged the receiver in its cradle. "Yes, Ms. Darcy?"

Eve raised her eyes from the magazine. Myers was looking at her impatiently.

Eve gave her a friendly smile and walked over to her desk. "I didn't want to disturb you. It's just a note for the deputy commissioner." She put the paper on Myers's desk.

The woman snatched the paper up as if it could singe the wood. "Not there!" she blurted. Then she laughed, a high, whinnying laugh that gave Eve goose pimples. "These things go in my In basket, here."

Myers lifted a paperweight. Eve saw a Virgo Maiden symbol on it. A nice one, the kind you could buy in an astrology store like Keiser's. "I'm sorry, Ms. Myers."

The secretary bristled. "It's Mrs. Myers, by the way."

"Mrs. Myers," Eve corrected herself. "Thank you."

Wondering what she was thanking the woman for, she left. What a world of difference there was between Myers and Clare. The secretary was the kind of Virgo cheap pop astrology touted—fussy, old-maidish, stingy of heart. Clare was the higher octave. Fastidious, organized, "crystal sighted" like the benign magician Merlin of myth.

But Eve forgot about Myers as soon as she was back in her office. Betty and Clare had returned from lunch. Eve told Iris to go to eat without her. It was time to talk to Betty.

Iris's conjecture proved out. Betty hadn't done a progressed chart for herself for six months. She confessed to Eve she'd planned to do one that night.

Eve handed her the printout. Her teammate's educated eye leapt right to the disturbing square conjunction of Pluto and Mars. "Oh, *no.*" Betty looked up at Eve. "It's a good thing I'm afraid of water." But her joke fell flat. Eve knew she was extremely upset.

Kane didn't drop in that afternoon, but Eve received a memo from him after the others had left. It said curtly, "Re DeLuise. We've got her covered. Same for Mrs. Rivers." The note made Eve feel officious. Betty's increasing tension didn't improve Eve's morale.

By Friday afternoon her spirits had hit a new low. The team hadn't uncovered anything solid. There'd been two promising leads, but both fizzled; one person had died of a heart attack and the other was discovered to have been in California for the last seven months with no indication of a return visit.

Before they went home Friday Eve asked if anybody felt like working the next day. Clare and Iris said they did, but Betty said she had an in-law commitment she couldn't get out of. Eve could hardly blame her. The recent information was enough to discourage anybody.

But I'm a target, too, Eve argued. And they needed all hands. Only three business weeks remained until the next scheduled attack. Christmas was coming, too, with all the usual obligations. A peace-loving Taurus like Eve hated crowds and hurry, so she generally had everything squared away by early December. She wouldn't this year—it was nearly that now.

To add to Eve's gloom a sloppy wet snow started to fall late Friday night, driven by gusty winds. On Saturday morning Eve was sorely tempted to take the subway into Manhattan, but told herself not to be insane. The trains would be too empty. And the Astro Killer's schedule wasn't engraved in marble. No one on earth could predict what a disturbed creature like that was going to do.

Her mood did not improve negotiating the slippery bridge, getting out of her car in the wind tunnel of Police Plaza. *It's like an airport,* she decided grouchily as she scurried through the entrance of the big white building. The wind had blown her hood back, and her wet hair stuck to her cheeks in strands. Damn, it was going to pop out into puppy-dog tails!

Seeing Iris already there, when she got to the office, made Eve feel even grouchier. Then guilty on top of it, because she liked Iris so much. Her Pisces team-member was absolutely glowing; Iris reacted to moisture like the fish of her sign, and she looked gorgeous.

Today she made Eve feel fat, and messy besides.

"Morning," she said briefly, and went to the mirror that the obliging Betty had installed for them, repairing her hair as best she could. "It sure is your kind of day," she added, trying to be pleasant.

"Yes, it is. The wind's awful, though." Iris grinned at Eve, her face impish above the collar of her orange sweater. Eve felt a wave of affection: Pisceans were such sweet people. Even in her pleasurable reaction to the hideous weather, Iris was making a valiant effort to be "normal," unable to feel good unless the people around her felt good too.

"You want some coffee?" Iris offered.

"Love it." Eve gratefully accepted her filled mug, asking, "Where's 'The Clock'?"

"In the jane, getting herself together. Eve, I got a flash last night—in the shower, of course." Iris grinned. "What do you make of the pattern of the victims' signs? I mean, the fact that the first was an Aries, the second a Taurus, and the third a Gemini?"

Eve sat down. "Iris, I didn't even think of it." She was devastated that she'd missed this obvious point. She was slipping. "That means each was murdered during the astrological 'month' of her opposite sign, the months of Libra, Scorpio, and Sagittarius. Which means," she speculated, "the next victim should be a Cancer, on the first day of

60

Capricorn. Iris, you're sensational. How I could have *missed* this . . ." Eve knew why. She'd been too damned distracted by Adam Kane.

"Don't you think this argues a certain closeness to astrology, as well as a highly orderly mind?" Iris asked eagerly.

"I certainly do. In a way it puts us back at square one: an astrologer. Or someone close to an astrologer. And if the next victim is a Cancer, then both Betty and DeLuise are in danger," Eve commented grimly.

When Clare came in Iris updated her. "This isn't my area," Clare admitted, "but it certainly sounds reasonable. While we're discussing patterns, what about others—boroughs they lived in, things like that?"

"Queens, Staten Island, and The Bronx," Eve supplied quickly. "Leaving Manhattan and Brooklyn."

"Betty lives in Brooklyn," Clare said, sounding tense.

"Let's get on this," Eve said. "We'll each take a victim. I'll take Asbury, the first. You take Baker, Clare, and Iris can take Cartwright. Let's go over everything again, with a fine-tooth comb. Try to establish other patterns. Okay?"

"And you're especially interested in 'feuds' with other astrologers, astrologer friends, relatives, and so on?" Clare offered.

"Exactly." They got into the project. All three were so intent that they forgot the time. At last Eve realized she was famished; she and Clare ordered lunch in. But Iris got into all her rubber gear to wade out into the slush; she said the wet air was good for her "fishy brain."

By four o'clock, however, none of them had come up with anything decisive. Adding it all up, the only thing they could conclude was what the intuitive Iris had already discovered—the murderer was an astrological thinker, a pattern person who was either an astrologer or close to one.

And the Cancer theory meant more bad news for Betty. Eve was going to have to tell her, and soon. Furthermore, this was a matter for Kane and Carlin. While the others wrapped up their tasks, she wrote out a memo and took it up to Carlin's office herself, putting it in Myers's In basket at her empty desk, with an extra copy for Kane, though she doubted that he'd show up this afternoon.

When she got back to the office, the others had gone. She leaned back in her chair, staring out at the wet, wind-driven snow, thinking about the new aspect of the case. In spite of her exhaustion she felt stubborn and strong again.

"Aren't you overtime?"

The quiet was broken by a deep male voice.

Swiveling around, Eve saw Adam Kane.

CHAPTER THREE

Eve's first reaction was totally feminine and irrelevant: she must look like a wreck.

But there was a friendliness in Kane's eyes she hadn't seen before. It chipped away at her icy defenses.

"I think we may have come up with something, Inspector." She dug out a copy of her memo and handed it to him.

With an impassive expression Kane sat down on the edge of her desk and began to read. She watched the dark, penetrating glance race over the page. "Interesting," he commented.

He looked up at her. "You've done quite a job here today . . . with the victim study, and all that. Very good." This time there was nothing indulgent in his voice, and she warmed with the compliment.

"But we're still no 'forrarder,' as the British cops say." Eve smiled. "I realize it's only a theory. And I know your team can come up with evidence we can't. I hope it'll help. I'm not too happy, though, about what it means to Betty Rivers."

"Everything helps, Ms. Darcy." There was a soft light in his fierce eyes that disarmed her. "And don't worry about Mrs. Rivers. We've got her covered. I'll ask Hansen to work on this new theory of yours. He knows more about astrology than the rest of us."

"Oh?" Eve lifted her brows.

Kane laughed softly, observing her expression. "Believe me, I don't like Hansen any better than you do. You might say we have very different . . . styles." This was another first: he'd never been this personal before.

She was more than ever aware of his imposing physical size, his big, competent hands, his aura of self-respect.

"That leaps to the eye, Inspector." Her comment was so ambiguous that he looked at her a minute, as if uncertain how to take it.

"Don't you think we can drop the formal titles?" he asked abruptly.

"With first names like ours," she retorted, "I don't think I could keep a straight face." But that sounded a bit snappish, so she hastened to add, "Why not?"

"Good. I'm glad that's settled. Eve. It's a pretty name." When his look lingered on her, she had a sudden need to do something with her hands, and straightened some of her papers. Adam Kane unsettled her even more with friendliness than with hostility.

"While we're at it," he said, "how about a

drink? The whole world's celebrating Saturday, and I'm off duty for a couple of hours."

It sounded lovely, but she still wasn't sure it was such a great idea. He might be a good man to stay away from; his appeal was immense, and she was feeling vulnerable. "You're off duty?" she asked evasively.

He understood the question. He hadn't come here for a work conference. "Actually, this is a personal visit. I wanted to . . . make peace. I was pretty rude to you, and I'm sorry."

Eve felt an absurd disappointment. That's all it was, then—more PR. Repairing fences with a colleague.

"I accept," she said lightly. "Why don't we have a drink?"

"Great." His black eyes gleamed at her, and he answered with more enthusiasm, she thought, than a man would who was just trying to sweeten an associate. He stood up and towered over her. He was a damned impressive man, she conceded. And so unusual looking, with those deep-black eyes in contrast to the sandy brows and hair. "Are you about ready to wind up here?"

"Very soon." She had to have some time to get herself together. "May I meet you downstairs, in about ten or fifteen minutes?"

"Sure."

When he'd gone out Eve went to the mirror to survey the damage. Not too bad, she judged with elation: her rather wild hair gave her a sensuous look, and her sleepy-lidded eyes were wide open, sparkling. Their gray picked up a pleasant turquoise cast from her vivid blue-green dress with its flattering asymmetrical collar. She was wearing Australian opal studs in her ears, the color of the dress.

Opal, one of the Scorpio birthstones. Quite a coincidence.

She tidied herself up rapidly, straightened out her work, and took the elevator down to the lobby.

He was already there, pacing a little, looking bigger and more powerful than ever in his overcoat and dark-brown hat canted rakishly on his head.

His stern face relaxed when he saw her.

"That was quick." He beamed. "Look, you stay right here. I'll get the car and pick you up in front. Only a husky could enjoy that." He nodded toward the wet snow that was still swirling down.

Waiting, she considered how nice it was to feel feminine, protected, taken care of for a change. Being strong and independent was lovely, a way of life with her. All the same, it was fun, now and then, to let a man take over a little.

His car pulled up and she got into the open passenger door. "Nice." She smiled at Adam Kane.

As he drove off, he asked, "What are your dinner plans?"

"Nothing special."

"Great. I know a nice place . . . if you'll have dinner with me." She murmured agreement, amused and gratified at the way "a drink" had escalated into dinner. Scorpios did love to be devious.

Driving with slow, one-handed caution, he spoke into his radio. "This is Kane. Taking Astro One till eight. I'll drop her at her car." Eve heard a brisk female voice answer, "Ten-four, Kane."

"So that's my code name."

"Yes. Appropriately." Eve reacted strongly to the implication that she was "number one." He was looking straight ahead, concentrating on difficult driving, but she felt he was observing her out of the corner of his eye.

The all-seeing "eagle" eye of the Scorpio. One of the Scorpionic symbols was that fierce, noble bird with its 360-degree viewing range.

She knew how significant a compliment from him was; Scorpios weren't known for their pretty speech. But it was disturbing how these vivid symbols sprang so easily to her mind, how seriously she took what he said. And she wondered if she should have come along at all.

Eve didn't say anything, and she felt him draw back. When he spoke again he seemed to be trying to keep it light. "This place is uptown a way. I think you'll like it. Especially on a night like this."

She knew what he meant the minute they walked in. The restaurant was called Chantelle. It was in a neighborhood she didn't know, that mysterious region between City Hall and Greenwich Village. Chantelle was small and plain, but wonderfully cozy. There were wood beams, shaded candles on each table, drawn café curtains of subdued, attractive orange.

While Kane dispensed with their coats, he called out, "Hi, Dave!" to a genial-looking man behind the small bar. The man waved to Kane and grinned, checking Eve out with interest.

"This is the first time I've been here with a lady," Kane confided to Eve when they sat down. They got quick VIP cocktail service.

Eve studied the hand-lettered menu, enjoying the warmth of the drink and the room. "Lobster with cider and apples? Scallops baked in pastry . . . fabulous."

Kane smiled. "You really like food. That's a treat. I thought all women were on diets."

"Only when I'm not eating." She listened to his big, full-bodied laugh with pleasure, and chose the scallops. He ordered lobster. Savoring the unique food, the fine chablis they had with the meal, Eve began to relax.

And suddenly they were easy with each other, talking and talking. Kane got her biography out of her, and surprised her by offering his—Scorpios loved to quiz others while keeping themselves dark. He'd grown up in Hell's Kitchen, on New York's West Side. Apparently it had left him with a passion for what his birthplace lacked—law and order on the one hand, space and beauty on the other. He was unusually knowledgeable about the arts and architecture.

She couldn't help thinking how much he'd appreciate her house on Sidney Place. On impulse she said so.

He responded, "I certainly would." His eyes were kind and level, with no suggestion of a leer, no prodding for an invitation the way another man might have prodded, making something suggestive out of her remark. That gave Eve a good feeling about him, but all the same, she thought it might have sounded like an invitation. Somewhat embarrassed she said the first thing that popped into her head. "You must have a big place."

Which didn't improve matters at all. She was putting her Taurean hoof in it, for sure.

He chuckled. "Not big, exactly. But one of a kind." She waited for a description; he didn't offer one. "I'd like you to see it sometime. You'll get a surprise."

His invitation had an intimate sound. She decided the conversation was taking a direction she didn't want to follow. Not yet.

So she changed the subject quickly, and he took his cue from her. But there was a glint of amusement in his sharp eyes, as if he'd read her mind.

Adam Kane is probably as skittish as I am, in his way, Eve thought. He'd suffered the deepest hurt and loss; he would not be likely to let himself go easily again. Scorpios were secretive and reticent, as a rule, slow to show their emotions because, once made, their commitments were total.

She also sensed his loneliness. He spoke with the eager, wholehearted rush of a solitary man who didn't get a frequent chance to talk about what mattered. It made her warm toward him, and she was sharply excited when their fingers brushed when they met over the little table.

The biggest surprise was what good company he was. She'd expected him to be as prickly as a porcupine.

"You're surprised, aren't you?" The question was so abrupt that it took her off guard. He *was* a mind reader.

"Surprised?"

"That I'm not the same ogre off duty as on." He pronounced it "oh-gree," trying to be funny, and it was. She laughed, feeling her face flush. Kane smiled at her guilty expression. "It was damned nice of you to accept my invitation," he said quietly, "considering that bad first impression. I hope you can forgive that." He looked so anxious that she warmed to him even more, and nodded.

She could forgive, all right, but it was hard to forget that he considered her profession a kind of joke. He'd adroitly avoided the subject all through dinner. It was an unhappy thought. Adam Kane had such a strong, intrusive personality, it was hard to relax with him for long. In fact, both of them were so hardheaded there could probably be nothing but collision between them.

She glanced at her watch. They'd been here almost two hours and it had gone by like a minute. He might be difficult, but he was certainly diverting.

Catching her glance Kane looked at his own

watch. "I'd better get back," he said with regret. "Where did the time go?"

His dark gaze locked with hers.

"Pleasant time goes fast," she said in a light, friendly voice.

He looked away from her, asked for the check. His friend Dave brought it himself. Kane held out some money.

"No good tonight, pal. Introduce me to this beautiful lady."

Kane did.

"It's a pleasure, Ms. Darcy. Make him tell you what I owe him."

Kane reddened, still offering money. "Big mouth," he muttered. Dave laughed, waving the money away.

Eve liked him. He was leonine in looks and had the Leo's expansive manner. "I might just ask him," she told Dave.

It had stopped snowing, but as they walked a strong wind whipped them, making talk difficult. Eve got in the car with relief. When Kane joined her, she asked, "What does Dave owe you?"

Kane started the car, his face deadpan. "Not a damned thing. He's a nice guy, but he embarrasses me when he does that." After an instant he added, "I stopped a holdup once and he thinks it's a big deal."

"Alone?" she demanded, impressed.

"Sure," he said dismissively. "Just doing my job."

How he reminded Eve of her closemouthed father, who had also been shy of praise. It made her

71

feel strangely close to Adam Kane. They were silent as they drove to her car parked at Number One, but it was a companionable silence now, not an awkward one. Kane's big hands on the wheel, the brush of his shoulder in the snugness of the compact car, gave Eve a sense of deep security. For the moment the car was a small world enclosing them from the threatening winter night.

When he braked in the plaza Eve said, "Thank you. I loved that place."

"I'm glad." Kane's eyes were bright. He leaned toward her.

Eve felt the pull of his nearness, so potent that her whole body responded, independent of her will. And she knew that the glitter in his dark eyes was an awareness of her feelings.

She studied his fine face with its hawkish nose and stubborn jaw, the mouth that no longer looked grim and tight, but excited, vulnerable.

"Do you know what's happening, Eve?" Even half whispering his basso voice stroked her like soothing hands along her back, and she quivered.

Mesmerized she nodded and moved closer to him. Right now her doubts seemed foolish. Nothing else in the world was relevant except the nearness of his mouth to hers.

His arms went around her, and he lowered his head slowly. His mouth took possession of her lips, cold from the night but soon so warm, firm and trembling all at once, seeking and demanding.

That kiss was shattering. She let herself respond in wild forgetfulness, no longer caring where they were or who might see, forgetting all that had divided them.

His hands were caressing her with hungry abandon; even through her heavy coat she was sharply aware of his fingers' heat and strength, and she could feel her stubborn resistance flow away. Her hands crept around his strong, hard neck.

When he raised his mouth she heard him breathing shallowly. "Eve, oh, Eve," he murmured, and pulled her to him again, overcoming her with the pressure of his eager mouth.

"Let me come to you tonight," he whispered.

Her whole self dissolved into assent: *Yes, yes,* her flesh cried out. It was all so simple and clear. She wanted him, wanted him more completely than she had ever wanted any other man, and his mouth, his arms, his body, melted her as the sun of spring did the winter snow. Her emotions were the rushing, melted torrent freed from its long-frozen state.

She looked up into his fierce, unreadable eyes.

Suddenly her whole past assailed her. This was exactly the way it had begun with Paul—a swift, sweet impulse that drew her to a man she hardly knew, a man who ultimately broke her heart.

And Adam Kane was even more dangerous. He was a hundred times the man Paul was, a man of such power he might be capable of uprooting her entire life and then go calmly on his way, leaving her even more devastated than she'd been before. She couldn't play with her life like that. Not now, not so soon.

Abruptly she pulled away, got out, and hurried to her car.

Adam Kane was too dismayed to move. For a long instant he stayed exactly where he was, indifferent to the freezing air that blasted through the open door. He'd been so lost in her fragrant sweetness, her soft warmth, that when she pulled away it was like a hard punch to his body. He was momentarily stunned.

But then his trained reflexes took over. He cleared his throat and spoke into his radio. "Take Astro One. She's driving out of the plaza."

Kane shut off his radio and leaned back. He closed the door and pulled out, heading north toward Greenwich Village. He was already late meeting Hansen for the checkout of the occult bookstores.

Driving uptown Kane found himself tangled in Saturday-night traffic, slower than ever because of the weather. But he couldn't think of much right now except Eve. And what a fool he'd been to speak so soon.

He should have known that she would get to him as no one had since Elaine. He'd walked around punch drunk for more than a year after his wife died, convinced he'd never love another woman. Love like that couldn't happen twice. Hell, really feeling for a woman, for him, took as long as a geologic movement. When he had finally fallen in love with his wife, it had been for good. It had never occurred to Kane that other women even existed, not in that way. He was resigned to the fact that women from then on would be random and purely medicinal. And that hadn't been too bad; he had his work to power him, to get excited about.

Until that day Eve Darcy walked into Carlin's office. She'd hit Kane like a ton of bricks. She had everything he admired in a woman—a real woman's body, not one of those half-starved little girl's; those deep, calm, sexy eyes that made him think of soft pillows, quiet places, perfect ease; beautiful hair with nothing "done" to it, so shiny it practically made him blink.

But most of all, that no-nonsense manner of self-respect and intelligence. She looked at peace with herself, and didn't try to knock a man over either with her looks or brains.

Accelerating a little in the crawling traffic Kane was disturbed to feel himself still ache a bit. Damn, it had been awful, letting her go. He'd wanted to ask her to dinner that first afternoon, but he hadn't for two reasons: One was that she'd probably have said no; the other was not wanting to feel like this. He'd figured all he could reasonably expect from the rest of life was comfort. And this sure as hell wasn't comfort.

He had a feeling she'd been burned too. She was cagey about certain aspects of her past. A woman like her, serious and choosy, had to have been involved in something deep at some time or other. Maybe with some dumb jerk who didn't realize what he had in her. Somebody like Hansen?

Could be. Hansen really pulled her chain. *He*

pulls mine, too, Kane ruminated. He couldn't understand a guy like that; he had a really lovely wife but he acted like a juvenile jackrabbit.

He was a good cop, though, Kane conceded, as his car crawled up the Saturday-night chaos of Sixth Avenue. *And I've got to remember I'm a cop and quit woolgathering.*

Kane pulled into a side street and parked, slipping his small cardboard notice under the windshield wipers to alert antsy guys in Traffic. He got out and slogged back to Sixth Avenue, leaning into the bitter wind. It was only a couple of blocks to West Fourth Street, and Kane enjoyed the cold.

That creep should be doing a land-office business on Saturday night in the Village. Turning into West Fourth, Kane shouldered past a group of high-looking teenagers and a small knot of fragile young men, striding toward the Satan Store.

What a name, he thought in disgust. How a bright woman like Eve Darcy could ally herself with such baloney stymied him.

Hansen's wife was into it too; otherwise she seemed perfectly sensible. "Handsome" must be inside already—it was no night to hang out on the sidewalk.

Opening the door to a jangle of bells Kane saw that he'd guessed right. Hansen looked around nervously. He was standing in a dim corner with a weird-looking girl who was wearing something that looked like a nightgown and not much under it. She had a wild-eyed gaze and so much stuff on

76

her eyes they could hardly bear the weight. Giving Kane an interested stare she seemed to forget Hansen.

Kane repressed a laugh. He supposed Hansen was jumpy, being in a place like this, never knowing when his wife might take it into her head to drop in on her own; they didn't live too far away.

"Well, well. Did you say Saturday or Sunday?" Hansen asked sarcastically when Kane approached him.

Kane gave him some rude advice, under his breath, ignoring the interested girl with the overburdened eyes. "Did he get here yet?"

"Not yet. Give it a while," Hansen advised softly. Kane caught a whiff of cheap wine on his breath. The store served prospective customers wine to loosen them up for sales. "Relax, Kane." Hansen smiled, and his smile included the bizarre girl. "Say hello to Annamaria. This is Adam."

"You're *kidding.*" Annamaria's voice oozed out, as if it were being squeezed from her. "That's sexy! What's your sign?"

Kane had no idea, and he was supposed to be another astrology buff like Hansen. Of course, in reality Hansen hated the stuff, saying his cuckoo wife drove him nuts with it.

But Hansen knew enough to save Kane right now. "Guess," he teased Annamaria.

The girl looked Kane over from head to toe. "Easy. He's Taurus the Bu-ull. So *big.*" She gave Kane a seductive glance.

"Wrong," Hansen said triumphantly.

Kane was getting a little tired of the whole

scene and started to wander around, looking at the items for sale. There were some racy posters on the walls that commented on the particular tastes of each astrological sign. Kane had seen many such posters, but these struck him as very unfunny. The books were no better, with mystical titles and high-falutin author names.

There was also a plethora of black candles, other junk Kane couldn't imagine a use for. He saw the proprietor, Andy Mephisto, approaching him. Mephisto was a middle-aged phony with a satanic Vandyke and thin moustache, and an avid eye for young girls. He always dressed in black trousers and a black turtleneck sweater; one of his protruding ears was pierced. "Can I help you?" he asked Kane in a deep, stagy voice.

"No, thanks," Kane muttered. "Just waiting for my friend over there." Mephisto pasted on his smile and walked over to a group of girls who'd just come in.

Bored and restless, Kane checked the door every time it opened. Hansen was still in low-voiced, earnest conversation with Annamaria, but his look jumped to the door, too, every time the bells rang.

An hour passed like eternity. Kane gestured to Hansen and, when he came over, said in a low voice, "I'm going to check out that second place, on Broadway. Relieve Reynolds. You can catch me there till closing."

Hansen nodded and raised his voice for the others' benefit. "Okay, pal, but this is where it's all at. See you later."

Glad to be out in the air, cold as it was, Kane went back to his car and drove west toward Broadway. At least there wouldn't be a parking problem in this weather, he thought sourly. Of all nights for their suspect not to show!

He found a parking spot with no trouble, but walking down Broadway he thought somebody had given him a bad address. There was nothing for miles that looked "occult"; in fact there wasn't much, period. A lot of tightly shut antique shops, a few random pedestrians trickling down from Fourteenth Street, eager to get out of the cold, messy dark.

Kane was surprised when he found the place. It was a plain, moderately lit bookstore; the few diehard customers had no resemblance at all to Mephisto's cultists. Cooler too.

Kane rapidly picked out Reynolds, glassy eyed among the books on yoga. Reynolds looked reprieved and slid a book back on its shelf. None of the clients was their suspect, whose features Kane had memorized. The store was divided into spiritualism, religion, and astrology. Kane zeroed in on the latter, passing Reynolds, who made a covert coffee-drinking gesture. That meant the coffee shop a block away.

Kane eyed him *Okay.* Watching the door sidelong he idly looked over the titles. This was another ball of wax. This, he supposed, might be Eve's kind of astrology. He felt another twinge, as if his whole body were one bad tooth. Damn it, he couldn't get her out of his mind.

A sudden draft of icy air struck Kane. His eyes

shot to the door. A sweet-looking older lady smiled her thanks to Reynolds for playing doorman. Meanwhile Kane checked books. One looked like serious business, a big hardback. The author's name was followed by a series of degrees.

His curiosity piqued, Kane slipped the book out and leafed the pages. What had Eve said he was—a Scorpio? Kane found the chapter on Scorpios and skimmed through it. The personality profile was so accurate he could feel the hair prickle on his forearms. Still alert to the door Kane read some additional passages. Could there actually be something to this malarkey?

He checked the price of the book and decided he'd buy it to read more carefully later. He was slipping a bill from his wallet when a red alert rang inside his head.

A guy at the counter, paying for a book, was a dead ringer, from his angle, for their prey. Where had he come from? Kane hadn't seen him at all.

He was at the cashier's desk in a few long strides. The suspect was already heading through the door and Kane hadn't been able to make out his face yet. But he thought he recognized the frame, and walk, from Hansen's description. Kane threw the bill down and, ignoring the cashier's cry of "Sir, your change!" rushed through the door.

The suspect was walking quickly down Broadway. Kane radioed to Reynolds, giving him their position. The suspect might be going home, Kane thought, elated. Now they'd have his address, which they hadn't been able to unearth before, because he had no name yet.

Kane heard a car slow down just behind him. It was Reynolds. He'd made good time. Kane waved him on, though; the suspect was turning west, and Kane was close enough to make it on foot.

Reynolds's car kept crawling down the wide street. Kane turned, too, keeping a comfortable distance between himself and Mister Ding-a-ling. He was pleased when the guy turned into a well-lit apartment lobby. Kane would really be able to ID him now. But when the fellow turned and greeted the doorman with an amiable smile, Kane saw that it wasn't their suspect at all, just a harmless-seeming guy who'd looked like the other one from the back.

Kane's adrenaline rush did a terrific reversal, leaving him cold and tired, almost dizzy. He walked back to Reynolds's car, making a no-soap gesture. He got in the car and signaled Hansen, giving him time to get out of the shop so he could talk to him without blowing their cover.

"Thought I had him," Kane growled. "A look-alike." It was time for the Broadway store to close. "What have you got?" he asked Hansen.

"A name tag," Hansen said quickly. "Annamaria just told me the ding-a-ling's home with the flu. She doesn't know where home is. But his name's Perry Martial. A friend of his called Mephisto to hold a book for him. The guy always pays cash. But at least we've got a name. I'd better get back. Taking Annamaria to the Monte

Carlo, a joint over by Sheridan Square. Her mob hangs out there. Maybe I can pick up something on Perry Martial."

"Go for it. Try not to pick up anything else," Kane rode him. "I'm heading back to Number One, see if we can find anything on that name."

"By the way, it's *M-a-r-t-i-a-l.*"

"Fancy. Watch your back."

"Ten-four, Scorpio," Hansen needled.

That reminded Kane of the book. He was looking forward to reading it. In a way it would be like getting to know Eve better, through the work she took so seriously. Maybe he'd get a break with her yet, the way they'd gotten a break on this Perry Martial.

Adam Kane was just getting started. This time, though, he wouldn't speed so much. He'd wait for her signal.

Eve turned up the TV volume to drown the party noise from downstairs. The racket wasn't unpleasant; it just made her feel so out of it.

A few hours ago, when she'd hurried in the entrance door, her downstairs neighbor Jean had poked her curly head out of her apartment, calling out, "Join us!"

"Thanks, Jean. I'm afraid I'm not in a party mood."

"We'll get you in the mood." Ed O'Malley, looking very smooth, had come to the door to add his invitation.

"Not tonight, Ed," Eve said firmly. "Thanks again." She went on upstairs to her own apartment, thinking how little difference Ed's presence made. He was pleasant enough, but a bit too sophisticated for Eve's taste. He'd pursued her at other parties of Jean's, but Eve smiled to herself, recalling a line from an old movie—"You're too smooth. I like my men a little bumpy."

That was Adam Kane to a T. Eve wondered if she'd made a big mistake, running off like that. No one had come close to affecting her like him, not since Paul. And she was a full-grown woman, with a healthy woman's needs.

The very fact of her uncertainty—she was always so sure of things—took the edge from her usual pleasure when she let herself in to her lovely apartment.

She put her outdoor things away and stood in the middle of the living room, looking around. The whole space breathed efficiency and ease, those qualities so dear to the practical, sensuous Taurean. In contrast to her country bedroom this room was starkly modern, yet very comfortable with its soft couch covered in a small checked fabric of gray, rust, and cream; the thick pale-gray rug inviting bare feet, the built-in cabinets painted ivory in agreeable contrast to pale gray walls. Color sang out from simple tables of redwood, touches of gold, green, and russet in pillows and spare decorative pieces.

Her corner office had more cabinets with sliding doors to conceal her computer and the other tools of her trade when she wasn't working.

It was a warm and gracious little house. But

now it looked so empty. She thought, *A house is asleep until it's shared.*

As she undressed and relaxed in a bath of rosy bubbles to calm herself down, Eve could feel the touch of Adam Kane. She still could hardly believe how much his kiss had aroused her. But she would have a very bad night if she lingered on that memory too long. Whatever else he was, he was also a stranger.

The thing to do, she decided, was to get to work. That was the one cure that never failed. She dried herself with new energy, got into a soft green robe, and padded back to the living room to her fat briefcase in the office corner.

She'd brought an enormous amount of data home, and now she was eager to follow up on the idea she'd had at Number One, just before Adam Kane had walked into the office.

She'd been considering a more extensive study of astrologers' records, one that went much farther back in time than theirs. Chicago's Star Slayer had nursed his grudge for twenty years. And, judging by the victims' youth and good looks, one could speculate that the murderer could be a jealous older woman . . . or an embittered older man.

Eve let the printout fall from her hands. Oh, sure, she ridiculed herself. Or an embittered *young* woman, or a jealous younger man. It was maddening that the murderer had given so little indication of sex.

She was suffering from burnout; her mind was going every whichway. She was getting nowhere because she was one tired, frustrated lady. She put the printout back into her briefcase, promising herself not even to think about the case again until Monday. Losing herself in TV was a good solution right now.

But the program listing was no help. She was offered a choice of an idiotic infidelity "comedy" —infidelity was about as funny to her as a fifty-car pileup on the highway—a cop show, and a tragic love story. She turned on the cop show; that would be the least of three evils.

It absorbed and relaxed her until a character appeared who reminded her somewhat of Adam Kane. And then, over the dialogue, she heard Jean, who was a talented musician, playing the piano downstairs.

She was playing one of those nostalgic Gershwin tunes, haunting as twilight. Paul had loved it. But it didn't make her miss him; she missed belonging.

And there on the TV screen was the actor who reminded her of Kane. Her sentimental, sensitive Pisces moon was at its full tonight.

Eve switched off the set, investigated her bookshelves, searching out distraction. Among the paperbacks she glimpsed the bright-blue cover of one of her favorite novels. It was usually a great escape.

It wasn't now. *The Seed of Scorpio.*

There he was again. It seemed to be inevitable. She might as well enjoy the discomfort of her attraction, Eve thought ironically. Looked like it wasn't going to go away.

She turned out the living-room lights, leaving one at dim night level, and went into the bedroom. Turning back the quilt she slid under it, hearing the wind strengthen and moan around the house's corners. *Give in,* she told herself. *Adam Kane's going to be around tonight in one form or another.* She tuned her bedside radio to a classical music station, heard the rainy sound of Rachmaninoff.

And began to read.

It was a unique novel about a mythical country where astrology ruled every area of life; it dealt with the "fated" love-opposites of the zodiac. Eve started with Taurus-Scorpio, "The Dove of Mars." Fiction paralleled reality—a Taurus woman hired by an imposing, prickly, close-mouthed Scorpio; the two hated each other on sight. There was even a murder in the plot.

The Scorpio was also a big man with a tragic past, a "lean, hawklike face," and penetrating eyes. It was eerie.

He felt, Eve read, *the familiar exhilaration of a Fluidian sniffing moist air.* She recalled Adam's reaction to the wet cold, mulled over a phrase about earth yearning for refreshing water, water's need to be contained. She and Adam each had what the other lacked: he was as restless as the ocean, she as calm as the land.

At the story's end the Scorpio said to his Taurean lover, *"You've tamed the very god of war."* Eve's sign was ruled by Venus, Kane's by Mars, the symbols of the female and the male.

She put the book aside, reliving the time since

they had first seen each other. The moment their glances met, she'd felt the deeper touch of his overriding temperament, stronger even than hers.

She felt now that his initial hostility had been a cover, much like the Scorpio's in that book. Kane had been hurt by life too. He was as cautious as she about getting involved again.

And yet he'd reached out to her, despite that. And she'd been too uncertain, too ungenerous, to reach back. She couldn't fool herself that it was because she didn't know him yet, that he was still "a stranger." She wanted him desperately, just as much as he seemed to want her.

Besides, she'd always believed that if you didn't feel something at once, you'd never feel it at all. At least that was the way it was for her, with her soft Piscean moon, her expansive Jupiter and impulsive Uranus.

She wondered when, and if, he would reach out to her again. In any case he would have to be the one who did. All she could do was wait. And see.

"Adam?"

Kane looked up from the big hardback. Deputy Commissioner Carlin was standing at his office door. "You were very intent," Carlin commented. "More homework?" He'd read the title of Kane's book with surprise.

"Yeah." Kane was only half lying. He'd rationalized that it couldn't hurt to be informed, since astrology was central to the case, and of course he wanted to be able to talk to Eve about it. What he hadn't foreseen was this damned fascination with the subject. "Have you moved in here too?"

"Not quite." The DC sighed and sat down on the corner of Kane's desk. "So we came up with zip on Martial."

"Right." Kane marked his place in the book, leaned back wearily in his chair, and put his feet up on the desk. "This flake doesn't seem to *exist,*" he complained, "except for his tax records. No car, no service record, doesn't even vote, for Pete's sake. This is the first time he's filed income tax in New York; must be a newcomer. Actor and model. Looks like we're going to have to do a lot more digging. Nothing but sabotage will work." Kane grinned tiredly. "I was thinking about driving back to the Village to see how Hansen's doing," he added.

"Come on, Adam." Carlin stood up, buttoned his overcoat. "He knows your frequency. He'd radio you with anything, you know that. You're getting more obsessive than usual. Why don't you give yourself a break? Go home."

"Is that an order?" Kane recalled saying he'd wrap up the case this week.

"No. Friendly advice." Carlin pulled his hat down over his brow and turned up his collar. "Make the Village scene, as they say, tomorrow. The weather's supposed to clear up a bit too." He held up his gloved hand to Kane in a parting salute.

Mockingly Kane gave him an actual one. "Aye, aye, sir." They frequently remembered they'd both been Navy, Carlin in Korea, Kane in Vietnam. An okay guy not to rub in "this week."

When Carlin was gone, Kane sat for a while staring out at the blackness of the night, listening to the wind. "Home" would be a rocky place tonight, in this weather. He sometimes wondered if he hadn't gone a little nuts when he'd chosen that place to live. Even for him it was a bit much.

But according to this maddening book—which had upset all his preconceived notions about his starry friends—that was just the kind of house he would choose.

Kane was getting hooked. He'd even checked out Perry Martial's birth date, which was exactly what he'd ask Eve's team to do on Monday, anyway. On the face of it Martial fell into a category that wasn't a Likely. But then the text had warned against such oversimplification. He'd have to leave that to the pros.

He was amazed with himself for checking out Eve Darcy's birth data, too. She was a Taurus—according to the know-it-all text, the "perfect match" for a Scorpio.

That was the only thing they'd told him he already knew. Kane packed it up and went down into the frozen night. The cold air was not stimulating now. Just lonely.

CHAPTER FOUR

"A whole new Eve. I like it," Iris complimented her on Monday morning.

Eve was armored in a sleek, all-business look to boost her confidence and morale. Her deep-black hair was smoothed back, and she was wearing her favorite black suit; with it her silk blouse, minutely checked in turquoise, magenta, and bright green, her flat silver earrings were striking.

"I *need* it," Eve confessed. "We might have a whole new problem."

"Betty."

"Too right, ducky. Clare called her yesterday to tell her what we've learned, then she called me. Clare said she took it very well; she's one gutsy lady. Betty said she's safer here than at home, which I agree with. But unfortunately she doesn't plan to tell her husband. And secrets like that, this early on, can make a lot of trouble between two people."

"Absolutely. So you think we haven't heard the last of it?" Iris asked.

"Not by a long shot. She's a typical Cancer—

more afraid of Bill's disapproval than a serial murderer," Eve remarked with a half-smile.

Betty came in a bit late, after Clare had returned from Computers. Iris went to her and hugged her, saying, "I think you're terrific."

"So do I," Eve added.

"I must admit I'm not overjoyed," Betty countered dryly, "but now I have an even more personal stake in this case." There was a determined glint in her deep-set eyes.

"Good for you." Eve squeezed her shoulder.

"So let's get to work," Betty said with a challenging air.

Going over the accumulated weekend mail, Eve thought, *I've got the cream of the crop working with me on this project.* She came upon a memo addressed to Eve Darcy from Adam Kane on a fresh suspect. *Maybe he's It,* she thought with renewed optimism. But she wanted to check it before telling the others. The memo was stamped *Priority* with Myers's careful blue stamp.

The memo contained birth date and available data on one Perry Martial, a new, hot suspect. Eve frowned in annoyance. The birth hour was missing, and he was born in Ames, Iowa. But he was evidently a steady customer of a Greenwich Village astrologer. Easy enough to check his chart with her.

She assigned that task to Iris. Clare and Betty were still deep in their own miniproject.

Martial was a Libra, Eve considered. And despite the dark aptness of his surname—probably made up, anyhow, legally changed to give an actor-model more glamor—she had a strong visceral feeling he wasn't right for a killer. Sure, it was unprofessional—plainly stupid—to assume too much from a sun sign, but her studies in astromurder had turned up damned few Libras.

Her inventive mind took off in another direction: murder methods according to sign. That, too, was quite an oversimplification, but it had helped solve the Star Slayings in Chicago. Virgos, for instance, inclined to poison; the sign was related to chemistry. Earth signs were more direct, preferring blunt instruments or strangling, Eve had discovered in the past. The fire signs were rash and impulsive, inclined to assault and battery, and the "firepower" of guns.

Water and air signs, especially Pisces, Cancer, and Gemini, were fonder of theft and fraud than of violence—except the violent, unforgiving sign Scorpio, who preferred sharp instruments to blunt ones.

She'd better keep it clinical, not go off on a tangent about one Scorpio in particular. But she kept harking back to Saturday night, to the feel of his arms around her.

Ironically she recalled a phrase from Piscean Elizabeth Barrett's poem to her Taurus lover, Robert Browning: "not death, but love." Eve Darcy's concern had to be the opposite: not love, but death. Violent death. And she made herself concentrate on the case again.

The Arien Star Slayer had beaten his victims to death. The Astro Killer chose to push his—or hers—to their death. Pushing suggested the directness of an earth sign, Taurus or Capricorn.

The earth sign Virgo, on the other hand, shrank from touching those hated. Poison kept a fastidious distance between a Virgo and a victim; that method was a Virgo specialty.

Yet the salient "weapons" in the Astro killings were the hands and arms. Gemini ruled those parts of the body. Sergeant Marnie Osborne was a Gemini, a strange, jealous, frustrated woman.

"Oh, for heaven's sake," Eve said, disgusted.

"What's the matter?" Iris asked as she took the readout of Perry Martial's chart.

"I'm riding madly off in all directions, like Don Quixote, finding suspects everywhere."

"Maybe that's the way to do it," Iris consoled her. "Besides, Quixote was a Pisces. He couldn't have been *all* wrong." She handed Eve Perry Martial's charts.

Eve looked them over. "Oh, swell. Aries rising, the sun sign's opposite. Really together." She flipped to the interpretation. "This astrologer's really sweetened the aspects, hoked it up. We can't go by this."

"I know her," Iris said fervently. "Heard her lecture. She made astrology sound like something the Easter bunny left in the grass for all good children. She's a Leo. Leos are more dramatic than accurate."

"Well, she sure laid an Easter egg here. A real show-biz job." In Eve's opinion the astrologer had smoothed over too much, invented strengths that just weren't there. "Let's go."

She and Iris combed the aspects, made corrections, did a thorough study of the stars.

Eve sighed when they were through. "I did her wrong. Martial *is* harmless."

"That's about what I make him." Iris sounded downcast. Betty was even more so. Naturally, Eve thought. A Probable would have been better for her morale than anyone's.

"I've got to get on this," Eve said. "The DC wants it by ten-thirty." She zipped out a report on the word processor and called Myers.

Angela Myers was apparently having a bad morning. She sounded grouchy and pressed. "I have no one to send right now," she snapped in her high, thin voice.

"Never mind," Eve answered calmly. "One of us will bring it up."

When she hung up Iris offered, "I'll take it to the old sourball."

Eve accepted gratefully. She wasn't looking forward to running into Kane. He was always in and out. And they hadn't said good-bye under easy circumstances. That was another very good reason for not getting involved at work, she told herself—one could never get away from the object of one's embarrassment.

She knew she was half fooling herself, though. Embarrassment was not what she'd been feeling for Adam Kane the last two days.

Then she made a firm resolution: no more wandering thoughts today. She was still haunted by last Friday's idea to investigate the old charts. It was just difficult enough to be daunting, even if it had been a decisive factor in nailing the Chicago killer. Eve was quite aware that New York was another matter—more than twice the population, consequently a much greater number of astrologers, more speed and pressure, and that old bugaboo, priceless physical space, so less old material and information was kept.

She almost dreaded bringing up the idea to Kane, but she would have to. She couldn't go over his head to Carlin, even if she'd wanted to. But he was already so opposed to her work she could imagine his reaction to a request for an additional mini-investigation to obtain the hard-to-get data.

Unless this project were carried out completely and methodically, however, it would have no value. They couldn't depend on random histories.

Damnation. Eve realized she'd already wasted the best part of the morning with all her worrying—the Martial thing had been accomplished with speed. She finally returned to the supply of new charts delivered Saturday afternoon.

At eleven-thirty her phone interrupted her work. It was Angela Myers, sounding almost chipper. "Will you hold for Inspector Kane?"

I did all weekend, Eve thought wryly. "Of course."

"I'm calling for Carlin, Ms. Darcy." His voice was quick and flat, and she was miffed that he hadn't even asked her how she was.

"Yes?" She answered in the same clipped tone.

"We're still waiting for the Martial report," he said curtly.

"Waiting?" Eve was so taken aback her tone climbed several decibels. "Iris brought it up to Ms. Myers at ten-fifteen," she added more evenly.

"What?" Kane's amazement was as obvious as hers. Eve glanced at Iris, who was staring. "Look here," Kane sounded abashed, warmer. "I'll check it out."

"Don't bother. Let me bring up another copy."

"I'll come down and get it myself," Kane said grimly, and Eve had a feeling that Angela Myers was in for a very bad time. Eve knew the Scorpionic temper.

Kane hung up before Eve could say anything else.

"Do you mean to tell me Myers lost that report?" Iris demanded, getting up and walking to Eve's desk. "I put it right in her stringy little hands."

Eve couldn't help laughing. Her Pisces teammate had a strong aversion to Angela Myers. Pisces and Virgo were zodiacal opposites, and could get on each other's nerves, unless they had a romantic, opposite-sex association, or a close friendship like Iris's with Clare.

"I believe you. You don't have to convince me." That was another interesting side to the Pisces-Virgo opposition: One would not think it of the dreamy Pisceans, but their sign shared Virgo's meticulous attention to detail. It was an astrological paradox that had always fascinated Eve.

Betty and Clare had heard the conversation

97

and had stopped in the midst of what they were doing.

"*I* think the witch lost it purposely," Betty averred. The most benign Cancerian had an instinct for malice matched only by Scorpio—and Betty could be right on target, Eve thought.

"It could be," she said reluctantly. "But that sounds so . . . freaky."

"She *is* a freak," Clare commented in her dry way. "I just *love* sharing her sign."

Eve was about to say something when she broke off. Kane was striding in. She immediately held out a copy of the report on Martial, and he took it from her.

"Thanks very much. Sorry about all the flap." Kane had not even looked at the others; his sharp, dark glance inventoried her swiftly, taking on an admiring gleam.

In spite of herself Eve felt her heart stop in her throat. She got her voice back in control. "Quite all right."

Almost before she'd spoken, he was gone.

He didn't check in with the team that evening, or the next, and Eve found that she had two more discouraging reports for Carlin. Kane phoned once to advise her that she'd been right about Martial. His men had checked the suspect out and he'd had unshakeable alibis for the times of all three murders. On two of the nights Martial had been at film "shoots" in the midst of an enormous crew; on the other he'd been onstage in a new off-off-Broadway play.

Eve's mild gratification was offset by her disturbing and continuing preoccupation with Adam Kane. She couldn't stop thinking of their abortive "date," the lonely weekend after. She knew in her very bones, from years of character study, that a man like Kane did not make overtures lightly.

She had hurt both his feelings and his mighty Scorpionic pride, dashing off as if he were something horrible in a cellar, full of clanking chains. He would not be likely to expose his feelings to her again anytime soon. And more and more she wanted him.

But she also had to remember why she was at Number One in the first place. They had only three weeks now before the next scheduled attack. That knowledge was getting to her, as it must be getting to the department. They must be working twenty-four hours a day—Kane had sounded exhausted when he phoned her.

In the interim there were plenty of other problems. Whatever Kane had said to Myers, it had made her even harder for the team to deal with. She continued to be obstructive in petty ways while taking care not to be actually remiss.

Myers began to say, "Hold on, please," automatically when any of the team phoned Carlin's office, to keep them waiting before she would talk to them. Simple requests, rare from the self-sufficient team to begin with, were treated as almost bizarre.

Eve wondered just what Myers had against them. She had nothing against astrology, that was obvious. Iris had noticed other tasteful Virgo artifacts on Myers's desk and once found her eagerly reading one of the "smarter" little manuals, as Iris put it.

On Wednesday Clare returned from a visit to the computer section looking indignant.

"What's up?" Eve demanded. Clare was so easygoing and self-contained, Eve knew that it took more than a trifle to upset her.

"It's so silly I'm ashamed to mention it."

"Mention it to me," Eve said tersely.

"It's that wretched Hansen. I usually just ignore him, but today he was really doing the lover-boy number. Well, I dealt with that"—smiling, Eve could imagine—"and then he said, 'I was just trying to be friendly. You can damned well wait for your job, then. I was going to let you go ahead of me.' And he said something to one of the other men about 'damned swellheaded broads,' that the whole bunch of us are 'trouble-makers,' and . . ." Clare flushed.

"And?"

"Really, something so unpleasant I can't even repeat it."

"Damn it, this is too much!" Eve's slow Taurean anger was coming to the boil. She'd heard a little off-color language from the blues in Chicago and learned to take it in stride. But it had never been directed at her and her colleagues. "I'm going to speak to Carlin about this," she said impulsively.

"Oh, Eve, *no.*" Clare was disturbed. "It's all so . . . trivial. We'll look like a bunch of babies."

Eve hesitated for a moment. "You're right. I

was going off half cocked," she admitted, grinning. "I'd just hung up with Myers when you walked in. I guess she lit my fuse . . . again. Let's just forget it, shall we?" *For the time being,* she added in resentful silence.

"Gladly." Clare shook her head and went back to work.

"How're you doing?" Eve was right in the middle of a thought when she heard Marnie Osborne's question from the door. She felt like answering grouchily, *As well as can be expected, with all the jerks we have to deal with.*

But she smiled, calling out, "Fine. And you?" There was something so childlike and needy about Osborne that Eve shrank from snubbing her.

"I've been better," Osborne offered, lingering at the door like a puppy. Her manner touched Eve, who remembered how friendly Osborne had been on that first day. Eve had meant to invite her to have lunch one day with Iris and herself, but there'd been so much going on it had slipped her mind.

"Come in and visit a minute," Eve invited.

"Well, *thanks,*" Osborne said. "I didn't want to bother you." She surveyed the office with her twinkly, curious blue eyes. Clare and Betty said hello, but Iris was so wrapped up in a chart she didn't look up. Eve saw Osborne's mouth tighten up.

Uh-oh. Eve wondered if Hansen was still pursuing Iris. Iris was so used to that she might not have mentioned it even if she noticed.

101

"Sit," she said agreeably to Osborne. "I'm ready for a little break, anyway. I came in an hour early this morning."

Osborne's avid gaze swept the charts on Eve's desk. "This must be fascinating."

"It is. But your work's not exactly dull, either," Eve said with a smile.

Marnie Osborne made a face. "I'd rather be out on the street. But the powers that be don't want me there. I flunked my inkblot test"—she gave Eve a stiff little smile—"for street duty."

"That's too bad." Eve offered her a cigarette. With a nervous glance toward the door Osborne took it and accepted Eve's light. "Isn't it pretty dangerous out there, though?"

"Sure." Osborne exhaled with pleasure. "But that's what makes life exciting . . . danger."

Probably what attracted her to the rotten Hansen, Eve thought. Uncertainty and danger. Osborne was a bit of a masochist, Eve decided.

"Angie says there's not much movement right now in the case," Osborne added. For an instant Eve hardly recognized the cutesy version of Myers's first name. So Osborne was on "Angie" terms with Myers, then. Interesting.

"That's about right. But we're still at it, slow and steady. Ms. Myers is in the center of things, though, isn't she?" Eve couldn't keep the ironic edge from her question.

Osborne studied her. "Has she been getting to you?"

"*No one* 'gets' to me, Sergeant," Eve said lightly. "Not when I have a job to do."

102

"Well, that's good," Osborne said, sounding doubtful. "Angie's all right, really. She's had a rough time of it. She . . ." Osborne looked at her watch. "Oh, I've gotta go." She jumped up. "Thanks for the smoke . . . and the talk, Eve."

"I enjoyed it, Marnie. I'll be seeing you."

Enjoyed it wasn't exactly true, Eve reflected when Osborne had gone. If she and Myers were so buddy-buddy, Eve wasn't sure she'd be a perfect lunch date for them. Her curiosity was piqued by Osborne's reference to Myers's "rough time." She'd certainly left a cliff-hanger, breaking off just when she did. And it was odd to consider danger the only thing that made life exciting. Eve couldn't help wondering what Osborne's inkblots had shown.

That afternoon Myers was again so savagely uncooperative that Eve made up her mind to have a private talk with her. She abhorred the tell-teacher gimmick of going over a person's head; she liked to face things head on, like an adult. Maybe she'd even surprise Myers by asking her out to lunch. That would be a barrel of laughs, Eve thought dryly.

But before she could arrange it, Eve was summoned to Carlin's office on Thursday morning. Maybe she'd be the one to be hauled up on the carpet; the team hadn't covered itself with glory, and perhaps the department had decided the team was a waste of money.

Eve was glad she looked especially nice, in a teal-blue suit and brick-red blouse, because it made her feel more on top of things, able to keep her cool. Why she thought she'd need it, she didn't know. But she had a feeling.

As soon as she announced herself to Angela Myers, Eve's feeling deepened. Myers looked as if she'd been dipped in bleach from head to toe, and faded. Her sallow skin and mousy hair were not enhanced by a dismal dress of gray-green.

Myers's sharp eyes swept over Eve, but she had a horribly cheerful intonation when she said, "Go right in. They're waiting for you." The implication that she was late was not lost on Eve, who was exactly two minutes early.

When she went in, she saw that Kane and Hansen were with Carlin. Two of them got to their feet; Hansen remained boorishly seated, and she saw Carlin shoot an irritated glance at him.

"Good morning," Carlin said genially, pulling out a chair for Eve. She smiled at him, sat, and said hello to the others. Adam Kane gave her an admiring and friendly look, and she felt a rush of warmth flood over her. It seemed like months since she'd seen him. She noticed Hansen's sensual lips curve into a smirk, and she looked quickly back at Carlin.

"Well, you and your team have been doing a fine job, Ms. Darcy," Carlin began. She could hear the "but" almost hovering on his mouth. "You've gone through an amazing amount of data. And you did a speedy job on that Martial matter." She waited.

"But," he added right on schedule, "Inspector Kane tells me there's some bad blood between your staff and mine."

"I'm afraid I don't understand," she said calmly. "Almost . . . everyone has been very cooperative." Eve glanced quickly at Kane. What was going on here?

"That's not what Adam said," Carlin remarked.

Surely a man like Kane wouldn't be petty enough to take out his personal pique on her professionally. That was more like Hansen, Eve thought in dismay.

"Damned right," Kane growled. "Myers lost that Martial report, not Ms. Darcy's team."

Eve understood then: Adam Kane was being the protective Scorpio, speaking *for* her. She didn't need any man to speak for her. He'd better learn that.

"But Ms. Darcy made no complaint, Adam. And I've never had any complaints about Angie before."

"That's because everybody gives her a wide berth," Kane retorted. "She's a"—Kane shot a dark glance at Eve and made an obvious amendment—"neurotic person."

"Come on, Adam." Carlin waved his hand. "I invited Ms. Darcy here to get her side of the story. What do *you* say?" he asked Eve.

This wasn't going to be easy. "I've always tried not to consider personalities in a job setting," she hedged. "As far as my team goes, we've gotten fine cooperation, generally. Ms. Myers has seemed . . . pressed lately."

"You should send her on a sabbatical, John

105

. . . for about ten years. She needs rest," Kane stated flatly.

Carlin ignored him. "Could you say that Angie Myers has been uncooperative, Ms. Darcy?"

"No, I couldn't," Eve said with reluctance.

"You've got a blind spot where that woman's concerned, John. I've told you that for years."

Carlin reddened with vexation after Kane spoke.

"The subject's closed. There is one other thing, Ms. Darcy. Lieutenant Hansen complains that your team members haven't been cooperative in the computer section . . . about priorities. That they've assumed their side of the investigation takes precedence over ours."

So that was Hansen's interpretation of the incident with Clare. Eve fumed. "That simply is not true, Commissioner."

Carlin looked at Kane, whose look said *I told you so.* The DC seemed uncomfortable. "I suppose there's just been a misunderstanding," he temporized.

"Misunderstanding, hell," Kane interjected. "Hansen couldn't score. That's the problem, that's what's behind all this."

Carlin was aghast. "I don't think there's any need to get so personal, Adam," he said repressively.

"Why not?" Hansen demanded angrily. "What we've got here is a personal problem. We can't all be monks, like the inspector here."

Eve looked at Kane. He was becoming very still. She knew that Scorpionic evidence of explosive anger building. He was like a snake getting ready to strike; she hoped he wasn't going to become physical. Kane didn't say a word. He just kept staring at Hansen, and Carlin moved restlessly in his chair.

"Besides," Hansen went on, "any 'trouble' is coming from that team. They've caused us more problems than any other consulting group ever did."

Now Eve was getting as angry as Kane. But she held on to her temper, and asked Hansen with a calm calculated to madden him, "Could you be more specific, Lieutenant?"

"I certainly can, Ms. Darcy. Angie Myers told me she can't get her regular work done, with all your unnecessary requests. And the guys in Computers reported your women don't know how to work their machines; there's always patch-in trouble."

"I'm afraid I don't understand the 'always,' Lieutenant." Eve was still managing to stay very cool. "I remember one incident, at the beginning, but that was neither the department's fault nor ours. The trouble was in the association's computers. I'd forgotten all about it," she needled softly.

She was surprised to see a look of sheer hatred in Hansen's blue eyes.

"And you should do the same," Kane snapped at Hansen. "It should be obvious, John, who's the troublemaker in this operation. Or the troublemakers. Hansen and Angela Myers."

Kane still looked as if he wanted to hit Hansen.

Eve devoutly hoped he wouldn't. Adam Kane was a lethal-looking man, with a heavyweight's build. He must weigh forty pounds more than the slender Hansen, she thought, all of it muscle.

"That's enough, Adam." Carlin looked extremely irritated. "I think we'll end this conversation right here. Thank you for coming, Ms. Darcy. I'm sorry I wasted so much of your time."

Taking his words as a dismissal, Eve stood up, murmuring a polite disclaimer. It certainly *had* been a waste of time. She heard Carlin tell Kane and Hansen to stay.

But when she opened the door and glimpsed Myers's face, she wasn't so sure the time had been totally wasted. At least Kane had brought Myers's enmity into the open.

Closing the door she caught a sharp question from Carlin, "What's eating you, Adam?"

And a quick retort from Hansen: "Too much monastery."

Eve shut the door softly. Through it she heard a thump, like a heavy chair falling over, Kane's deep voice raised in a pungent epithet, Carlin trying to smooth things over.

Avoiding Myers's eye, Eve walked through the outer office. At the door she glanced back.

Angela Myers was leaning forward in her chair, trying to take everything in.

She must have felt Eve's observation, then, because her narrow head, with its wispy hair, jerked around.

Their eyes met.

Angela Myers's pale gaze was vindictive and

triumphant. It said as plain as words, *You have no business here. And this proves it.*

Eve gave her a calm, deliberate smile and walked out.

The whole conference in Carlin's office had shaken her up thoroughly, but Eve was proud of her bland exterior. She considered that as she rode down in the elevator. Studying in England had taught her more than astrology. It had also taught her the value of a poker face.

Eve was practically grinning when she walked back into the office.

"Was it a good canary? What's up?" Iris queried. Clare was out of the office. Betty looked up from her printout with interest.

"God save the Queen and poker faces," Eve said enigmatically. When she sat down she filled them in on the conference.

"What is the matter with Myers and Hansen?" Betty demanded.

"Come on, Betty," Iris teased her. "We don't have enough time to list all their problems. You've got to go to lunch at noon."

Eve and Betty laughed.

"It's all a pack of nonsense," Eve said. "Anyway, I have a strong feeling Carlin's going to straighten out Hansen, one way or the other."

In a little while the very silliness of the whole thing made Eve dismiss it. They were doing a more intensive study of another angle to the case —the cultist leanings in both clients and astrologers—and she found it fascinating.

What she couldn't dismiss, what kept intruding on her thoughts, was this other Adam Kane who'd revealed himself in Carlin's office. Angry and outspoken, he certainly didn't watch his words with his superior. She liked that.

Protective toward her and the team, just as strongly as he'd first opposed their hiring. Kane was extraordinarily complex, even for a Scorpio.

The thing she remembered most vividly, though, was Hansen's obnoxious comment about a "monastery." Clearly Kane had to be a very selective man.

And he had selected her. Hansen must have guessed that, considering the way he'd smirked at them in the conference.

The whole idea filled her with warm confusion. She had a strong desire to thank Kane for his defense of her; at least she could do that.

Suddenly she wanted to be alone, out in the sun, not to be lunching indoors with Iris today, much as she enjoyed her company.

"I'm feeling a little cabin fever," she said to Iris. "Mind if I skip lunch with you today?"

"Not at all. I wanted to do some shopping anyway."

"Great. I think I'll go out now." Eve got her coat and went out, comfortably ahead of lunchtime crowds, and walked to City Hall park, the big green space studded with old trees which was a favorite resting place for downtowners.

The mercurial New York weather was warming again and Eve unbuttoned her coat, feeling less restless already when she smelled the grass and trees. The park was a piece of country right in the midst of the exciting city; beyond the grass she watched busy traffic stream up Broadway, lifted her gaze to the tall Gothic beauty of the Woolworth Building.

She realized she'd been too pressed and hurried lately to look at much of anything.

For no light reason: the Astro Killer was still free. He could be sitting on one of these benches now, and Eve would not even know. The dark, oppressive notion chilled her, took a little brightness from the sun.

The ever-cautious Betty had reminded Eve not to stand too near the curb when she was about the cross the street. The killer could just as well shove a victim in front of a truck or car, despite the previous pattern of murder on public transportation.

Eve remembered she hadn't reported to her "shadows." And even though Iris would, Eve hadn't told Iris where she was going.

This was ridiculous. It was broad daylight and there were always policemen around City Hall, the city's heart, where people demonstrated against something or other all the time.

Nevertheless the park had suddenly lost its appeal. She looked around. A big, tall man in a tan overcoat and dark-brown hat was walking in her direction.

When he got nearer he smiled at her and raised his hand. She returned his wave.

"Inspector." Eve looked up at him, smiling, shading her eyes from the sun.

"I thought we'd passed Go," he retorted, as he sat down next to her on the bench. "It's Adam. Remember?"

"Adam." His huge shoulder was just at the level of her eyes. She looked up again at his face.

"That's a lot better." His hat brim shaded his dark, penetrating eyes, but where the light struck his skin, she could see fine lines around his mouth that she hadn't seen before. He looked even more rugged and impressive in the light of day, and his nearness was as reassuring as a safe house. "I followed you," he said abruptly. "I figured you might need to be alone for a bit, so I've been loitering. Several women found me very suspicious."

He grinned and she laughed out loud. If she had expected anything, it hadn't been quite this.

"You handle yourself very well at curbs." He sobered, and suddenly things weren't laughable. "I know you must feel pent up, restricted," he went on. "But please, try not to run off without letting someone know. It was the sheerest luck that I found you. As far as I'm concerned, there are no guarantees, or schedules, in murder, Eve. I feel better when I know what you had for lunch and where you went shopping." He was trying to be light, but his tone was serious.

"I'm sorry," she said, meaning it. "As a matter of fact, I was thinking about that very thing when I saw you. And I'm very glad to see you."

His expression did not change, but his eyes glittered. "Glad to see a friend with the difference?" His overcoat was unbuttoned, thrown back, and she was conscious of the bulge under his jacket. "Difference" meant a gun; he wore his on a snap holster on his belt.

Eve felt her face warm up. "Glad to see a friend, period." He made a sudden, restless movement and she wondered if that meant he wanted to touch her. She had a very overpowering desire to touch him. Steadying her voice she added, "I wanted to thank you for . . . speaking up for us in the DC's office."

"Oh, Lord, *that.*" He chuckled, raising both hands and bringing them down on his knees. "Of all the idiotic . . . you were great. Very cool and collected, veddy English."

She was surprised at how much his compliment pleased her. Touched, also, that he'd remembered her telling him she'd studied in London. She'd only mentioned it once.

"What a memory, Inspec—Adam."

"Good, you're learning," he teased her, and grinned. The smile made him look much more open. Vulnerable. Human. "I remember everything about you, Eve." His quick seriousness moved her. "You know, you just thanked me— for nothing much—and I came here to make my third apology." His intonation was self-mocking. "The first two were for being a bear, the third is for being an ape."

She had to laugh, in spite of his earnest expression. "An *ape?*"

"That night, after dinner. Just because you were sweet enough to let me kiss you, I . . . I assumed a bit too much. I'm sorry. I got very

113

carried away. Do you think we could start again? If I promise to act like a civilized human being?"

She looked up into his eyes, and they had no resemblance to hard coal, as they had that first afternoon. And they were not hot and bright with greedy wanting. They were deep and tender, and in the brightness she saw golden-brown shadows in them.

She wanted to say, *I'd like to kiss you right now, and civilization be damned.* But she didn't. In the first place she was far too conservative for that, and in the second, she was sharply aware of his Scorpionic fastidiousness, his proud need to be the prime mover.

So she merely smiled, and nodded. "I think that's a lovely idea."

"That's great. That's wonderful." He took her hand. Her response to the simple touch was astonishing. She could feel a dart of hot lightning shoot up her arm, just from that slight pressure of their two gloved hands, and her entire body felt like liquid sun.

Nothing in her life had ever happened just like this before. It was positively astounding; she was almost frightened of being moved so much. *But it's too late now,* she reflected. *It's happened. We've hardly known each other any time at all, and yet already I can't imagine not touching him, not being near this man.*

"What would you say to a real old-fashioned 'date'?" he asked her eagerly. "Will I be lucky enough to hear you're free tonight?"

"Perfectly."

114

"Fantastic." He squeezed her hand. "Even a cop gets time off for bad behavior, and tonight happens to be my night."

"I take it that has something to do with Hansen. I heard."

He twinkled at her, looking caught out but very pleased at the same time. "Carlin said *I* need R and R, not Myers."

"What did you *do?*" she demanded, smiling.

"Just emphasized my point. Nothing much. But let's get onto a pleasanter subject. For some reason—probably hope—I bought two tickets to a piano recital. Rachmaninoff . . . Chopin . . ."

"Oooh . . . and Copland! Ferrau is playing."

He beamed. "None other. You *would* like it, then."

"*Like* it? I'd slipped up, didn't get tickets." She loved music so much, and this was another bond between them.

"Now, about dinner . . ."

"*Light,* please. I hate to feel like a stuffed crocodile when I'm trying to hear Chopin. Don't you?"

"Yes." He looked at her. "I can't believe this."

She knew what he meant. "Neither can I." Eve had a feeling that her eyes were saying all the things she hadn't.

They agreed to go to dinner direct from Number One, and he walked her back to the office. The encounter in the park seemed to have opened a kind of floodgate in both of them; they couldn't stop talking.

Adam left her reluctantly at her office door and hurried back downstairs.

Betty and Clare were gone, Iris intently at work, when Eve walked in glowing.

"Well, *that* was quick," Iris marveled. "What was lunch, a peanut?" She studied Eve intently. "No . . . a *makeover*. What happened to you? You look reborn."

"One thing that happened was forgetting lunch." Eve had totally forgotten it, and so had Adam. Shaking her head over her own giddiness she phoned for a sandwich.

"You can't *do* this to me," Iris protested.

"Do what?"

"Leave me hanging. When a woman looks like that, there's got to be a man in it." Iris was observing her with eager, friendly curiosity. She was such a total romantic, Eve thought with amusement. "Wretched, closemouthed Taurus Mercury," Iris scolded.

Eve couldn't withstand her. "All right, all right. Maybe there *is* a man," she admitted.

"Kane?" Iris prodded. There was nothing officious about her inquisitive guess—it was too enthusiastic and childlike to offend. "It's *Kane*. Goodie. I think he's fabulous. He reminds me of a big, young Humphrey Bogart. I was bowled over by him myself, at first, until I met Pete."

"Pete? Iris, I can't keep up with you." Eve grinned at her teammate.

"I've just met him, and he's delicious. A Virgo. You can't imagine how long I've been waiting for a Virgo, Eve."

116

"I think I can," Eve said softly, thinking of her own "opposite," Adam Kane. It was pleasant to let go of her reticence a little, with the affectionate, sympathetic Iris. Eve had always been "closemouthed" about her private affairs. "I'm glad for you."

And glad for me, she added silently after Iris had gone out and the others had returned.

She went back to her project in a kind of absentminded wonder: right at that moment the Astro Killer didn't seem quite real.

The only thing that did was the coming appointment with Inspector Adam Kane.

CHAPTER FIVE

There were times, Eve decided, when life and the city lived up to every expectation. And tonight was one of them.

She and Kane were heading down the FDR Drive, with its dark, shining vista of the East River, its heart-stopping view of the castles of Lower Manhattan glittering in charcoal and silver at the end of the Drive.

Neither Eve nor Adam had said a word after the dazzling concert. They'd just looked at each other, glowing from the music in silent and companionable agreement. Their silence now had another quality, an aura of excitement, anticipation; she had felt those emotions building in both of them the whole evening.

Eve could almost touch the tension-edged quiet. Their conversation had been spare, weighted with feeling they had not expressed. She remembered how dark his eyes had looked against the restaurant's rosy walls lined with gilded cages full of doves . . . the symbol of Venus . . . the "dove of Mars"; Ferrau playing Chopin, a water sign like Adam.

They were nearer the shining downtown castles. Eve wanted to break the silence, but she was shy of repeating her thoughts just then. "New York is on its best behavior."

He nodded, glancing at her. "When New York is beautiful, it's beautiful enough to . . . break your heart."

His openness, his gentle intonation, stirred her.

They slowed for the exit and it was quieter in the car, quiet enough for her to answer softly. "It must be hard for someone who loves the city to . . . do your job."

Kane slowed. They were driving almost lazily toward Number One.

"It is, Eve. You're very sensitive to see that. My job brings me in contact with the worst of the city. But I feel that I'm . . . fighting to keep it the way it should be. Like tonight."

He pulled up beside her car in the plaza, looking down at her. The light glittered in his intense black eyes.

"It was perfect," she said.

He was silent. A half-smile curved his mouth, and she could swear she heard him thinking, *Almost:* they were going to say good-night.

Then he said it aloud. "Almost. I'll see you to your car."

He'd meant it, about acting "civilized," and she was sorry. More than anything at that moment she'd wanted him to kiss her.

He got out and opened the door for her,

walked close beside her to her car, looked in the back and even in the trunk. Stooping down he ran his hands over the tires.

Looking for what—an explosive?

Eve shivered. In the midst of her pleasurable excitement, the twinge of their imminent parting, she saw the shadow of the killer. For hours and hours Kane's presence had exercised such magic over her senses, she had totally put the murders from her mind.

"All right," he said, standing. "You're perfect." Kane smiled, staring down into her face. "In more ways than one, Eve Darcy." She couldn't take her eyes from his. "Look here. Why don't I shadow you home?"

"I'd like that." She was growing more and more reluctant to say good-night.

His smile lit up his austere face. After she'd gotten into her car, she saw him take out a small radio, speak into it.

He was "taking Astro One."

Indeed, he already had, in many ways. Eve smiled to herself as she drove away and onto the bridge. Adam Kane had taken her by storm. All the way over the bridge she could glimpse his car in her rearview mirror; she was feeling light and high as a new balloon, and the view of downtown Manhattan, scintillant in the dark, was a perfect extension of the dreamlike evening they had spent together.

By the time she parked on Sidney Place, he was already out of his car, walking toward her.

And she knew, with utter certainty, how the night must end.

"Please," she said when he opened her door. "Come in."

"I was planning to. I want to check out your place for you," he said matter-of-factly. "Nice," he added, glancing up at the façade of the small white house.

Eve smiled to herself. He assumed she'd invited him in just for protection.

When they stepped into her living room, he looked around with an appreciative eye. "This is lovely." Then, he asked, "May I?"

"Of course." He opened the closet doors, looked in the other rooms. When he came back, he said, "It all looks fine."

"May I give you a drink . . . or must you go right away?"

He hesitated an instant. Eve was amused at her own perversity; when he had pleaded with her to be with him, she had run away. Now that he seemed less eager, she was eager for him to stay. "Thanks. I'd like that. Bourbon, if you have it. Anything." He smiled, taking off his hat and coat, resting them over a chair.

She registered that gesture—it meant he wouldn't be staying long. Eve slid back one of the ivory doors and made him his drink, pouring a small glass of sherry for herself.

He stood with his drink in his hand. "Make yourself comfortable," she said. "I'll put on some more Ferrau, if you'd like that."

"I'd love that." He didn't sit down yet, but

sipped his drink standing, surveying her pretty, serene living room. "I like your taste in everything," he murmured.

When she sat on the couch, he joined her. He ran a big hand over his sandy hair and then rested it on his leg, careful not to touch her. "Thank you for a beautiful evening," he said softly. "It's been years since I've . . . enjoyed anything so much."

"It was good for *me*, Adam. Very good." She leaned back, letting the sweetness of the Rachmaninoff concerto wash over her senses, languid but aroused.

Her hand lay on the couch by her side, near Kane's. Their fingers brushed, and she felt his strong hand enclosing hers, holding it tightly.

The same swift fire, the turbulent feeling that had assailed her in the afternoon, sang in her flesh again, and she knew that he could feel in the very submission of her hand to his the greater, more total submission of her body.

Kane raised her hand to his mouth. Turning it over slowly he kissed the palm, and her skin ignited; her whole heart seemed to fill her throat. She could not have uttered a word even if she had wanted to. It was the most total feeling she had ever known. She was swept along on the feeling, overwhelmed by it.

She turned her head to look at his face. In the dimness, which she had not brightened, his eyes were openly pleading. The eyes no longer glittered. They blazed, blazed with the rushing hotness that infused her veins, and she made a sound of hopeless longing, moving close to him.

Kane let go of her hand abruptly, closing her in his powerful arms. Her languorous lids descended, and with half-blurred vision she perceived his black, mesmeric eyes grow larger, larger, blotting out the room, the world, the light, until she drowned in them. Her mouth was under his; he was kissing her with a new and wild, triumphant hungering.

This kiss was nothing like the first, not tentative or pleading: it possessed her, as if their bodies were already meeting, in the final and explosive joy.

He raised his mouth, and said her name, just once, in slow, bedazzled wonder.

Then he drew back slightly, looking down into her face, and his eyes were anxious, solemn. "Eve, I don't want to come on like a Hun again . . . the way I did before. You mean so much to me, already, that I'd hate to . . . scare you away."

She shook her head. "You can't . . . not now."

The tenderness of it moved her to slide her arms around his warm, hard-muscled neck and run her fingers up the back of his proud head. The feel of his brief, soft, prickly hair aroused her strangely, and she moved nearer into his embrace while his hands stroked her trembling sides and found her breasts.

Now there could be no turning back: she was driven by a sweet, wild need, a scalding demand, stronger than anything that she had ever known or even dreamed of, and her hands seemed to assume a bold life of their own, stroking, discovering, caressing, until he cried out her name again.

"Come, darling. Eve. Come with me." Holding both her hands in his, he coaxed her gently to stand, walking close by her side into the shining bedroom, as dimly lit as the other. Smiling, he turned off the single lamp and with even gentler hands took off her darkly vivid jacket and put it on a chair. Then he stood back to survey her in the soft light streaming in from the other room, letting his gaze wander over her curving body in its silky blouse and narrow skirt. "Don't move," he ordered, kneeling down to remove one shoe, and then the other, rising to take her close to him again.

With careful touches he unfastened her skirt and she let it fall. Then he unbuttoned her blouse and laid it over her jacket, drawing in a delighted breath.

She was wearing a brilliant satin slip the color of terra-cotta, and he whispered, "You look like fire. So warm . . . so warm." He peeled her pantyhose away.

His caressing hands urged her to the bed; she sat down on its edge, looking up at him in wondering pleasure while he stroked her shoulders, persuading the tiny straps to descend.

Her slip fell away from her vibrant breasts, and he took another hasty, indrawn breath. Sitting beside her he lowered his head and let his shaky mouth meander over their richness. The soft slip fell below her waist. She lay back, trembling as he lifted her body to free her of the satin.

Eve closed her eyes, listening to the swift rustle of his discarded clothes. When she opened them again he stood above her naked.

His body was massive perfection: not an ounce of spare flesh marred it anywhere, from the breadth of the shoulders to the corded waist and narrow haunches, from the hard belly to the powerful legs.

She raised her eyes to his proud, shapely head, and in the half-light the dark stare gleamed upon her own bare body. "So beautiful, you are so beautiful," he breathed, before he lowered himself slowly down.

He took her body in his big hands, holding her with a firm yet careful strength, with a superb control that made his grasp viselike and still incomparably gentle. His mouth began a titillating journey over all her skin, and she almost cried out with yearning until his journeying lips had found her center, beginning a long and skilled caress that evoked unnamed desires. He brought her surely upward, to a height of such sharp pleasuring, of such ecstatic power, that she could not contain the cries of joyful wonder torn from her body's profoundest depths.

Resonant, shaken, she perceived that his urgent touch upon her was a signal of his pained and unappeased desire; his fingers had a fever in them. With sweet haste she drew him toward her, until their bodies clasped and blended. His rhythmic madness was arousing her, to her amazement, to still another transport of irreversible and tender lusting. This time, this magic time, they approached and longed and found at last their joy together. His cries of pleasure, the shattering release of a gigantic need, moved her to an even greater tenderness. They lay close together, and he enfolded her in his massive arms. She had a sense of utter fulfillment, complete and total peace.

It was glorious, how big and sheltering he was. She was not a little woman, by any means, but his size and power were so great that now for the first time in her life she felt small and fragile. It was intoxicating.

He kissed her brow and hair with many small, tender, grateful kisses, as if to thank her for the wondrousness of what she had given. The caresses deepened her melting tenderness, and with every touch upon each other they seemed to grow closer and closer in their minds.

"The marriage of true minds," she murmured. Her face was buried in his chest. She could sense the quick reaction of his sensitized flesh to the warmth of her lips and breath against it.

He pressed her closer to him and fondled her head. "What did you say, my darling?"

Eve raised her head a little and repeated it.

"Oh, Eve." Adam kissed her with slow sweetness, making her feel like vapor. "I thought that from the very first, from the minute you walked into that office, and I saw your beautiful, stubborn face, and those cool, sexy eyes. I thought,

That's exactly my kind of woman." He chuckled softly, and she burrowed nearer, and his arms tightened more.

He was still exercising that controlled strength that he had before; she found it remarkable. "So did I. So did I," she said.

"What? Think that I was just your kind of woman?"

She laughed at the acerbic Scorpionic humor, realizing, too, the tribute in his teasing—he felt close enough to her already to do that. "You know what I mean." She struck him playfully on his bicep with her fisted hand—and it hurt her. "Oh!"

Alerted, he asked her anxiously what the matter was.

"That hurt my hand. Do you believe it?"

"Oh, Eve." He lifted her hand in his and kissed it. "That's awful." He kissed the hand again.

"I'll have to be careful with you, I see that. It's like hitting a rock." All of a sudden she was newly aroused by his massive strength; it was thrilling. Astounded, she realized that she was excited all over again.

Something strange and wild in her made her press her body against his, and she was speaking to him without a single word; her flesh called out to his, and she could sense his eager response.

This time they came together with a sharp, swift hunger different from anything that had come before. And yet in this one crowded hour she felt their bodies had become familiar, that they knew each other deeply, prematurely, in a way that made it all seemed fated, meant to happen.

Overcome, they lay apart a little, holding each other's hands, allowing their swift breaths to slacken as the breathing slows from drowsiness to velvet sleep.

Before their sleep washed over them like a rhythmic tide, she felt him draw her near again and fold her in his arms.

When Eve woke it was still dark beyond the curtains, sometime in the middle of the night. Adam was propped on pillows, staring at her fondly through the gray haze of smoke from his cigarette. A small, dim lamp was on in a far corner; by its rosy light his face was as familiar and dear as that of someone she'd known her whole life.

"My darling. You're so pretty, asleep." He put out his cigarette and leaned toward her, kissing her.

"It's wonderful to wake up and see you there, Adam. I feel as if . . ." She stopped, feeling shy.

"As if we belong here." His dark eyes were softer than she'd ever seen them, profoundly serious. "We do, Eve."

When he said that, she was sure, sure of him as she had never hoped to be. For him, as for her, this was far more than the encounter of one impetuous night. The depth of his emotion was plain in his voice, the touch of his big fingers on her face, the brightness in his deep black eyes.

"Yes. Yes, Adam, we do."

"Oh, Eve." He gathered her into his embrace.

"I was thinking . . . I should leave you, let you sleep. It's very late, and I've got to get up so early. I hate the thought of waking you. But I don't want to go. I can't imagine being away from you."

"You mustn't go. I couldn't bear it. Stay, Adam. Stay with me. Things like that don't matter, you must know that." His thoughtfulness of her, the deep yearning in him to be with her, moved her unbearably. "I can't imagine, either," she confessed.

The solemnity of their kiss, after that, was so profound and heavy it was close to pain, and when his arms held her, they were desperate with feeling.

"Besides," she said, smiling, to lighten the moment, "you're starving . . . aren't you?"

He leaned back. His eyes brightened and his face relaxed. "How did you know?"

"Because I am too."

He gazed at her, and ran a finger lightly down the side of her face. "How did you know I was feeling so much, just then, that I couldn't have taken any more . . . that one more minute of that would just have . . ." He paused, and she could see a film of moisture over the darkness of his eyes.

She cupped his cheeks with her hands; he turned his head from side to side, kissing one hand, then the other. "I just . . . knew," she whispered.

"That book was right." Adam shook two cigarettes from his pack, offering her one.

She nodded and leaned for his light. "What book?"

When he told her about the book he'd bought at Keiser's, she was flabbergasted. The skeptical Inspector Kane, actually giving some credence to astrology!

"I can't believe it!"

"Believe it. I couldn't argue with evidence like that." He balanced an ashtray on his stomach and gestured to her to lean against him. There was something so companionable between them now that he felt like her husband.

She told him about her discovery of the planetary laws, of her own early skepticism, as obdurate as his. "I demanded evidence," she teased him. "Which should appeal to you, Inspector."

"It does." He laughed. "But I don't need any more evidence than this." He kissed her lightly, then his mouth lingered.

"And we're still starving. If you'll get me something to wear, I'll make you something to eat." She wasn't used to this; she felt absurdly exposed.

"Something to wear?" he mocked her. "What's wrong with what you have on, now?" He leered at the hollow between her quilt-covered breasts. "I'm teasing you. I like your shyness—it's very sweet. Where do I find something?"

She indicated the closet. "This end."

He got up at once, and she admired his hard and powerful body in his briefs as he strode to the closet and chose a terra-cotta robe. "I'm always going to have a thing about this color." He

131

grinned when he handed it to her. "After seeing you in that little shiny red thing for the very first time."

She giggled at his male description of the slip and got into her robe. "Now, with your permission, I'll shower first."

"Go right ahead. I'll just lie here and count my blessings." Before she left the room, Eve glanced back at him, sprawled out on the bed, following her eagerly with his eyes.

When she came out of the bath and went into the kitchen, she heard him turn on the shower. She was starting the coffee, breaking eggs, and preparing ingredients for an omelette, when he started singing. She smiled.

His voice, so beautiful in speech, was horrendous singing.

The coffee was ready and she was just putting the omelette mixture into the pan when he came into the kitchen, filling the compact space with his size. "If you can survive my singing, we've got it made." He came up behind her and put his arms around her waist.

"If you molest the cook, I'll never get *this* made," she retorted fondly.

"I'll behave." He sat down at the table. "Is this my coffee?"

"It's not for my shadows."

There was a brief, significant silence. As she served their omelettes, she looked at him questioningly. "What did I say?"

He looked a little abashed. "I was just thinking —the cat's out of the bag now, for sure. When I

132

said I was 'taking Astro One,' I didn't hope for anything like this. I just hope it won't . . . embarrass you with the 'shadows.' "

He sounded so concerned that after she'd set his plate before him, Eve took his head in her hands. He leaned against her, and when she stroked his head and brow he sighed with deep, grateful pleasure. "I don't embarrass easily," she said. "And the business of my heart is no one else's but mine . . . and yours."

"Your heart." He raised his hands to cover hers. "You're quite a woman. You make me feel so damned . . . fortunate. I can't tell you. I just can't *tell* you."

There was another poignant silence. "I can't, either, Adam Kane." Eve thought she was going to cry.

To save them again she added quickly, "Eat your food." Patting him she walked around the table and sat down.

With the first ravenous bite he said, "This is fantastic. You cook *too?*" His expression was comical.

"Doesn't everybody?"

"No," he said fervently, wolfing the rest. She made more toast and got out more jam.

After they finished eating, he shook his head. "I don't believe you, lady." He reached across the table and took her hand.

"I can tell you now," she confessed abruptly.

"What?"

"One of the first things I wondered was what it would be like to cook for you. Of course, the

Columbine's a hard act to follow." And she told him about the doves, and their symbolism, about "The Dove of Mars" in the novel she'd reread the night she'd run away from him.

"That's beautiful," he said soberly. "In fact everything about you, about this, has been beautiful. I still can't quite believe it's happened, that we're sitting here." His face darkened. "Or that it was . . . murder that brought us together."

"It just struck me how strange it is, Adam—when we've been alone together, we've never talked about the case."

"I've never wanted to," he admitted. "We can't escape the fact that you're intimately involved." His smile was ironic. "My main concern now, as far as *you* go, is just taking care of you." Adam reached across the table again, stroking her hand, her wrist, her arm. "Protecting you. Not only from . . . danger." She felt he was reluctant to say the other word, just now. The ugly word "murder."

"I've wanted to protect you from ugliness," he went on in an earnest way that made her feel tender all over again. "To . . . keep this apart from everything that's sick and brutal in the world. Maybe I've had enough of it myself." That sounded so weary she felt new compassion for him.

"I understand. I really do, Adam. And you must be tired—you haven't had much sleep."

His eyes were tender, but at half-mast. "I am tired," he admitted.

Eve got up and went to his side of the table, pulling at him. He laughed.

"You'll never make it," he teased her. "You'd need a crane."

"Go to bed. Right now," she ordered. "I'll be right with you."

He got up, looking really tired. "Alone? Never."

"Not for long," she promised.

"I think I will, then."

Rapidly she cleared the table, put the dishes in the dishwasher, and followed.

"Now I can sleep," he said drowsily, smiling at her from the bed. She turned out the one dim light, slipped into a nightgown, and got into bed beside him.

His arms enclosed her, drawing her close to him again: she felt the most perfect happiness that she had ever known.

When she woke a couple of hours later to dim, gray morning light the first thing she saw was a pair of bright black eyes. Adam was bending over her, fully dressed, about to kiss her. She smiled, putting her arms around his neck, returning the kiss with fervor and delight.

"What time is it?" she murmured drowsily. He sat down on the bed.

"Time for me to leave."

She couldn't believe how energized he looked; they'd slept very little, but he was showing that Scorpionic vitality.

"I hate like hell to go," he added, bending to her for another long kiss. "Go back to sleep, dar-

135

ling. I'll call you later. Maybe with luck we can go to lunch."

"I'd love that," she murmured drowsily.

After a swift touch on her tumbled hair he got up with reluctance and walked to the bedroom door, where he turned and kissed his fingers to her.

The bed seemed very empty without him. But after she heard the front door close, listening to him try it to be sure it was locked, Eve's sleepiness overcame her, and she drifted off again.

When her alarm woke her, she felt positively reborn, her whole body calm, her mind alert and happy. She padded to the window to check the day: it was dark and gray, with the promise of more snow.

But she couldn't care less, not this morning. Everything had a new brightness because of the night before. As she went about her morning preparations, she relived every moment of their sweet, close time together, feeling fresh energy pour into her body just as it had into his.

She put on her apple-red dress again, and its warm matching coat, with dark-gray accessories. Appropriate, she decided, smiling. Apple-red for Adam and Eve. It was amazing how the hokey happenstance of their first names was suddenly not a joke—a comedy when they were adversaries —but sweetly apt now.

At Number One her good-morning to the others practically sang. The clear-sighted Clare and the romantic Iris observed her with warm empathy. But Betty was in one of her moody lunar phases and seemed uneasy. Eve had a feeling Betty wasn't going to last, but even that thought couldn't disturb her.

She was elated when their cultist study turned up some promising leads and immediately prepared a memo for Adam and Carlin. This time when she phoned Myers, a young blue appeared almost at once to pick up the message; this made Eve feel even more elated. There must have been a mild shakeup in the DC's office, all very much to the good.

About eleven-thirty Adam phoned. "How are you?" His voice was so quiet and tender she could feel it on her skin, like his hands.

"Absolutely splendid. And you? Walking in your sleep?" Eve was speaking very low. She heard his deep chuckle.

"Just about. I'm afraid lunch is no-go, and it's all your fault. Carlin liked your cult clues so much they're going to be followed up right now. Which means I'll be eating pizza in the Village, if I'm lucky."

"Sorry about that, Inspector."

"Lady, you don't have to be sorry about *anything*. You've made my year." Her heart swelled; he sounded so happy.

"You've done the same."

"Darling, I may be very late tonight. I want to see you so damned much, but I don't want to leave you hanging. Maybe tonight I should just call you?"

"I want to see you. Whenever," she answered boldly. "Don't just call, Inspector."

137

"You're great. The whole day has just turned around. I will call you at home, though, to give you a ball-park figure." His tone carried a smile.

"I'm looking forward to it."

She hung up in a glow. For the first time since she'd started the project, the day seemed to drag. When at last it was over, and she was back in her own neighborhood, she decided to cook something very special that could be kept warm to welcome him with.

The evening had grown quite wild: a strong wind swept in from the harbor. Her place would have a special coziness tonight.

Eve noticed a clean-cut man following her on her errands; he had to be one of the watchdogs. She glanced at him covertly, not wanting to blow his cover, and gauged his air of competent alertness. Her shadow, for sure. She was sorry he had such a detail—following her around in such weather—but she wasn't going to cut any corners, not tonight.

She bought the ingredients for her special salad and her famous stew. She lingered over the choice of red wine, and then picked up some bright-gold candles and an enormous mass of greenery with berries the vivid color of bittersweet, and drove back home.

She had a grand time arranging the berry branches in the living room and bedroom—they looked magnificent with the bright star-burst quilt and pine-green pillows. She put the new gold candles in brass and pewter candlesticks and plunged into her favorite avocation, preparing salad, starting the hearty stew. After arranging petit fours on an ivory plate, she lazed in a long bubble bath and washed and blow-dried her hair.

Surprised that it was already nine-thirty, she glanced guiltily at the stuffed, zipped briefcase in her home office. The idea of work had never seemed so uninviting.

I'm entitled, she told herself. *It's been too long since I've had the fun of being "just" a woman.*

So she put the briefcase in one of the ivory cabinets and firmly slid the door closed. Back in the bedroom she looked over her lounge dresses and chose one of medieval simplicity, with a soft cowl neck, in vivid teal. Then she slipped Australian opal ear-studs into her lobes. Paying careful attention to her light makeup and her hair, she judged herself ready.

When the phone rang about ten-fifteen, she was stretched out on the couch reading.

"Hello, sweetheart." Her heart lifted when she heard his deep voice. "How are you?"

"Very eager to see you."

"Wonderful. I'll be there in a half hour. I'll give you three rings."

Her warm glow, when she hung up, had a tarnished edge. For all those happy hours she'd totally forgotten that ever-present danger. They must stop the Astro Killer soon, put an end to this horrible dread—not only hers but all the others'.

Still, when she heard his three sharp rings at the door, Eve resolved to think of nothing else but this lovely night, and Adam.

She lit the candles and went joyfully to the door. When she opened it he towered there above her, looking exhausted but also very glad. His hat and coat were dusted with melting snow.

"Eve, you look *beautiful,*" he murmured as he closed the door. "I'm so wet. Let me get rid of these things." His eyes shone at her. He leaned forward and gave her a swift, warm kiss.

He took off his things and put them in the closet. Turning back to her eagerly, he grabbed her in his arms, holding her so close she could feel every contour of his hard, vital body. It seemed to resonate with new desire.

"I thought of you all day," he whispered against her hair, "everywhere I went. Eve, everything I saw reminded me of you."

She felt her own body's melting response and whispered against his neck, with soft teasing, "I take it, then, my beautiful dinner will have to wait."

He drew back, smiling down at her. "Dinner? You're too good to be true. But as a matter of fact it could wait a little."

With his arm tight around her waist they walked into the bedroom, where she turned out all the lights except for the candles. Their love, this night, had a familiar sweetness under the high excitement.

Afterward they dined with lazy enjoyment, savoring the rich red wine by candlelight, and he observed the beauty and the peace around them with deep contentment. She saw that he was heavy lidded with sleep.

"How would you react," she asked him languidly, "to a little decadent ease? Like watching television in bed. I'm exhausted."

"It sounds great. But first there's something I have to take care of." He got up and went to the living-room closet, reaching into the pocket of his overcoat. He came back grinning, his big hand fisted around something.

He held out his hand to her, opening it to reveal a velvet box. "I ran across this today in the Village. The fellow told me it was your symbol."

Eve opened the box. On a background of dark-brown velvet she saw a delicate red-gold chain formed of tiny Venuses, the circle surmounting the cross and, hanging from its center, a larger Venus in the same bright metal. Venus was the ruling planet of Taurus, and copper—the same color of the red-gold—its metal.

"Oh, Adam." She unclasped the chain and put it around her neck. The chain was long; the symbol rested between her breasts, vividly beautiful against the teal-green of her robe.

"Adam, it's exquisite. I've never seen anything like it. Thank you." She smiled into his dark eyes. "Where on earth did you ever *find* it?"

"In the wilds of Christopher Street, practically in the river. Full of guys with one pierced ear." He grinned. "A ripe source of investigation. Your cult idea may lead to something, Eve. But we've still got some distance to go."

He did not seem eager to go into details at the moment, and she was not eager to press it. "We

141

never talk about it much . . . the case, I mean. And tonight I'm glad. I'm very glad, Adam."

She could see gratitude in his tired eyes.

"In fact, I think it's lazy time right now," she added. And then they were totally relaxed, a little high on lack of sleep, luxuriating in TV as they watched her small bedroom set. In hardly any time at all they were drifting off into oblivion, close in each other's arms as the freezing wind blew outside the small warm house.

Adam complained the next morning about having to leave her "as soon as he'd gotten there," bemoaning the fact that cops had no weekends to speak of.

They began to talk about the case, at breakfast, however; it was too much on their minds to set aside any longer. Adam said there were two Probables whose birth data wanted checking, and Eve turned to the job that day. The results were discouraging.

But once again they managed to have their night together, a repetition of the night before. And Sunday, at last, belonged to them completely. It was a heavenly day. They slept late, and Eve made an extravagant brunch. The weather was bitterly cold that morning, so it was even more pleasant to stay inside.

Unavoidably their conversation reverted to the case. The target date was growing ever nearer.

Late that afternoon the sun appeared and the winds calmed. Adam said, in a tentative fashion, "I should get back to my place for a bit, pick up some clothes."

Eve ran her hand over his hair. "Perhaps you'd like to . . . leave some here."

"Do you mean that? You wouldn't mind?"

"*Mind?*" She put her arms around his neck and drew his head down. He kissed her slowly, gently.

"I will, then." They both knew that it was a kind of commitment, and she thought, *I love him. Already I love him, and it's unimaginable not to be with him.*

"Come with me," he urged her. "You can see where I live." His smile was mischievous, and she recalled his saying that he had a most "unusual" place.

"I'd love it. My curiosity's killing me." She dressed in a warm copper-colored sweater and matching pants, pleased at the effect of her Venus symbol with the color.

He drove them to that mysterious point near the Brooklyn Bridge where she'd let him off that first evening.

"I don't see any apartments," she said, looking around curiously.

Adam just smiled. "Come with me."

He led her through a strange underground passage. "What on earth . . . ? Are you really the Phantom of the Opera?" she teased.

"You've discovered my sinister secret." Their voices echoed eerily in the tunnel. "This is one of the old tunnels that hasn't been used for years. I had to sell my soul to the city for the rights of passage."

They emerged on the waterfront, and he led

143

her onto a small houseboat. *"This* is it?" she asked, delighted.

"This is it. And you're the very first lady to board her."

The boat was trim and cozy, very clean but sparsely furnished. Almost monastic. She remembered Hansen's nasty comment about "too much monastery." New tenderness warmed her. Adam Kane was a rarer man than she had realized. "Most appropriate for a water sign."

"So I've discovered . . . since I've been living with the stars." He took her in his arms. She glowed at the double entendre and kissed him soundly.

"Umm." After a moment he got up, saying, "Relax, while I look up my gear." He served her an excellent cup of coffee from his trim galley, then began to throw clothes into a small bag.

Eve put down her cup and saucer on a shelf by the bunk, leaning back to watch him. He zipped up the bag and looked at her. "What a picture."

"What's your hurry, Inspector?"

"None. None at *all."* He knelt down on the side of the bunk and gently started removing her sweater. The gentle brush of his fingers on her exposed skin aroused small ripples of pleasure in her flesh. Through half-shut eyes she observed him put the sweater aside, saw him smile as his hands slid down her sides toward the waistline of her soft wool trousers.

He reached above her to draw the curtains; the sunset filtering through splashed the cabin with a fiery color, and Eve felt as if the orange warmth had sweetly invaded her skin. Her pulses raced. Her whole body felt expectant and eager and receptive.

Adam was still staring at her hungrily, his dark eyes studying her face, her tumbled hair, her body scarcely covered in wisps of russet satin. Then she was not wearing the satin anymore, and he was baring his massive, splendid body.

He slid back the covers and lay down beside her, drawing her close until their bodies were aware of every contour of the other's. He lowered his mouth to hers.

At that very instant a parting vessel's deep, titanic horn resounded, lingered. Eve opened her eyes and stared into the black profundity of his, rocking to the rhythms of the harbor water underneath their mobile floor.

And by the time the great horn faded, followed by the peeping whistles of the tugs, the mournful crying of the creaking gulls, she had drowned again in his enchantment; entering the dreamworld symbolized by the sea, the fascinating element of Adam Kane.

CHAPTER SIX

That Monday morning Eve woke up when Adam did, so she arrived at the office well ahead of the others. It was very different from the Monday before, when she had been arrayed in sleek sartorial armor to mask her emotions.

Combing her hair she saw that even it looked bedded, in "sweet disorder," and she didn't mind at all. Eve smiled at her reflection. Adam had made the weekend so magical that for hours together she'd been able to forget the case, the dark fact that someone might want to take her very life from her.

The office, with its closed door, was quiet; a vagrant beam of morning sun struck her desk calendar. The big red number nine stared back at her: Monday, the ninth of December. The first day of the month of Capricorn was exactly two weeks away.

Eve sat down and started to go over the weekend's new material. She'd almost forgotten the case for the last two days. But Adam hadn't; in the midst of their happiest moments she'd been surprised to see a thoughtful look in his black eyes.

The quiet bore down. Eve felt an odd unease scurry over her flesh. She'd be glad when the others came. But it was still only ten till nine. Quickly she opened a sealed manila envelope. Another chart, with an apologetic covering letter from a Bronx astrologer whose client had "balked" at signing a release, told her to "forget the whole thing." The astrologer was torn between ethical practice and a fervent desire to help the police. Suspecting the client's attitude she'd cast his horoscope anyway from the available data and sent it.

Apparently fear was winning out these days over people's professional standards. Eve wondered darkly if clients would ever trust any of them again.

When her team arrived they gave her an interested once-over; the weekend must show, she decided. When Iris came to her desk she admired Eve's pendant. Betty didn't notice. She looked awful.

Eve wondered if she should ask Betty to lunch with her today, try to talk to her about what was going on at home. There was no possibility of lunch with Adam. He'd picked up a lead on some alleged Satanists on Long Island and was involved in a stakeout that could go on into the night. But Eve was not too optimistic about getting Betty to talk. She knew the Cancerian temperament, moody and withdrawn, at times closemouthed as a clam, another mollusc related to the Crab of Betty's sign.

Well, she'd give it a try.

The next time there was a natural opportunity to say something to Betty, Eve asked warmly, "How are you today?"

"All right," Betty answered flatly. Eve knew that was Cancerian for "awful," but didn't say so. Cancerians didn't react well to prodding—much like Scorpios—and would simply scuttle back into their metaphorical grottos and peer out, threatening to pinch any intruder.

"Why don't we have lunch together?" Eve suggested. "I haven't had a chance to really talk to you in all this time."

Betty gave her a tight smile and looked at her a little suspiciously. "Thanks, but I'm meeting Bill today."

"That's nice. Another time, then."

It might not be just "nice," Eve reflected anxiously. She suspected that Betty's husband, a conservative, impatient Capricorn, was probably getting antsy about Betty's staying with the team and had assigned himself as her unofficial watchdog.

Then Eve remembered her promise to Osborne to lunch with her one day. This was as good a day as any. She phoned Osborne, who accepted at once, sounding very pleased.

They walked to a cozy Italian restaurant east of the Federal courthouse. When they sat down at a small, pleasant table opposite the bar, Eve smiled at Marnie Osborne. She looked thin and narrow-shouldered even in her uniform, and Eve noticed that her short, tow-colored hair was very poorly cut. Osborne could be very attractive, she thought, if she got a good cut and played up those huge blue eyes. Osborne's features were small and fine but appeared indeterminate without artifice.

"I'm not a lunch-cocktail type," Eve admitted, "But you go ahead." She'd caught Marnie Osborne's darting glance at the bar.

"I think I will, for a change." Osborne ordered a martini and Eve a small sherry. With the first few sips Osborne began to relax a little.

"Do you wear makeup?" Osborne demanded with the sudden directness of a child.

Eve recovered from her surprise. "Oh, yes. Quite a bit, as a matter of fact."

"It sure doesn't show." Osborne gulped her martini, studying Eve.

"It shouldn't." Eve smiled. "You know, you have great skin . . . and lovely eyes. You could really play up both."

"Could you show me?" Osborne's eagerness touched Eve.

"Of course. Did you bring any makeup with you?"

"I've got a whole bunch of stuff, back at the office. A woman told me what to buy, and I bought it. But I'll be damned if I can make it work." Osborne looked doleful and finished her cocktail. She held up her glass to the waitress, who brought her another one promptly. Eve wondered if it were a habit.

150

A blue went by and raised his hand to Osborne. "Hi, fella." The sergeant flushed and took a sip of new martini.

"Did you hear that?" she demanded.

Offended for her, Eve consoled, "The man's an idiot."

"I don't know. I'll never be able to look like you."

"So much the better," Eve kidded. "You can eat anything your heart desires. Some men like the delicate type."

"Not this 'delicate type,'" Osborne countered. "That makeup woman told me I should cut my hair real short, too, it's so curly, but Hans"—she broke off, reddening—"the man I'm interested in hates short-short hair."

"That's too bad. With your fragile bones it would do a lot for your face." Eve consulted the menu.

"That's just what that woman said." Osborne ordered indifferently and the waitress went off. Eve passed up wine with the meal, but Osborne had ordered a split of Chianti. That was quite a lot for a lunch. "But then, his wife . . ."

Osborne looked at Eve, abashed. "He's married. I guess you wonder what kind of jerk would fall in love with a married man."

"No, but I wonder why you'd want to be hurt," Eve said frankly.

"I don't know." Marnie Osborne sounded miserable. "I just can't seem to see anybody else. We . . . we had an affair. If you can call it that. Just

151

once. It was like he wanted to . . . give me a break, or something," she finished resentfully.

"Give you a *break?*" Eve repeated.

They were silent as the waitress set their lunches before them, then Osborne resumed, "Yeah. I don't know why I put up with that either. He said I should let my hair grow. Susie, his wife, has long hair, and . . ." Osborne took the last sip of her drink.

And it hasn't kept Hansen from pursuing every other woman, Eve thought nastily. She thought of Iris, with her short-short hair, and how interested Hansen was in her. That phony. He didn't give a hoot about hair; he just wanted to manipulate, control. Eve recalled one of the Sagittarius symbols—the chariot, "sign of the overriding will," the desire to be the driver. In an unevolved person that need translated into petty malice.

"Is the man a Sagittarius?" she asked.

Osborne stared at her. "You *are* good. How did you know?"

"A shot in the dark," Eve punned on the Centaur's bow and arrow. "If you'll excuse the expression."

Osborne grinned. "You're some potatoes. Have you got a Gemini Mercury?"

Osborne was pretty conversant with astrology, Eve noted. "No, but thanks for the compliment."

Marnie Osborne looked more at ease. "I can really talk to you. You know it's Hansen . . . don't you?"

"I gathered that. And I'm sorry. From what I've heard he's not the nicest man around."

"That sounds like Killer Kane."

"I heard it from others," Eve said casually. "Who gave the inspector his nickname, anyway? Hansen?"

"Right again. It's not just because of 'Cain.' " Osborne spelled it. "It's because Hansen thinks of the inspector as a 'passion killer,' an absolute monk. You see, a lot of women come on to Kane, and he hardly notices. Like that girl on your team —*Iris.*" Osborne said the name with emphasis.

"Iris doesn't have the slightest interest in Hansen, Marnie. Believe me." Eve was still distracted by Osborne's history of Adam's nickname. If that's what it was about, she felt even better about him. Additional evidence, if she'd needed any, that everything he'd said to her was sincere. She *was* special to Adam Kane.

"I guess not. And she is nice. She's been nice to me." Osborne nibbled at her lunch, studying Eve. Eve's expression must have given her away, because Osborne asked, "You like him, don't you?"

"Who?" Eve hedged.

"Kane. He sure likes *you.*" Marnie Osborne grinned, and Eve warmed to hear that. She thought how charming Marnie looked when she smiled. She said so.

"Well, *thanks.*" Then she laughed. "You sure *don't* have a Gemini Mercury. You're as twisty as a pretzel, changing the subject on me."

Doing it again, Eve conceded, "Taurus. Close-mouthed."

That started them off on a discussion of astrology and Osborne's chart. She volunteered the information, too, that Hansen hated astrology. His Scorpio wife doted on it and it drove him "bananas," Osborne said.

That was very interesting.

"He must hate working on this case," Eve commented.

"Oh, he *does*. Except for the fringe benefits," Osborne added darkly. "I'll bet he's just dying to meet those Satanic types tonight. They're into all kinds of weird things, things he'd probably just love." Her bitterness was plain.

"I really don't think Satanists are involved in this case," Eve said. She couldn't stand them; they gave her the creeps, and she deeply resented any remote connection they might be considered to have with astrology. "They wouldn't kill by pushing somebody in front of a bus or train; they'd use some horrible . . . ritual, or something."

"That's just what Kane said to Hansen," Osborne admitted. "But I guess it's desperation time."

It certainly was, with the target date two weeks away, Eve thought. To distract them both she said idly, "Scorpio and Sagittarius. That's a 'heavy rap,' as your customers would say." She grinned.

"Isn't it, though? But I'm supposed to be a real soul mate for Sagittarius. The laugh of the year," Osborne said sourly.

"You didn't ask me, Marnie, but if I were you, I'd take some medicine," Eve offered.

"Medicine?" Osborne raised her untidy brows.

"A whole makeover. Get that haircut and let 'em do everything—makeup, eyebrows, the whole schmear. Let Hansen, and the world, know you like yourself. And take a look at some of the single men."

Osborne stared at her. "You know, I might just do that. Tonight. All the stores are open late for Christmas, and . . . I just might."

"And if Hansen makes a crack about your haircut, tell him to go home and look at his *wife's* hair." Eve chuckled. "That was one of my better lines in Chicago."

"I bet no man ever walked all over you." Osborne looked admiring.

"Don't bet on it. I've done my doormat duty. Only once. That was enough."

"Maybe once'll be enough for me too. Thank you, Eve. I guess I've been needing someone to say all these things to me. And you did. I'm grateful."

Embarrassed but pleased, Eve made light of it. "We'd better get back to Number One. Maybe we'll have time to do a makeup job on you in the women's room, if we hurry."

Osborne quickly agreed, and they did have time. Already Marnie Osborne was looking prettier.

Eve got back to the office a bit late. Clare was waiting for her.

When Eve apologized, Clare said, "No problem. I've been addressing Christmas cards, and had lunch in. I thought I'd do some shopping over on Broadway."

Christmas. Clare had reminded her of something she'd hardly thought of lately. It was one of Eve's favorite holidays, and this would be her first Christmas in New York. What a very different holiday she'd pictured—early, pleasant shopping in midtown with careful choices for the relatives and friends she would gift; lingering in Rockefeller Center in the evening to look at its giant Christmas tree, decorating her apartment, giving a party.

All of that seemed faraway as fantasy right now. The Astro Killer was scheduled to strike the day, or night, before Christmas Eve. It was hard to remember nice things like Christmas with that shadow over her, day after day.

Suddenly Eve began to feel depressed. The sun had fled and the air was a somber gray. To help shake off the unwelcome mood she reexamined her interpretation of the Bronx chart she'd done that morning. That, too, seemed a total loss; the chart was that of a person full of resentments but far too weak and diffuse, in her opinion, to be capable of the act of murder. Eve wondered why his own astrologer hadn't concluded that for herself. But then all astrologers were running a little scared these days, and it might be affecting their judgment.

What about her own, for that matter?

It wasn't the same. She was, after the Chicago triumph, considered one of the best in forensics.

One of the best. And she still hadn't uncovered any leads to the Astro Killer. But neither had Adam, nor the department—nothing solid. And she remembered his heartening disclaimers about how long it had taken to catch other killers in the past.

In any case she should do a memo for Carlin on the latest chart. She did, succinctly, and had it delivered to the DC's office.

She turned to the other material, but something was nagging at her, making concentration difficult. Maybe what Osborne had said about Hansen's wife. Her astrology "drove him bananas," Marnie claimed. Why, specifically?

Perhaps Susie Hansen relied too heavily on her astrologer; there were clients like that. Dependent in all things, they too often forgot that an astrologer was not a psychiatrist or savior, that astrology impels, does not compel, showing what people might do, never stating must or will. It was also possible Susie Hansen went to an inferior astrologer, like Perry Martial's.

Eve started putting clues together: Adam had mentioned that the Hansens lived in Greenwich Village. Susie probably went to a neighborhood astrologer; most people did. And ten to one her astrologer had done a synastry of the Hansens' two charts that pointed up problems, which Susie might nag Hansen about.

With the team's computer clearance Eve could get the data in minutes. She hesitated. Here again it wasn't strictly ethical; neither Hansen nor his wife was an official suspect. Still, Eve was empowered to investigate, too; and it was certain Susie Hansen had signed a release, anyway, since her own husband was involved in the case.

157

Of course, out of the standard "MOM"—means, opportunity and motive—Hansen so far had only the "MO." With his mobility and schedule, his training, he had means and opportunity. But motive was another matter. Would a man commit serial murders just out of irritation? It seemed absurd.

Before she could talk herself out of it, Eve went to the computer and checked the team's own data, allowing for every possible variation of the last name. But there was no Susie Hansen.

Eve took a deep breath and patched in to Starmain, the association's master computer. She hoped that no one would catch this inquiry; it would not help her professional reputation to be accused of harassment and improper procedures.

She entered *Susie Hansen, Manhattan,* and waited.

The data flashed onto the screen: Susie Hansen's Greenwich Village address and birth data. Eve asked for synastry and progressed horoscopes, requesting a printout.

Eve erased the data from the screen, hurried back to her desk with the flimsy sheets, and dived right into them. The indications were very negative.

The Hansens' Suns and Ascendants were in quincunx aspect, contributing enormous strain to the marriage. Hansen's Sun squared his wife's Saturn, wet-blanketing the whole relationship. And, although it was one of the most dangerous forms of oversimplification, the jarring notes of their inimical Sun signs could always be heard:

Susie Hansen was a jealous, possessive, passionate Scorpio, her husband a freedom-loving, fickle Sagittarius. Eve had always had a strong regard for simple factors, and she'd always been ninety-five percent correct in following her native intuition.

She was so deep in the comparative charts she hardly looked up when Iris, and later Betty, came back; was almost unaware of their quiet and busy presences.

Right now it was the husband half of the comparative chart that fascinated Eve. It showed a bent toward extramarital affairs; the progressed chart indicated a period of extraordinary crisis in the autumn of this year—the time of the first three Astro murders.

Quite a leap, she ridiculed herself, from marital crisis and bad aspects to serial murder. However, Hansen did have a very badly aspected "Mother" House, a sign of possible enmity toward women in general, and his Venus was perverse, according to the present reading. But something wasn't quite right, Eve calculated. There was an error in this chart too.

The only way she could satisfy herself was to cast his chart afresh at home, study it with more detachment. Right now other work pressed her, and she was beginning to question her own judgment. She would have to be severely objective . . . and that wasn't easy, with Hansen.

She shelved the project and was getting back to other work when Adam phoned. He sounded wired. "I only have a minute, darling. I just wanted to hear your voice, check up on you. Everything all right?"

Eve answered silently, *Just great. I'm after your lieutenant.*

"Fine," she said. "Will you be very late?"

"Probably so late I may sleep at the office," he answered. She could hear his savage frustration. "Word is now these loony tunes may meet late, or may not meet at all. I'm ready to strangle Carlin. All we can do is wait. I'll call you at home, the next chance I get. Damn, I miss you, darling. But I'm in touch with your guard."

"I miss you too. I'll help you strangle Carlin," she added, trying to lighten Adam's mood.

"Appreciate it." His voice had a smile now. "Talk to you later."

"Later," she murmured before he hung up.

It gave her a lift, hearing his voice, being conscious of his concern. The fact that he was always "in touch with her guard" gave her an extra sense of security. But she knew how lonely she would be tonight if he stayed at Number One. It was astonishing, almost scary, how accustomed she'd grown to his massive presence in her house, her bed.

But tonight it was consoling to know that she'd have a very absorbing project to keep her occupied.

Back in the apartment on Sidney Place she found herself impatient with the dinner ritual and made herself a quick scratch meal. It wasn't long at all before her briefcase was emptied, her home computer going.

Going more deeply into Hansen's individual astrology Eve found shocking aspects—the most heavily tenanted house in his chart was the eighth, symbolic of death, sex, and peril. Hansen's impulse to love was manifested in sadism; his chart reflected both guilt and grandeur, a dangerous combination.

Surprisingly Sagittarius was the only fire sign in Hansen's horoscope; all of the others were earth and water. The heavy earth signs gave one the desire to adhere to a fixed plan, a schedule . . . like the schedule of the killings. And Hansen's Saturn was in conjunction with the malefic fixed star, Scheat, found in the charts of many murderers.

And there, she discovered, was Lilith, that satellite so prominent in the chart of the Star Slayer and so many others.

When Eve's mantel clock chimed, she realized she'd been sitting in almost the same position for hours, she'd been so intent. She was positively aching, and blurry eyed.

She shut off the computer and leaned back. Even with all that data, she had just begun. It was one thing to find the indications, even hints as grave as these, and another to find the evidence to clinch them.

And how on earth could she freely investigate Hansen, a member of Adam's own team, a New York City detective judged a "fine cop" by his superiors, without having her sanity questioned? Of course there were "bad cops," now and then. But this was a good one, according to all indications, no matter how juvenile he was with women, no matter how distasteful, even obnoxious. Infidelity was wrong, by her standards anyway, but it wasn't a crime.

If this were an ordinary suspect, the police would quickly check his alibis for the murder nights; his habits, acquaintances, psychological profile, everything. But he wasn't. So how could she find out what she needed to know?

There weren't any answers right now, and she was mentally exhausted. So much so that she was beginning to question her own intuition.

Deciding to wrap it up for the moment, she left the work where it was, took a long bath, and watched television with only a small part of her attention. The more she thought of Hansen, the more impossible it seemed to pursue the matter.

And yet she was still haunted by certain memories—the almost sadistic pleasure he took in hurting Osborne, the glance of naked hate directed at herself during the conference with Carlin, his enmity toward astrology and astrologers.

It took a lot of enmity to commit murder. What Osborne had said might apply to Eve Darcy: it was "desperation time." All this could be a feverish conclusion based on nothing but hysteria.

The sound of the phone was more than ever welcome. But Adam sounded anything but happy.

Eve glanced at her watch. It was nearly midnight.

"Damn it, it looks like I'll be bedding down at

Numero Uno. Just what I was afraid of. At least I've got a little more time now."

"What happened?"

"The ritual hasn't come off, and the main ding-a-ling, the one we really had our eye on, never showed up in this area. We've got to hound him elsewhere, leave this affair to the locals. They want the group on other charges, you see." Adam sighed deeply. "So now we're taking off for another county. Even with the best of breaks, it'll be daylight by the time we check him out and get back and get the report written up."

"How awful. You must have Carlin's noose wound already," she kidded gently.

"It's *been* wound, baby, since this morning. Eve, I'd like to be there. I can't believe how much I miss you, after just one day." His voice was caressing.

"It's the same for me. But I've been consoling myself with homework."

"I can think of better ways to spend an evening. Try to relax a bit. I'll see you tomorrow, darling."

"Tomorrow," she repeated softly. After their good-bye Eve looked at the Hansen material again.

She could imagine what Adam would say if he knew her "homework" concerned his right-hand man. He'd think she'd short-circuited from overload.

And she was tired, she admitted. Her mind was running like a caged squirrel. She got ready for bed, deciding to watch some TV to unwind.

Without checking the schedule she turned on the set; the movie was an old one—about a woman serial murderer.

Eve gave up and, half following the movie, let her mind drift and range.

Another person who had an animus against the team was Carlin's sour secretary, Myers. She was right in the middle of the case. A plain older woman who might hate young, pretty ones, whose thin, unfeminine body could look very unisex in coat and trousers. A Virgo with a penchant for patterns.

This is too much, Eve concluded. *I'll be suspecting Carlin next, or Adam.* If Myers were a killer surely all those able, experienced men would have found it out. Eve turned off the TV set and tried to fall asleep; she didn't succeed until very late.

Tuesday was another Monday, but worse. Eve was fuzzy from lack of sleep, and the team was flooded with new material on the Satanists.

They were a distasteful bunch to begin with and doing their charts did little to improve Eve's morale. She was convinced that cultists had nothing to do with the murders; her forensic studies had invariably turned up ritualistic M.O.s.

When her phone rang in the middle of the morning she answered with a snappish Hello.

"Bad day?" It was Adam.

"Not now." She smiled, hoping he could hear the smile in her answer.

"Good. Mine just improved too." His tender

inflection warmed her like the sun, and suddenly everything was all right again.

"How's it going with you?"

"The formation of rock would be faster," he retorted, "and just about as much fun to watch. Nothing to report. I'd bet my badge you've turned up the same in your morning's work."

"How right you'd be," she said wearily.

"Enough of that, lady. I miss you. Something awful."

"I miss you, too, Adam. So much." She wanted to see him that very minute, have him hold her, kiss her.

"I'll tell you something," he promised. "I'm going to see you tonight if I get busted to patrolman. If you're free, that is."

"Am I, ever."

"I'll call you again later," he said exuberantly. "Say four-thirty? I don't know about you, but I feel like a real city-type dinner . . . I've got suburbitis, bad."

"We'll cure it. I promise. That sounds perfect to me."

After their good-byes, Eve hung up in a glow.

My mother was right, she thought. *There's nothing love can't overcome—even a king-size case of murder.*

Kane hung up the pay-phone receiver and walked slowly back to the booth he shared with Hansen. If there was one thing he detested, it was hanging out at a bar in the daytime, especially on a day like this, and in a bar like this one.

165

And with this particular partner, he added to himself when he sat down again opposite Hansen. Kane had had it up to there with Hansen's histories of exploits with women. He had a strong feeling most of it was fiction. If it weren't, Kane wasn't too crazy about the characters described, in any case. Hansen should have gotten that out of his system twenty years ago.

"What's up at HQ?" Before he'd talked to Eve, Kane had been checking in. He wanted to save her for last, so he could walk away from the phone with her soft, seductive voice echoing in his ears, to give him a boost. And that's just what she'd done.

"Nothing new."

"That was a lot of talk for 'nothing new.'" Hansen surveyed Kane with his blue, hyper eyes. The guy was as curious as a gossipy old lady, Kane thought, and his look prodded in an unpleasant way.

Kane didn't answer; he swallowed the rest of his beer. It tasted flat and stale, like the whole damned stakeout.

Hansen held up his mug to the waitress. "Want another?" he asked Kane.

"Hell, no. I'm floating." When the waitress undulated over to them, giving Hansen the eye, Kane ordered a Coke.

"What's got you so sour, Kane? You've been like a sore-tailed bear ever since we started this." He was actually miffed because Kane hadn't told him whom he was talking to. Hansen was the last man on earth Kane could talk to about Eve, even if he talked about his private life.

"I can't stand these jerks," he said tersely, glancing at the Hell's Angels at the bar. "The Satanists and the Angels are a bunch of juvenile psychos." Kane's voice was audible only to Hansen: they were supposed to be hangers-on who had no objection to either group. It was easier for Hansen. He seemed right at home in his gear. But Kane's wig was itching him, and he'd never had any fondness for cruddy clothes.

"Of course you can't stand them, buddy. That's because you've never gotten with it. Just because it's different, it's no good, right?"

Kane was silent.

Hansen dug at him again. "These people have a ball. Sure, the ritual's a lot of garbage, but who cares?" His eyes gleamed. "There's the fun part, man. That's what I want to get into." He waited for Kane to say something. Disappointed that he hadn't gotten a rise out of Kane, he went on, "Now, those guys." He nodded at the Hell's Angels. "They've got it made. I envy them. And they sure know how to treat women. They keep the broads in their place, all right."

"You're sick, pal." Kane swallowed some Coke and observed the scruffy characters at the bar. They were noisier than the video games; most of the men had their arms around each other's shoulders. The women with them were mostly ignored. One of the women cast longing glances at Hansen and Kane.

"Why did you ever join the force, Hansen?"

167

Kane demanded. Hansen's face changed; he looked cornered, uncertain. But Kane already knew the answer to his question. Hansen had joined the force because it gave him a sense of power he couldn't have otherwise. He liked to throw his weight around as much as he could with the force of the law behind him.

"I'm sick?" Hansen countered, evading the question. "What about those nutty broads on that astrology team? Now, that's a bunch of sickos. I hate those damned astrologers . . . running everybody's life, getting women all riled up, giving 'em big ideas. . . ." Hansen's voice trailed away. He upended his mug.

"You didn't seem to hate the ones in the Village," Kane remarked.

"Hell, that was different. I was trying to get next to that crazy broad on Fourth Street. It's this witch my wife goes to I'm talking about. We got along pretty good until Susie started listening to her."

This was very interesting to Kane. Hansen had never opened up quite so much before. Perhaps he'd had one beer too many.

"What do you mean, exactly?"

Hansen gave him a wary look. Kane wasn't generally this sympathetic to his ideas. "Well, hell, she . . . she got Susie all hotted up about me running around."

Kane lit a cigarette, eying Hansen with sardonic amusement. "Well, she didn't need a stargazer to tell her that, did she?"

"Yeah, she *did,"* Hansen snapped. "Susie never

started checking up on me until she went to that loony . . . I think that broad's got it in for men. Hell, Angie's mother offered to do Susie's chart for nothing. But, no, she had to go spend good money for some nut to tell her I'm a lousy husband."

Kane's ears pricked up. "Angie's mother? Myers's mother is an astrologer?"

"Sure she is. You didn't know that?"

Kane shook his head. The less he'd known about Myers, the better.

"Of course. The old lady offered her services to Carlin, too, and he went and hired those other uptight broads instead."

Kane held on to his temper. The detective in him was on a new scent: Hansen hated astrologers, and probably women, despite his bragging; Myers had a reason to hate the team too. Could that hatred extend to other astrologers? Myers might have a subconscious enmity toward her mother which could include other women who practiced that discipline.

To camouflage his interest Kane turned his head and made another visual sweep of the bar. "Our target's late today, I see."

Hansen studied Kane. "Yeah. So relax. Think I'll have a game." He jerked his head backward at the video games in the corner. "How about you?"

"Later," Kane said. "I need some cigarettes." As Hansen headed for the video games, Kane got up and put some change in a cigarette machine, went back to their table, and glanced impatiently at his watch.

The next time the waitress passed he ordered another Coke. This time he noticed some of the patrons eying him, so he responded to the woman's flirtation. It might be a good idea to give the impression that the waitress was the reason he was hanging around. He saw that the ploy had worked; the people who'd looked at him relaxed.

Hansen was avidly making believe that he'd just shot two dozen elk on the video machine. When he came back to the table he looked brighter.

"So what do you think?" Hansen asked. "Should we give it a little longer?"

"I could use some air. Tell you what, I'll get Johnson, check out that wood site again, send you Gardner."

Hansen smiled, and it wasn't a pleasant one. "Anything to change partners, right? You're still burned over that meeting with Carlin, aren't you, Kane?"

"See you later," Kane evaded. "I'll send Gardner over."

He got up, putting a bill on the table. Winking at the pleased waitress Kane walked out to his car. *Damned right,* he answered Hansen in silence, *anything to change partners.*

As he got into his car and made the necessary radio contacts, Kane analyzed his increasing overreaction to Hansen. Obnoxious as he was personally, Hansen was still one of the best cops on Kane's team.

170

Kane drove down the road, passing a bank and a line of stores; suddenly the highway became a blacktop and the town had become country. Not such great country, either, he decided sourly. The trees were mostly bare, desolate looking, and there wasn't enough snow to make a pretty scene. It just looked spare and lonely.

Driving into deeper woods Kane passed a tavern-hangout of other locals; a dozen Harleys were parked outside.

Good thing it wasn't summer, Kane thought. People would be hanging around outside, checking out every car that passed. But now, with everyone inside and the head-splitting rock music blaring, his passage would be unnoticed.

He pulled up in a strategic spot that had served them well before and lit a cigarette, waiting for Johnson. Knowing Johnson, he'd be there before it was half smoked. And right now Kane needed an extra couple of minutes to get his thoughts together—to picture what it would be like tonight with Eve.

Watch it, Kane warned himself, smiling. Once he started on beautiful ideas like that he'd forget the matter of Hansen. And he had to do some thinking about that.

There was definitely something different about Hansen these days. He used to play it cooler with his hostilities. In fact, that had been Kane's major divergence with him—the guy had always been sly in his malice, needling instead of confronting. Two faced as well. With Myers, for instance.

Kane, disliking the woman, simply avoided her as much as possible; Hansen seemed to hold her in utter contempt, and yet he knew a great deal about her, including the information that her own mother was an astrologer. That certainly explained Myers's attitude toward Eve's team—not only was she jealous of their age and looks, but she probably resented the fact that the team was "doing her mother's job."

Damn it, he was right back to square one again—square Astro One. All his thoughts led back to Eve.

For the first time in years she'd made him feel as if he were really living, instead of just functioning. Her place was the closest thing to home he'd had in a long, long time. But it wasn't the place, so much, as her. Kane admitted to himself how starved he'd been for that—a woman who was home, a base, solidity, yet stimulation, excitement, satisfaction, all at the same time.

Kane heard a car approaching. It looked like Johnson's, but nothing could ever be taken for granted. He stubbed out his cigarette and reflexively put his hand to his gun.

Recognizing Johnson, Kane relaxed, sliding his hand away from his belt.

As Johnson got out of his car Kane lifted his hand in greeting. He let his thoughts linger a moment longer on a certain lovely face framed in gleaming black hair, a ripe, sweet mouth, and gray, provocative eyes.

Soon, lady, he promised in silence. By the time he opened his car door, Kane was practically grinning at the respectful but puzzled Johnson.

CHAPTER SEVEN

On the morning of Wednesday, December eleventh, Eve didn't just walk into her office—she practically danced. Adam's quick good-bye kiss a moment before in the empty hall was warm on her mouth, the bow on the package of last night.

As she walked in, Eve's memory saw it again, in quick, successive slides: dinner in the magnificent pool area of the Four Seasons restaurant; walking in the light, powdery snow towards St. Patrick's and Saks on decorated Fifth Avenue; watching the skaters at Rockefeller Center.

The magic had continued in the drive to Brooklyn to the warm, welcoming house; their hungry kisses, the long night of talk and love.

"Good *morning!*" Eve beamed at Iris, Betty, and Clare. Even the colors they were wearing accorded with her mood: Clare had on an uncharacteristically bright blue dress, Betty's sweater was the shade of her vivid hair and Iris wore a Christmasy red. "Great colors."

"So is yours," Iris said when Eve took off her coat, uncovering a dress the tint of a peeled nectarine that looked wonderful with her Venus pendant.

"Somebody's feeling good." Clare smiled at Eve.

"Somebody's feeling terrific." Eve sat down at her desk. "What's *this?*" She saw a memo on top of the other mail, from Angela Myers to *All Staff.*

"A Christmas card list, no less, from Ms. Scrooge herself," Betty answered in her driest tone.

"Will wonders never cease?"

"And she was here to deliver them when I got in," Iris added.

"Nothing like the season to work miracles," Eve commented, looking over the new charts that had come in. She saw Betty pick up the full coffeepot and head for the door.

"Where are you going with that?" Eve demanded. "I'm hurting." She was not only floating from happiness, but also from too little sleep. They'd talked until the small hours of the morning.

Betty paused. "I wouldn't. When I was heating it, it smelled awfully stale. I'm going to dump this and make a fresh pot."

"*Heating* it?" The team took turns making fresh coffee every morning.

"Somebody must have made it for a Christmas present," Iris conjectured. "Somebody who can't make good coffee."

"Well, let me have one cup before you throw it out. I'm desperate."

"You *must* be. Taurus really is the stubbornest

174

sign," Betty teased her, setting the pot on her desk. Before Eve could pour some coffee into her mug, her phone rang.

"Ms. Darcy?" It was Angela Myers, sounding friendlier than Eve had ever heard her. "How are you this morning?"

Myers really seemed to be interested. *St. Nick's here already,* Eve thought with puzzled amusement. "Just splendid. And you?" she added politely.

"Fine, thank you. I just wanted to make sure you got the Elliott chart . . . with the new material." There was a subtle change in Myers's high, thin voice. It was all very odd. She'd never bothered to check up on anything like this before.

"Just a second. I'll look." Eve rapidly thumbed through the manila folders. "Yes. It's here."

"Very good. I was . . . afraid that one might have been omitted. Thank you, Ms. Darcy." Myers hung up abruptly, cutting off Eve's civil "Not at all."

"Well, well," she murmured.

"Pour your poison, lady. I want to get rid of this stuff," Betty prodded.

"Sorry." Eve poured. Betty started out the door again.

She was right; the coffee smelled terrible. But Eve needed the stimulation so much she drank it anyway.

At once she felt a path of flame run down her throat; her stomach was bladed with an awful shooting pain. A cold sweat was breaking out

175

over her entire body, making the soft wool dress feel like a heavy, sodden blanket.

She gasped. "Oh, my God!" Her voice came out in a croak. Iris and Clare were staring at her.

Clare ran out in the hall. Eve heard her shouting at Betty, "Don't pour it out! Bring it back!"

At the same time Iris was running to their small refrigerator, snatching out a carton of milk, racing back to Eve with it, tearing it open, shrieking at her, thrusting the carton at her mouth. "Drink this! Right now!"

The fresh milk smelled revolting, but Eve obeyed. In a swift, startled second she knew what had happened: the coffee was poisoned.

She made herself swallow and was overpowered by nausea: she was helplessly, immediately, getting sick; horribly, over everything. But nothing in the world mattered now, except to stop the dreadful pain, the burning.

Her eyes were blurred. She could not speak or move. From far away she was aware that Clare was telephoning, that Iris had rushed out, somewhere.

Betty was standing utterly still, with the coffee maker in her hand, just staring.

That was the last thing Eve remembered.

On the afternoon of Thursday, the twelfth of December, Adam Kane paced the corridor of the hospital taking nervous drags from his cigarette.

Rage was always his response to anxiety, and resentment tore through him when he heard the doctor's curt "Not yet," and saw the man's unreadable expression when he went into Eve's room.

He paced some more, kneading the tissue-wrapped stems of the flowers in his other hand. Finally the doctor came out, saying in the mild voice that rankled Kane, "All right, Inspector. You can question her now, but only about ten minutes."

Question *her?* Kane protested in silence. *Jerk.*

The man's glance caught the bunch of roses and his expression changed. He smiled a little, looking more human, and walked away.

Kane was already opening the door. Eve smiled at him from the bed. He crossed the room in a few long strides, dropping the roses and bending over to kiss her.

"Oh, Eve. Dammit, Eve, I was scared to death." She raised her soft hands to his cheeks and pulled his face down to hers again for another kiss; it was the sweetest sensation he'd ever had in his life. "How are you feeling?"

"Fine now, darling." Her voice sounded weak. Kane burned with new anger: the damned thing had happened right at Number One, under their very noses. And to her. Her, of all people in the world! But he wiped the anger away; he didn't want her to see that expression on his face, not now.

He took her hand and looked at her for a long moment without speaking. She was pale, but if anything she was prettier than before. Her pallor emphasized the deep blackness of her shining hair, made the light gray of her eyes into smoky quartz. She'd put on lipstick too; it looked very bright against her paled skin. An admiring tenderness melted Kane's anger; she was pursuing her womanly business-as-usual in spite of the fact that she might have died the day before.

"I love you, Eve," he said solemnly. "Maybe I didn't really . . . know until this happened. Not for sure. It hit me like a bomb. All I could think of was that I might never get a chance to tell you, that . . ." He stopped. The weight of his feeling was so immense that for a minute his voice could not carry it.

But he saw a new brightness behind the slight glaze on her eyes, the sedative effect of that rotten poison. A smile trembled on her mouth. "Oh, Adam. I thought you'd never say it. I love you. I think I must have loved you from the first, but I couldn't admit it." She caressed his face tenderly.

Her touch overwhelmed him. He covered the hand with his own, drew it gently to his mouth, kissed it again and again. Keeping her hand in his he ran his fingers up her arm, delighting in the satiny feel of her live and vibrant flesh.

She looked at him with such love that his heart almost turned over.

He pulled his chair a bit closer to the bed, and leaned to stroke her hair with light, careful fingers. It felt like filaments of warm, fine silk thread.

"I was on the way to the Island when I got the news on my radio," he remarked softly. "I nearly went berserk until I got here. Talk about a 'cowboy cop.' " For the first time since he'd come into

178

the room he could feel himself smiling. The smile didn't last. "But then, when I finally did, you were still unconscious. They wouldn't even let me see you. If only we were—"

Married, he'd started to say. But he'd bitten off the word. That was too much to spring on her now. He couldn't take advantage of her weakened condition.

"They weren't even sure you were going to make it," he went on in a low voice. "If you hadn't, Eve—" His hand cradled her face. Such a small face, he thought. She was a good-sized, healthy woman . . . all woman . . . but right now she seemed so terribly fragile. "If you hadn't, I couldn't have taken it." Eve turned her head and kissed his fingers. It made him shiver.

"But I did, Adam. I *had* to. Yesterday morning I was feeling so alive, so happy. For the first time in . . . so long. I couldn't lose that. My life is just *starting.*" She smiled at him widely, and he was heartened; it was a stronger, braver smile than the others.

"I hardly remember what happened," she went on, "between the office and here. There I was, being horribly sick at my desk, and then I woke up here. And saw the wonderful red roses. Thank you."

Roses. He'd completely forgotten the others. Where in hell had he tossed them?

"What's wrong?"

He gave her a sheepish smile, bent over, and retrieved the bouquet from the floor, handing them to her.

She unwrapped them and exclaimed, "Oh . . . how beautiful! *Sunburst* roses." The flowers were an unusual, almost orange color. The florist had told him they were "very rare." Kane had retorted, "Good. So is the lady I'm taking them to."

"Bring me that vase," she ordered gaily.

"Wait a minute," he objected. "You're not supposed to be doing anything. Let me ring for somebody to take care of them."

"Don't give me a hard time, Inspector." He grinned at her and reluctantly brought the vase from the windowsill. He put it on her bedside table, watching as she arranged the new roses among the others. That was another thing he admired about her: she always liked to do things for herself.

"Now. Isn't that marvelous?" She gestured at the vivid mixture of color.

"Nice. Makes me feel warm just to look at them," he said. He picked up the vase and put it back on the windowsill, where the flowers were framed against the thickly falling snow.

"Did you know that roses are a Venus flower?" she asked softly. "They're a flower of my sign. Taurus is ruled by Venus."

"No. But it's certainly appropriate that you're ruled by Venus." He looked at her, and her eyes glowed back into his. Kane loved her so much at that moment he couldn't think of a single word to say. All he could do was feel it, just keep looking at her.

Then, swiftly, her glow faded a little and she

looked very serious. "Things must be . . . rough at Number One."

"That's the word," he said grimly. "We've vacuumed your office for clues; the whole damned building's being interrogated. Uniform, civilian, door guards, deliveries, workmen. You name it. Last I heard, nothing's turned up. But we've only gotten started."

She nodded. "And you've been talking to the team, I know."

"Talking and talking." His policeman's mind had reacted very negatively to what the redheaded one had said to Eve: "Pour your poison." The little one, Iris, had let that slip. If you listened to people long enough, Kane knew, you eventually heard it all. But he could hardly go into that with Eve. It might also bring up the other awkward matter—that he wanted her off the case. And she mustn't be upset.

"Adam? Aren't you going to tell me about it?"

"No," he said firmly. "Not now. You've had enough for one day." He reached for her hand again, engulfing it with his. "Shock and fear, physical trauma. You're supposing to be relaxing. I must tell you one thing, though. There's a news blackout on you, darling. Only the medics concerned, and the department, know you're getting out of here tomorrow. The press thinks it's Monday. That's for two reasons, which I'll tell you later."

He smiled at her. "Right now I'm overtime on my time allowed with you. You're supposed to get some rest. I'll be back for a little while tonight. Okay?"

"Okay. But there's still a lot I don't understand."

"Plenty of time for that. This weekend." He got up, hating to leave her. At least she was safe. Blues outside; he'd checked the staff out down to their freckles. There wasn't going to be any of that stranger-within-the-gates malarkey, where some creep dressed as an orderly sneaks in to waste the patient. Carlin had spoken to the administrator and Kane had practically given a minicop course to the nurses. What's more, Kane was going to replace one of the blues tonight himself.

"I love you, Eve." He looked at her with tenderness. She had nearly lost her life yesterday—the thought still chilled him—yet now she was living in the moment, enjoying, sharing, looking forward. She was the picture of courage, of pulsing life.

And he was going to cherish that life. For her . . . and for him.

"I love you, Adam." He kissed her one more time, quickly, and made himself walk away. At the door, though, he had to turn back for just one more look.

Eve lay back and watched Adam turn his proud head. She loved the look of his big, muscular body, the set of his shoulders. And his eyes looked just the way they had after their first night together. The dark, fierce glance was gentle. She kissed her fingers to him.

When the door closed she thought languidly, Adam had a point. She *had* had enough for one day.

Nearly being murdered yesterday, today being told that the man she loved felt the same about her. For a man like Adam Kane that declaration meant forever.

She knew very well why he hadn't wanted to talk about the case. It was to spare her. And he was probably right—she felt weakened again, drowsy. Too lazy even to read, too languid to move.

Eve closed her eyes, resolving for now to put yesterday out of her mind. The important thing was to get well enough to be discharged tomorrow. And she was good at the exercise of "happy thoughts" which often helped her fall asleep in ordinary times.

She reviewed the brief time of her knowing Adam—the first amusing, irritating moment she had looked into those savage, penetrating Scorpio eyes.

She smiled. It was incredible to think that she'd felt hostility between them. What it had been was the crackle of the "polar opposites," the strongest of attractions.

She remembered their first tentative entente, that first dinner. The first time he had kissed her. Measured against the sweet, familiar closeness of the present, all that seemed so long ago.

And yet it had been only two weeks. Astonishing. She felt as if she'd known him all her life.

He loved her. He made her feel so cherished and protected.

Overprotected?

Eve wondered where that had come from. The happy-thought routine wasn't working as well as usual. Maybe she was a little nutty from her isolation.

Adam had said there was a news blackout on her; apparently the blackout was very effective. She noticed there wasn't a word about the poisoning on TV. The telephone had been silent all day. They must be holding off her calls.

He'd said only the medics and the department knew she'd be released tomorrow. Adam hadn't even mentioned the team. There was no reason to keep the information from them. That was very odd.

It occurred to her now that none of them had phoned or visited. Not that she needed anything. The aides and nurses had been terrific; the nurse had had her dress cleaned, an aide had even washed out her underthings for her, which was "above and beyond the call of duty."

But then, she wasn't exactly an ordinary patient. She surmised that there was a certain glamor attached to caring for a near-murder victim. Eve had read that in some of the attendants' glances.

As for being overprotected, that was a silly notion.

The killer hadn't succeeded. There could be another try. Eve shivered involuntarily.

She thought, *I'll be glad when Adam comes back.* It would be good to talk with someone right now.

Eve hoped that the absence and the silence of the team was the doctor's idea, not theirs. It seemed strange to be out of touch with them, she'd gotten so used to seeing them every day. But maybe they were frightened out of their wits. The coffee hadn't been meant just for her.

Maybe there wasn't going to *be* any more team. That couldn't happen. They couldn't give up now.

She had a good mind to phone Carlin. But she couldn't do that. He and the whole department had to be up to its collective ears. It could hardly be otherwise, after a murder attempt on the premises of Number One.

Eve felt her face getting warm.

The pleasant day nurse came in. "How are you doing?"

She was studying Eve's face carefully.

She put her fingers to Eve's wrist and stuck a thermometer in her mouth. "That must have been some visit," the nurse said dryly. "You've had a bit too much excitement."

Eve's captive mouth was forced to stay closed around the offending thermometer, but she hummed a protest.

"No humming," the nurse teased her. "I don't wonder. He's gorgeous." She took the thermometer out. "That's it. You'd better stay quiet or you may not get out of here tomorrow. More fever, more lockup."

"Heaven forbid," Eve grumbled.

"Do you need anything?"

"A good long run along the halls."

"Uh-uh. Inspector Kane said no-show until you're out of here. And I know I can't trust you to stop at the elevator." The nurse grinned at Eve. "The doctor's going along with him, I'm afraid."

"Okay. If that's it, that's it," Eve responded dryly.

The nurse left her dinner form to be checked off and said an aide would pick it up shortly. Eve checked without much enthusiasm; the choices were very bland indeed.

She told herself not to be a baby. It was just one more night, and she was extremely lucky just to be alive. She resigned herself to the fashion and women's magazines and to the few paperbacks volunteers had provided. Now she noticed *The Seed of Scorpio* among them; the nurse must have taken it from her handbag. Eve had brought it to lend to Clare. She hadn't read the whole book in ages, just the Taurus-Scorpio story.

She got so absorbed she barely noticed when the window turned to black from gray and the night-lights were turned on. She'd forgotten that sinister personality woven through the plot like a somber thread—the vengeful poisoner.

A Virgo.

Angela Myers. A likelier suspect than Hansen. The MO hadn't fit before; it did now. The Virgo's favored murder method was poison. Myers wouldn't have had the chance to administer poison to the other victims.

But what would she have against astrologers? She had nothing against *astrology,* for sure, surrounded by personal possessions marked with the Virgo glyph and expensive books a professional would read.

Angela Myers exhibited the most negative Virgo traits—abnormal, compulsive tidiness, a hypercritical manner, an almost neurotic prudery.

As if someone had told her she was "supposed" to be like that, and she was living her life to some twisted standard. People's characters, Eve reflected, were formed not only by astrology, but to an equal extent by their parents. She'd give a lot to know more about Myers's mother, a real nudge, she'd bet, in the light of that overheard phone conversation.

Eve summed up: Myers knew astrology, was in the midst of the Astro case; was a trusted, long-time employee "above suspicion," a frail older woman who didn't seem physically able to murder young women.

More significant, she'd acted totally out of character yesterday morning. Instead of conveniently "forgetting" the team when the Christmas lists were passed out, Myers had actually brought them to the team's office.

After having made, and poisoned, a pot of coffee.

And phoned later, not to check on some missing record, but to see if anyone would be alive to answer.

Eve shivered, feeling chilled, then quickly feverish. Her skin had that uncomfortable, prickly feeling that sometimes accompanied a fever.

Damn. She was just dying to get out of there, at that very moment, to start checking up on Angela Myers.

Her mental researches were not doing her much good: the nurse had warned her that if she had a fever, she might not be released tomorrow. That poison must have brought her down more than she was willing to admit.

Feeling inordinately thirsty she drank some water.

No wonder Adam and the doctor had forbidden her the news. If they'd known about her thoughts, she judged, they'd censor those, too, if they could.

She returned to the puzzle of Myers.

The most bothersome point was the breaking of the pattern, the ignoring of the scheduled date —the first day of the month of Capricorn.

This attempt could be entirely separate from the Astro murders. Myers could easily be responsible for the poisoning, but not the three successful murders.

An unhappy choice of words—"successful."

Eve's head began to ache and she was feeling awful. She had to stop this right now, she resolved. The important thing was to get out of here tomorrow; she'd never be able to do any detecting from a hospital bed.

She had a gloomy feeling that the team might not want to be involved, not anymore. She wouldn't blame them.

Maybe Adam didn't want *her* to be involved. Eve had a strong feeling about it.

Adam.

Inevitably the thought of him lifted her drooping spirits, cleared her mind. It was silly to prejudge him.

She turned and looked at the roses, burning against the rectangle of the dark.

No matter what else happened, he was now the one glad, glowing constant of her life. He loved her. She loved him. They would solve this thing together.

The brightness of the roses blurred, and faded. Eve gave herself up to swift, unquestioned sleep.

"Ms. Darcy?"

Eve opened her eyes and blinked, astonished. Sunlight was pouring through the window; the snow had stopped falling.

She'd slept away the night. Slept through Adam's visit.

"How are you feeling now?" the nurse asked.

"Incredibly good." It was true; she did. She felt much more energetic. "But I can't believe it. I slept through . . . everything."

The nurse was a sharp woman. "Not really. He was here, right on schedule; he didn't want to wake you. That sleep was just what you needed. From the looks of you it'll be checkout time in a few more hours."

Eve's watch was in the safe downstairs. She glimpsed the nurse's, flabbergasted at the time— eleven o'clock!

"One more checkup, though. The doctor'll be here in a few minutes. We'll let the Inspector know. He's getting a little sleep now himself. He was outside your room all night," the nurse volunteered before she went out.

Poor Adam. He must be dead on his feet. Eve pictured him on guard, grim and unrelenting, and she was overcome with tenderness.

In a little while the doctor was checking her out, pronouncing her ready to be discharged. Eve was amused at her own reaction: for the first time she really liked him, now that he had given her good news.

When she got up she felt fairly steady on her feet and was allowed to take a shower. What with her late breakfast, and her preparations, the discharge hour arrived before she knew it.

She was seated in the obligatory wheelchair with the roses in one arm when Adam walked into the room, beaming.

There were dark shadows under his eyes, but the eyes themselves were bright. Whatever sleep he'd gotten had done him good.

"I'll do the honors," he told the nurse, and wheeled Eve into the hall.

There was so much Eve longed to say, but she couldn't; the nurse was in their wake, handing Eve's coat to Adam.

At last they were downstairs, and bundled into her coat, Eve was walking slowly beside Adam to his car, being helped in like something infinitely precious and fragile.

When he was beside her, he said softly, "Come here to me," and pulled her toward him, kissing her with gentleness and hunger. "This is one good day, Eve," he murmured against her hair. "Now, let's get you home."

They drove in happy silence across the long bridge toward Brooklyn Heights. Eve was too full of his presence, too elated with her release, to give a thought to the case right then. The downtown skyline of Manhattan was a silver-gray splendor in the sun-washed light; it was one of those bright, cold days of dazzling clarity. She had never felt so glad to be alive.

He, too, seemed content with silence, but when they pulled up near the small white house, he seemed to tense. His eyes darted up and down the block. She saw relief on his face.

"Looks like we've lucked out," he said. "It hasn't leaked. I was afraid we might be rushed by reporters. Come on, darling. Let's get inside. First things first. I don't want you standing around . . . visible."

The way he said it made her feel uneasy. The air was freezing cold, but the house looked welcoming. Like a little fairy-tale house with its snowcapped roof and the white drifts around it.

The stairs left her slightly winded, but she was careful not to let Adam know. The last thing she wanted was to really be back in the hospital.

He unlocked the door with his key. She

couldn't remember ever being quite so glad to be at home again.

The place was in the same shining order she had left the day before yesterday; sunlight filtered through the creamy curtains.

And she saw that something lovely had been added—masses of yellow roses, lovely in the gray and ivory and earth-colored room. Adam had used his key.

"Oh, Adam . . ." she began. But he was checking out the bedroom, bath, and kitchen. She could hear him opening and closing doors.

"Sorry, sweetheart." He was back again, taking her in his arms, hugging her close. "Sit," he ordered.

"My flowers. I've got to—"

Adam took them gently from her and laid them on the coffee table. "Don't move. Tell me where you keep your vases. I'll bring you one."

She started to protest but knew that she was glad to sit down. So she told him.

He went to the kitchen, returning with the vase filled with water. After she arranged the roses in it, he asked, "Where to?"

"The bedroom. On the big chest."

When he was back again, he said, "How about some coffee?"

She shook her head. "How about just you, Inspector?"

Adam grinned and sank down beside her, pulling her close. He leaned his head back, caressing her hair with his big hand. She looked up at him and saw that his eyes were closed. They looked deeply shadowed. "This is so nice . . . so nice," murmured.

"Adam, you're so *tired.* I have a feeling you've hardly had a wink of sleep lately. And still, you came here to fill the house with roses. I love you, Adam Kane."

He opened his eyes then, leaning down to kiss her upturned mouth. "I love you, Eve. Love you so damned much I was nearly crazy until I knew you were going to be all right."

He loosened his hold a bit, sat up on the couch as she put her hand on his knee. "How are you feeling now, darling? A little more together?"

"A lot more together." Eve squeezed his hard leg.

"Then we've got a lot of things to talk about."

"I think it's time we did. I've had enough of my little ivory tower." She smiled at him to take any sting from the remark. "I know it had to be that way."

"It did. I'm glad you can see it. But I wasn't talking about the case, Eve. There's another . . . item I wanted to bring up. Now that you're *compos mentis,* feeling better." His penetrating eyes twinkled at her.

He sat forward, reaching in his jacket pocket, bringing out a small square box of dark-green velvet.

He held it out to her, snapping open the lid with his thumb to reveal a beautiful ring against ivory satin. Eve had never seen anything like it; it was starkly simple, composed of two rectangular gems, nestling as close to each other as yang and yin—a rich emerald as clear as water and green as grass; a vivid honey topaz the hue of sherry with candlelight behind it.

Their birthstones, emerald for Taurus and topaz for Scorpios of November. The ring was set in a narrow wave of gold whose shape suggested both the leaves of earth and form of water. Like the marriage ring in *Seed of Scorpio.*

"Will you put it on?" he asked her softly.

Looking into his eyes she nodded. He slipped the ring from its lip of satin and put it on the fourth finger of her left hand. Then, raising the ringed hand to his mouth, he kissed it, keeping his dark glance all the while on her happy face.

"I had to know that you'd say yes to what this means," he whispered. "You do . . . don't you, Eve? Please say it."

"Yes. Oh, yes, yes, yes, Inspector!" She felt she was babbling, high and giddy with her declaration.

"Eve, I'm so glad. I wanted to give you this yesterday," he confided. "But it didn't seem . . . fair. You looked so weak, so . . . confused. I couldn't ask you then, somehow."

"I'm glad you didn't give it to me then. I want it on my hand, not in a hospital *safe.*" Eve held out her hand to admire the glowing colors of the gems in the gentle light. "Our birthstones. It's such a perfect symbol, Adam. You've become very knowledgeable about these things."

He hugged her. "I've been reading about it, during the long watches of the night. More and more your art makes more solid sense." He kissed her nose. "I've become conversant with medicine too," he added dryly. "And you're not following doctor's orders."

She shrugged. "Oh, *that.*"

"Yes, 'that.' " He got up and took her hands. "Some more bed rest this afternoon, and tonight. I know you hate it, honey, but you've got to."

He picked up her bag and hung her coat in the closet, walking her into the bedroom. "Get yourself undressed and into bed," he directed. "Then I'm going to bring you every single thing you need and stay here with you until your watchdog comes."

"My watchdog?" She turned from the closet, where she was withdrawing a nightgown and slippers.

"That's something else I want to discuss with you." She sat down on the bed. "For the time being I've assigned a policewoman to be here with you when I'm away. But I was wondering" —he put his hands lightly on her shoulders, smiling—"if you'd let me take the night shift?"

"I couldn't imagine a better arrangement. Nothing in the world would please me more."

His dark eyes brightened. "I was hoping you'd say that." He kissed her again, then straightened, suddenly all business. "Okay. I'll let you get yourself ready for bed, while I make some tea." He raised a sandy brow. "That wasn't the most tactful suggestion a while ago . . . about the coffee."

Wonderingly she said, "I didn't even think about it."

195

"Don't think about it now. Just get yourself comfortable."

While she got into the gown, Eve heard him whistling in the kitchen. After a while she heard another whistle—the homey sound of the kettle's small siren. She smiled to herself in the cozy bed. The bright roses flamed on the shining chest, the vivid gems in her betrothal ring echoed themselves in the colors of the star-burst quilt. At that instant even the shadow of her brush with death was gone. When Adam came in with the tea, she hoped her welcoming eyes were eloquent enough: her heart was too full for her to say how much love she was feeling.

They must be, she decided. Adam's dark and piercing eyes had never looked so happy. She held out her hand for the tea but never made it. She was sinking into sleep again.

When she woke the light was brighter, golden. It must be dark outside, she marveled. Her mind felt clear as glass.

A woman's voice, then a man's, reached her from the living room. Adam, of course. The woman said something else.

Osborne. Marnie Osborne.

Her "watchdog" for the interim would be the woman on first-name terms with Myers. Eve's thoughts raced: if she intended to investigate Myers, she could hardly do it around Marnie Osborne.

But she could. She could start by doing it *through* Osborne. Now she might be able to find out what it was that Marnie Osborne had twice

196

started to say and left unfinished, once when she ran out of time, the other when Hansen was the topic of conversation.

Osborne's presence meant Adam had to leave. And there was still so much Eve wanted to ask him. First, the department's intentions toward the team. On the other hand Eve was not at all sure how much she wanted to tell him. She might be way off base in suspecting Myers; there was no point in bringing it up until she had a lot more to go on.

Eve made a restless movement with her hand, rocking a metal ashtray on her bed table. Adam was suddenly walking through the door; his sharp ears must have caught the slight sound.

He closed the door and walked over to the bed. "How do you feel now, baby?" He sat down on the edge of the bed and put his hand on her arm.

"Like getting up this minute," she retorted.

"No way. You stay put. Marnie'll be here till I get back. She can fix you something to eat, help you with anything you need. And I've got two men outside." He peered at her. "Marnie is okay with you, isn't she? I thought she'd be the best choice. She said you two had lunch together, that you'd been terrific to her. I figured you two had gotten pretty friendly."

He'd taken so much trouble to please her that she said warmly, "We are. It was sweet of you to bring her." She raised her hand to his face and petted his cheek. Lowering her voice a little, she murmured, "All the same, she's a poor substitute."

Adam pressed her hand, ran his fingers slowly down her arm.

"And work's a damned poor substitute for this." Leaning over he kissed her chin and nose, her brow and cheeks, then lingered on her mouth. "But I've got work to do. Another lead on . . . Wednesday."

She had a feeling that was going to be their code word for what had happened to her. Adam seemed to be avoiding the bald words—*the poisoning.* It saddened her to think their little moment of escape was over. The next time they talked, she knew it would be about every aspect of the case.

Eve nodded, clinging to his hand. "I hate it, honey, but I've got to go. Remember, you'll be fine with Marnie Osborne, and the other two. Everything's been checked to a fare-thee-well. She'll fill you in some more. Meanwhile"—he stood up, still holding onto her hand—"I'll miss you like the devil. I'll be as early as I can."

Reluctantly his fingers let hers go and he walked out. She heard him call out, "Marnie. Shift change," and Osborne's cheerful answer and light, approaching footstep on the varnished floor.

"Eve." She came in smiling.

Eve looked at her in surprise. "You look wonderful!"

Marnie's thin face brightened at the compliment. She'd had her promised haircut: her pale, curly hair was short and frothy, showing off the pretty shape of her head. She was wearing light

198

makeup but she'd done a lot with her big, sky-colored eyes. Even in her usual uniform she managed somehow to look much more appealing.

"I can't get over you," Eve said warmly. "You're a whole new woman."

"It's all because of you, you know. You got me started to . . . like myself." Marnie grinned. "Mind if I light up?"

"Mind? I'd love it. I had nicotine fits in the hospital." Eve lit one of her own cigarettes. "Sit down."

"Not until I get you something to eat. The inspector clued me in about your diet. He's laid in a stock of all the thrilling items . . . soup and milk and pudding."

"I can't wait. I really can't wait until tomorrow, when I won't have to be waited on."

"Nothing to it. What'll it be? There must be fifty kinds of soup out there and eighteen puddings." Marnie wriggled her newly tamed brows, making Eve giggle.

She named a flavor for both. "You've got it. I won't be two minutes."

Adam had thought of everything, it seemed. Eve decided to wash up a bit before she ate and went into the bathroom. Something looked different, although everything was still the same. Strange.

It was all new—toothpaste, shampoo; in the medicine cabinet, new medications. "Everything's been checked to a fare-thee-well," Adam had said. It certainly had. A typical Scorpio . . . he hadn't missed a thing. He'd probably replaced all the food in the kitchen, too, and not just to provide her bland diet.

Eve washed up and, feeling shaky again, went back to bed.

Smiling, Marnie came in with a tray. Eve felt new guilt: Marnie was such a darling, not only guarding her but nursing her with an absolute zest that shamed Eve when she thought of using Marnie further by picking her brains.

But she couldn't pass up a chance like this. Marnie, with her curious and confiding ways, was just the one to fill Eve in on Myers.

Marnie sat down as Eve started eating her soup. "Look here," Eve said, "if you're missing anything on TV, don't be polite."

"I'm not, until later."

"Good. It's nice to have you to talk to, after being in solitary." Eve grinned at her. "Not about the case either."

"That's a relief. The inspector said he'd bust me to a meter maid if I let you talk shop tonight."

"Do you like Scrabble?"

"*Love* it," Marnie assured her. Eve told her where the set was, and after she'd removed the tray Marnie brought in the game.

"What's happening with *you?*" Eve demanded while they were getting set up. "I never saw you look so good."

Marnie beamed. "I never *felt* so good. I've told Hansen to take a walk."

"Great."

"And there's someone new, just the way you

predicted." Marnie's eyes sparkled. "A Sagittarius . . . and *single.*"

"You sure got that horse on the wrong end of the wagon," Eve teased her. "But I'm really glad, Marnie."

Marnie caught the gleam of Eve's ring. "New?" she asked inquisitively.

"*Very* new. Today." Eve thought, *Why am I so damned closemouthed? Marnie's always so open.* It seemed ungenerous not to respond in kind. "From Adam."

"Oh, that's marvelous. I think he's sensational. He's always been so nice to me," Marnie confided. "And I think he's got more respect for me now, since the Hansen thing's over. Kane seems to know *everything.*"

"That doesn't surprise me."

They were soon into an intense and friendly game; Marnie was a sharp competitor, which made it even more fun.

Adding up her score, Eve remarked casually, "Things must be chaos in the DC's office."

"You've got that right." Marnie turned over her new tiles. "Angie's worked off her feet."

It was the perfect opening. Eve was jubilant.

CHAPTER EIGHT

"That's nothing new," Eve commented. "I've never seen her otherwise. She must have a tough job."

Eve won herself a triple word score, building *deception* on Marnie's innocent *ion*. All too apt. She played her last tile, conscious of her partner's glance. Eve's remark had been very kind, considering she'd never expressed any liking for Angela Myers.

To justify it Eve added, "I guess I feel bad about disliking her so much. You said she'd had a hard time of it."

Eve called herself a hypocrite, as soon as she said that. But no snooper with blood in her veins could have resisted an opening like that. "Are you two . . . close?"

She was relieved when Marnie Osborne said, "Oh, *no*. Not close. I don't think Angie's close to anybody, except maybe her mother."

Eve absently totted up her score. While Marnie started playing, she asked casually, "What's her mother like?"

"An absolute monster, frankly." She built two short words on Eve's *deception.*

"Really?"

"Oh, yes. I only met her a couple of times, but that was enough. It's obvious who made Angie such a mess, poor thing. She's an astrologer, you know."

An astrologer. "Who? 'Angie' . . . or her mother?"

"Her mother. As a matter of fact—" Marnie flushed. "I do have the biggest mouth in New York."

"No, you don't." Eve smiled at her. "I *asked.*"

"Well . . . say, would you like to scrap this game? You're winning, anyway, and I'd just as soon talk." Eve grinned at Marnie's rationale.

"Sure. So would I." Indeed she would. This was getting more interesting by the minute. "Aren't you hungry, though?"

"Not yet. I'll build myself a sandwich when it's time for my 'night soap.' Would you like anything?"

Eve shook her head. "No, thanks. Give me that." She indicated the Scrabble set. "I'll put it back together. So Mrs. Myers is an astrologer," she prompted.

"Mrs. Duluth. Myers is Angie's married name."

"Yes, I remember." Eve dismantled the board and started putting the tiles away.

"I don't think she's a very good one. Not like you," Marnie commented. "She's kind of rigid,

204

and mean as a snake. A Virgo, with Scorpio rising, Angie said."

"That *is* a combination. Why were you so antsy before, Marnie, when you said she was an astrologer . . . and then commented on your 'big mouth'?"

Marnie looked abashed. She lit another cigarette, taking the Scrabble box from Eve. "It's embarrassing. You see, she was really teed off when Carlin hired you and your team, after she'd offered her own services to the department, for free."

"I see." So that's what Myers and her mother had been talking about that day Eve overheard the phone conversation. She told Marnie about it.

"Poor Angie. Her mother nags her all the time. Why she keeps on living with the woman I'll never know."

"Good heavens. She and her husband live with her mother?"

"Her husband? Oh, *no.* Angie's been divorced for a *long* time," Marnie offered.

"But she insisted that I call her Mrs. Myers," Eve said, bewildered.

"Poor thing. Her husband's divorced. Angie's never been. If you know what I mean." Marnie raised her brows.

"I know what you mean, Marnie. That's sad."

"Peter left her, actually. For another woman." Marnie was warming to her subject; she seemed relieved that Eve wanted to discuss personalities rather than police business, because she was looking more relaxed now. Apparently Adam had

205

clued her in about introducing "upsetting" topics.

If he only knew. Eve's brain was going a mile a minute now. She just had to keep Marnie talking about Myers.

When Eve remained silent, Marnie looked at her and asked, "You're not getting tired, are you?"

"Oh, no! Never. You can't imagine how I'm enjoying this," Eve assured her. She felt like a witch, but it was partly true, after all. She'd had her fill of silence and isolation at the hospital. "He left her, you said. That's a pity."

"It certainly is. They'd been married for eighteen years, then he picked up and ran off with a girl who hadn't been alive much longer than that. A client of Mrs. Duluth's, no less." Marnie made a face. "Peter came over to pick Angie up at her mother's one time . . . this sexy kid was just leaving after a consultation. And the rest is history."

"How awful." Eve lit a cigarette for herself. "You wouldn't think she'd want to live with her mother after that, would you? The 'scene of the crime,' and all that," Eve added dryly.

"*I* wouldn't. But that's the strange thing—Angie's got some kind of . . . weird attachment to her mother. She's way too old to be that dependent. I'm crazy about my mother, but there's a time to leave the nest . . . you know?"

"I certainly do. My mother taught me to 'fly' very early on." Eve smiled, thinking back fondly.

"So did mine. And I'm glad."

206

They were getting off the subject. "I see now what you mean . . . about Angie having a hard time." The nickname came very naturally now to Eve's lips; she felt she knew Myers, more and more. But with her compassion she continued to feel something else—increasing suspicion. It all hung together so well. "How did you two get to be friends?"

"It's the strangest thing. I can't even call us friends. More like friendly acquaintances. What we had in common was an interest in astrology. You know, Eve, it sounds . . . kind of awful. But I'm about the only person who ever took the trouble to talk to her. She turns people off, with that prissy, stiff personality. But I felt . . . sorry for her."

"So do I, Marnie. So do I. Terribly." Eve leaned back and blew a smoke ring and watched the misty grayness break, disappear.

I must be going mad, she decided. *I think it was Myers who tried to kill me.*

Marnie went on, "It must be awful . . . living with that mother in that creepy house. Like that Brooklyn witch in the movie."

"They live in Brooklyn?" Eve felt apprehension scurry over her flesh.

"Way out in Coney Island."

The farther out the better, Eve reflected darkly.

Misreading her expression Marnie said, "I've been talking your ear off. How are you feeling? You look a little pale."

"I'm fine. A little tired, maybe. I might try to take another nap." That wasn't strictly true, but

207

Eve was eager to be alone for a while, put together all the fascinating information Marnie Osborne had supplied.

"Do that." Marnie looked at her watch. "I can't believe what time it is—eight-thirty already. My program comes on at nine. Are you sure it won't bother you?"

"Not a bit. Go. Get yourself some food, and enjoy."

Marnie went out with the Scrabble set under her arm and closed the door.

Eve let out a sigh of relief. It had made her very nervous to pick Marnie's brains like that in the guise of friendly conversation.

But she was elated over the harvest of data: most of it added up to an A-one motive for the deaths of three pretty young astrologers.

Myers had a love-hate relationship with her astrologer-mother, likely to make her both obsessed with and hostile to astrology. And she had another reason to hate it. Astrology had brought Myers's husband together with her young rival.

If she had killed those astrologers, she had been able to murder two women each time—her mother and a young, beautiful woman. Eve thought, *I'd give a lot to know the signs of Myers's husband and his lover.* Ten to one the girl had been an Aries. That was the sign of the first murdered astrologer. On the other hand what about Libra? Linda Asbury, an Aries, had been killed on September twenty-fourth, the first day of the month of Libra.

If Myers's errant husband had been that much

attracted to an Aries, he could well have been a sign incompatible with Myers's Virgo; and her "monster" mother would have been quick to remind Angela Myers of that. Another source of rage and frustration.

Of course, Eve was building a whole structure on a base of speculation. Yet her sheer intuition had led to the capture of Chicago's Star Slayer. If instinct had worked then, it could work now.

Eve leaned back and let her intuition take over. If something worked, she thought wryly, why fix it?

Her theory was still suspicion without evidence, however. She needed to get hold of Angela Myers's chart. With an astrologer for a mother she was bound to have one, likely a synastry, too, charted before and after Myers's marriage. Astrologers generally kept family charts separate from their other records. That meant Myers's chart might not be available through the association's data patched in to the department.

I might have to do some burgling, Eve decided. It was a wild, improbable idea. But in her checkered forensics career she'd actually come across some positively likable burglars—unarguably felons, but people who shrank from violence, proud of the fact that they had always been "only" thieves. Paul had used one for an informer in Chicago, been taught the tricks of his trade. For a gag once Paul had shown Eve how to pick locks; she hadn't forgotten. It wasn't exactly the kind of thing she would use for dinner conversation, but it was a handy skill on the occasions when she'd locked herself out of her own place.

Eve took a pad and pen from her bed-table drawer and began to sketch out a rough plan. In the midst of it she almost laughed out loud. Poor Adam had taken pains to shield her from upset these last few days, even from news. And here she was jumping headfirst into an actual violation of law.

There was an astrology conference scheduled for Wednesday, December eighteenth at a college in Brooklyn. Angela Myers would be at work; her mother was bound to be at the conference. It was an important one, and the next wouldn't be held until late spring.

Eve cussed the happenstance of having to turn down an invitation to speak there; lecturing on the Star Slayer would have inevitably led to the Astro Killer, and all that was top secret at the moment. That would have been the perfect escape. And she'd have Marnie sticking to her like a cocklebur. Well, she'd just have to think of some way to give Marnie the slip. Check the conference registration, too, for Duluth. If she'd already paid, she was likelier to be there.

She had to get into that house. Unless Myers had a copy of her chart, and the comparative chart done on her and her husband, at the office. Many people did.

That was no good at all: Eve could hardly rummage around in Myers's personal files under the very nose of Carlin's staff. Besides, she had a feeling Angela Myers rarely left her desk. Every time

Eve had seen her she'd looked as if she'd been sculpted as part of her chair.

Eve put the pad and pen on her table.

She could hardly believe what she had been planning—the commission of a technical crime to check out an unfounded idea. Breaking and entering, for heaven's sake; the theft of another person's property, which the chart assuredly was.

Eve shook her head. There must be a better way. But if there was, she couldn't find one.

Faintly through the closed door she heard the music heralding the finale to Marnie's prime-time soap. Then the music went off and she heard Marnie approaching the bedroom, opening the door.

"Hi! How was the show?"

"Fabulous," Marnie enthused. "The perfect escape. All kinds of new and juicy things are going on. Do you follow it at all?"

"I'm afraid I don't."

"I won't tell you, then. You'd need a scorecard to know who's what and who. Would you like anything from the kitchen?"

"I'd like to get up and get it myself," Eve said ruefully. "But to be more polite I'd love a soda."

"You've got it." The good-natured Marnie went off on her errand. When she returned with the soda, she remarked, "The inspector should be along pretty soon. He said he was only going to work half a day, since he hasn't slept in about six."

For the first time since she'd come to love Adam Kane, Eve had mixed feelings. On the one hand she couldn't wait to see him; on the other there was still a lot she wanted to find out about Angela Myers. But she said, "Good. Then your long day will be over."

"And yours will start." Marnie grinned, but she seemed a bit embarrassed over the personal remark. "Would you like some company?" she asked hastily.

"Love it. Unless you'd rather watch some more TV." Eve smiled warmly at Marnie to show that she hadn't been offended by the remark, that she wasn't totally the austere self she'd presented before. After all, she'd confided in Marnie about the ring. And Adam's taking the "night shift" left no doubt about their status, anyway. "Aren't you drinking?"

"I already did. What have you been doing with yourself?"

"Just taking some notes for . . . work," Eve responded, hoping that Marnie's sharp eyes hadn't deciphered her rather illegible notes, lying under a stream of lamplight on the table.

"Oh." Marnie Osborne looked positively dismayed. The team's work must be another forbidden topic. Eve was convinced of it now—Adam must have persuaded Carlin to take them off the case. But she certainly wasn't going to press Marnie; she was only following orders.

So she said quickly, "I've been thinking about our conversation about Angela Myers. That poor woman has had an awful time of it." She hoped she wasn't being too heavy handed; Marnie might wonder about her sudden interest in someone

212

she'd made no secret of disliking. "I'm afraid I'm getting to be an awful gossip. Confinement, you know. Before this I was literally never bedbound in my life."

"I haven't been, either, knock on wood." Marnie rapped her slender knuckles on the bed table, almost touching the damning notes. "You're a very compassionate person, Eve. You know that?"

Eve felt worse than ever, but her desire to pursue the subject was stronger now than any guilt. "Not so very," she said dismissively. "I think it was more of an astrological interest. I was wondering what sign her husband is."

"Libra. Not too great for Virgo, right?"

"*Too* right."

Libra. Eve was getting goose pimples.

"Was his . . . girlfriend an Aries, by any chance?" she asked Marnie.

"You're *fantastic!* I think you're as big a witch as Angie's mother," Marnie teased her. "Except that you're a 'good witch.' The girlfriend *was* an Aries."

Under ordinary circumstances Eve would have laughed at Marnie's comment and her expression, which approached awe. But she did feel witchy, manipulating Marnie like this.

"You are absolutely psychic," Marnie declared.

"I've just had practice. A lot of practice." Eve made light of it, but she was delighted with the accuracy of her educated guesses. That made the first murder all the more significant—the time was that of Peter Myers's sign, the victim was the same sign as the destroyer of Myers's marriage.

Eve was so excited she could barely contain herself. But she knew she'd better simmer down: Marnie was a bright woman, and a policewoman at that. If Eve revealed the true depth of her interest, her suspicions might not be a secret much longer.

"Well, enough of all that." She tried to sound as if she were getting bored with the subject. "We haven't talked a bit about you. I want to hear about *the* Sagittarius."

"Don't get me started," Marnie warned her, laughing.

"I think I already have," Eve kidded. "Go on."

And Marnie proceeded to describe her exciting new love in great detail. Eve tried to listen, but she was constantly distracted by her plans of research and pursuit.

Marnie was in midsentence when they heard the key turn in the front door. "That's the inspector."

Eve recognized his step, heard him call out, "Osborne?"

"Here, Inspector, with the perpetrator."

Adam's big laugh filled the hall, and Eve felt her heart quicken. All of a sudden her obsession with Myers began to wane: when she saw his massive frame fill the doorway, and he asked, "Has the prisoner been behaving?" every other consideration was dismissed.

While she groped for a witty answer, all Eve could do, for the moment, was to stare delighted into his dark, gleaming eyes, savoring the welcome sight of his tired but joyful face.

Eve opened her eyes to the gray morning light; her body felt warm and sheltered. She was cradled in Adam's arms, with her back to him, and could hear his deep, steady breathing.

Amazing, she decided: that doctor was right on schedule. She felt exactly like herself again. If she had been alone, she would have leapt out of bed, enjoying the return of her well-being.

But she wasn't. Not by half. Eve smiled, snuggling closer to Adam; she heard him murmur, felt the strong arms tighten around her.

"Ummm." He held her more tightly, kissing the back of her head. "How's the prisoner's health?"

"Perfect." Eve turned slowly and slid her arms around his neck.

"Absolutely sure?" He was more awake now, speaking against her lips. The sensation was pure torture, she suddenly wanted him so much.

"Never . . . surer . . . in . . . my life." Deliberately she said each word against his mouth, feeling his breath quicken, sensing the swift arousal of his need. "What about you, Inspector?" Eve turned her head and whispered in his ear. "Marnie said you hadn't slept for a week."

"That was last night." He chuckled. After Marnie's lieutenant had picked her up, Adam had gone out like a light. "This is morning." He slid his arms down her sides, pressing her waist, running his fingers over the curves of her, making sounds of yearning and expectation.

"So it is." She moved nearer to him. "A wonderful morning. And I'm better than new, Inspector. Back to rude health. Shall I show you just how rude my health is?" She was caressing him boldly.

"Oh, Eve. Eve." He wasn't smiling anymore; he was solemn, almost desperate, with the intensity of his desire. His naked skin was firm and heated, heaven to stroke, to touch.

"Freeze," she ordered, smiling. She held him close, sliding down his body.

"What . . . what's the prisoner doing?" He was trying to match her lightness, but not succeeding very well. His deep voice was shaky with excitement and surprise.

She gave him no answer other than a fresh caress, letting her half-open mouth wander over his tense, hair-roughened chest; she kissed the pounding flesh above his heart, the vibrant hardness of his solar plexus, the excellent flatness of his stomach.

"Eve . . ." he whispered. She could feel the quaking of his body as she began the boldest, light caress. He was crying out, and the smell and sound and taste of him were driving her to an abandonment that she had never imagined, a wildness she had never known, or dreamed of knowing, with anyone. It drove her on to madder and wilder acts, thrilled her as if it were *her* flesh that was the recipient of delight. At last he cried out half in pleasure, half in protest, slowing her with sudden strength. With passionate delight he began reciprocating all the joy she had given him.

Now they rose and soared together to that glorious peak of ecstasy, and her body broke in warm and flowing fragments of sun and rocking waters. Like the widening rings of ripples in a still lake, she at last grew calm.

Breathless, they were still for a long instant stroking each other, too overcome to say a word.

Then leisurely, at last, they were lying again, face to face, and his big, still-shaky hands traced the softness of her body.

He pulled her to him, urging her head onto his wide chest, and she could hear the rumble of his voice when he said, at last, "Never . . . never was there anything like that. For me. Not in all my life."

"Nor for me, Adam. I don't . . . know what . . . happened to me," she whispered, becoming irrationally shy.

His arm bound her and his strong hands stroked her side. "It doesn't matter. I'm just so glad it *did.*"

Eve raised her head to look at his face. It was like none of the several faces he'd worn before: his dark, sharp eyes were heavy-lidded, his mouth unutterably tender, and some of the lines of strain and exhaustion were gone.

She could not find the words to express her wonder, and yet she struggled for them. They must not go unsaid.

"Every time you're . . . this close to me," she

murmured, "I feel like your phoenix, renewing itself from its ashes."

He hugged her close, with his chin brushing the top of her head, and she could feel his warm breath when he asked gently, "*My* phoenix?"

She told him then about the various symbols of Scorpio, among them the phoenix, for the sign's power of regeneration; the eagle, for potency and triumph.

"Strange," he said. "I've always had a special feeling for the eagle. Now you show me why."

Eve looked up at him, suspecting he might be indulging her a bit. But his face was quite serious, and his eyes looked at her warmly.

"I mean it. I had no idea how much there was to what you do, or how close it comes to the way people are. Like the same numbers turning up again and again." She was listening intently, pleased by what he was saying. But all of a sudden she had a strong desire to be up again and doing.

Involuntarily she stirred in his embrace.

He chuckled. "Someone wants to get up. I don't blame you."

"Oh, Adam, it's not . . . this is . . . wonderful."

"The most wonderful thing in the world." He kissed her forehead. "But it's just as well. I've got to go soon." He took his watch from the bedtable and slipped it on. "Marnie'll be here in about . . . twenty minutes."

"Ohh." Eve sat up in bed. "I wanted to make your breakfast."

Adam was getting up. "No *way*. Maybe tomorrow." He stood there smiling down at her, and once again she was struck by the extraordinary power of his body; he looked Herculean in his narrow briefs with his wide chest and shoulders, his big biceps, his lean hips and middle, and his stalwart legs. "Marnie can make yours."

The devil she will, Eve thought, but didn't say so. Instead she made a face at Adam. "I'd better enjoy the view, then, while I can."

"I like the way you think." He grinned at her, slipping into his undershirt, getting the rest of his clothes on. "Why don't I make us some coffee—if you'll excuse the expression?"

His words reminded her that he still hadn't told her a word about the case. Of course they hadn't had a chance last night. Or this morning. "All right, Inspector. I accept."

He went off toward the kitchen and Eve showered and put on a bright striped shirt and gray denim trousers, glad to be in real clothes again.

"Hey, you look good," he approved when she entered the kitchen.

"I *feel* good. I feel fantastic. Thanks." She sat while he poured their coffee, feeling an affectionate amusement for his masculine awkwardness in handling things, noticing that with a man's erring instinct for dishes he'd managed to give them soup spoons. That touched her deeply, the way little things could. "You are so sweet, Adam Kane."

"Big deal," he teased her, beaming at her over the rim of his cup. "Oh, Eve, I wish we had more

219

time. I hate to rush off like this. This morning was . . . I can't tell you."

"I know. You don't have to." She reached across the table for his hand, which closed around hers, squeezing it hard.

"I hope I can be earlier tonight. And then tomorrow . . ." He said the word with hope, anticipation. "Look here, darling, I know we haven't talked about the . . . attempt. We're going to. We've got to. You understand why I wanted to wait."

"Of course. For me," she said gently.

"That's it. Tonight, tomorrow, we will, Eve. There's a lot to get squared away." She thought, *My role in the case, for one.* But they couldn't get started on that now. "And today I don't want you to knock yourself out, all right? Your system took a hell of a whack. But more important, Marnie's got to be glued to you when I'm not here . . . for a while longer." He spoke with a grim inflection. "We're getting closer, but—"

The doorbell cut him off. He kissed Eve and went to let Marnie in.

Eve was already plotting: she had to start checking on Myers. And she couldn't let the police know, especially the ones named Kane and Osborne. She went out to the living room. Adam was already gone.

"Join me in breakfast?" she invited Marnie.

"Had mine, thanks." Marnie was rubbing her hands.

"Come on. I'll give you some coffee."

After breakfast—and Eve enjoyed the "real

food" for a change—she and Marnie wandered back to the living room. "Can you hack this confinement?"

"*Hack* it? I'll wallow in it," Marnie declared. She took off her shoes and stretched out on the couch with a book she'd brought along.

Eve was glad her work area was a comfortable distance from the couch, and that Marnie's back was to her. She got her computer going, punched buttons, looked at the screen. LILAH DULUTH, 1223 MERMAID COURT, SEA GATE, flashed on.

Lilah. One of the variations of the name Lilith, the "dark moon" and "mother of demons." Mother of demons. Spooky.

Eve took out a Brooklyn map: Sea Gate was at the very end of the borough, past Coney Island, a projection of land into Gravesend Bay.

The name *Gravesend* also had a gloomy ring.

She could end up in her own grave by going to Gravesend Bay alone. But if she started thinking like that, she'd never follow through. And her feeling was so strong that she knew she was on the right track. She just knew it.

Fervently wishing she was at Number One, where she could get driver-license info on Lilah Duluth, Eve recognized one very important aspect: if Mrs. Duluth drove to the conference, it could take her a lot longer to get back home. Maybe she'd drive *with* someone. No astrologer willingly took a train or bus right now.

Eve dismissed that question for the moment, asked for Lilah Duluth's chart, and got it. But

221

when she requested Angela Myers's, she got *No Record*. She tried Angela Duluth; *No Record* appeared on the screen.

Marnie shifted on the couch, turning her head slightly, and Eve's heart jumped up in her throat. She erased the screen and said casually, "Put on some music if you like. When I get busy I don't even hear it."

"Thanks." Marnie turned and smiled. "But the quiet's nice. Quite a change from Numero Uno."

Eve didn't answer, thinking, *I wish I were at Numero Uno right now.* That reminded her of Iris and the team. It still seemed strange that Adam hadn't wanted them to know she was out of the hospital. She was going to ask him why tonight, for sure.

One thing at a time, though. She was wild with curiosity about Lilah Duluth's chart and went over it quickly. What an overpowering one it was —a preponderance of planets in Scorpio and Capricorn, indicating relentless, impermeable strength. The aspects of a prima donna.

Eve leaned back in her chair, fired with excitement. Placements indicating enormous power and domineering qualities . . . an overwhelming mother with a repressed, apparently impotent daughter.

She examined the chart again: the placement of the dark moon Lilith at Duluth's birth, that enigmatic satellite without the luminosity of the larger earth Moon, was such that it marked difficult childbirth. If Lilah Duluth had had unusual difficulty in bearing Angela, she could unconsciously wish to punish her daughter.

Now Eve was almost wild to see the chart of Angela Myers.

She expelled a loud sigh.

"What's the matter?" Marnie put down her book and swiveled around on the couch. "Tough problem?"

"Don't ask," Eve retorted, wishing she could share it. But that was about as impossible as it was going to be to evade Marnie on Big Wednesday. When she looked at the clock on one of her shelves, she was surprised that she'd been at it for more than two hours. She'd been so lost in thought, so engrossed in Duluth's chart, that the time had sped.

What she'd told Marnie was true: she did have to catch up on private charts. Putting the Duluth material aside with reluctance she started to do so.

Later she fixed some lunch for herself and Marnie. Then, while her bodyguard napped, Eve went back to her postponed horoscopes, working straight through until it was dark again.

After she'd showered and washed her hair, Adam phoned.

"Going stir crazy?" he asked her tenderly.

"Not a bit," she said, meaning it. "The guards have let me work in the kitchen and the shop."

He chuckled. "You're a model inmate. Can you stand another night behind bars . . . with a plain cop?"

"I can serve a term like that *standing*," she boasted, putting on a tough accent.

"That's not exactly what I had in mind," he retorted, "but whatever turns you on."

"You're disgusting," she scolded, but the way she said it made it sound like "You're wonderful." She lowered her voice. "I love you, anyway."

"I love you." Now his voice had no laughter in it. "And I can't wait to see you. Be there about seven."

She hung up in a glow, remembering too late that she hadn't said a single word about dinner.

When he walked in at seven, the first words out of his mouth were, "I didn't say a word about dinner." They caught each other's eye and laughed. He was laden with heavy-looking paper bags. "Do you like Chinese?"

"I *love* Chinese."

"That's a relief." He started toward the kitchen with his burden. "Marnie? How about you? There's enough here for the squad room."

"No, thanks, Inspector." Marnie, freshly made up, looked eager to leave. "I have a capital *D* Date. If he's not outside you can bust him."

"I'll do that. Good night."

When they were alone, Adam grabbed Eve in his arms and kissed her, hugging her close; he was still wearing his coat and hat.

She reached up and took his hat off, caressing his hair. "Welcome home, Inspector."

He still held her, gazing down into her face.

"That's just what it is, Eve. Home is where you are."

"It's just like that for me," she whispered, raising her face for another kiss.

Then suddenly they were light and easy with each other; he was taking off his coat, asking her if she was hungry, and she was saying she was starved, delighted to be off Pablum.

They dished out the food together, eating cozily in the kitchen; sat replete over coffee, looking at each other.

"I'm sorry it's had to be like this, darling. I know you feel like a bird in a cage."

"A bit," she admitted.

"You've been so sweet and patient. Not even asking me anything. I appreciate that, Eve." He took her hand. "But I know there must be a hundred things you want to ask now. Ask them."

She nodded, lighting a cigarette. "There are. I wondered why the team has to be kept in the dark."

He met her eyes levelly. "Because, for one thing, I suspected one of them. Betty Rivers."

She was appalled. *"Betty?* But Adam . . . why?"

He told her what had come out in his conversation with Iris—Betty's remark about "pouring your poison."

Eve had totally forgotten until now. "Good Lord. But it was just . . . a manner of speaking."

"I know that now. She's been checked out. I couldn't tell you a thing like that when you were

225

feeling so low. Surely you understand, darling. There was another reason: I could hardly tell you before we'd cleared her."

"No," she answered slowly. "I guess you couldn't. It's just so . . ." She shook her head. "But what's been happening, Adam? What have you got?"

She thought she saw his eyes grow secretive. But he said promptly, "Nothing definite. And a hell of a lot of work behind us already. We've interrogated hundreds of people since Wednesday afternoon, investigated them down to their tooth enamel. It doesn't look like an outside job." His face was grim. "It could be someone in the department, Eve."

Her heart lurched. *Someone close to Carlin,* she answered in silence. She lowered her eyes a second to hide the excitement in them, wishing she could come right out and say it, wanting to be open with him.

"We're tied into your association's computer," he went on, "comparing staff names with astrologers' client names."

Oh, my God, she thought. Could her computer inquiry have been seen at Number One? These computer breaks did happen. Vaguely she heard him add something about eliminating two thirds. She looked at him a little blankly.

"Two thirds of the department's staff," he repeated, studying her. "Are you okay?"

"Of course. I was just thinking—I'll be glad to get back to give you a hand." Now he really looked uncomfortable.

"Eve, listen . . ." He reached for her hand again, and she let it lie limply in his big fingers. "Honey, this is the thing I hated, most of all, to tell you. You're off the case. There isn't going to be any more team."

Even though she'd half expected it, she repeated numbly, "Off the case? You can't mean it, Adam. You can't *do* this."

"It's already done. It was done last Wednesday afternoon, right after the . . . attempt was made on you. It's too dangerous now. You can't be a sitting duck for some lunatic. Didn't you listen to what I was saying?" he demanded, sounding defensive. "It may be someone in the department. You can't go back there now. Do you think I'm going to allow that?"

Allow. She felt her hackles rise. This was a bit much.

"I didn't know I needed your permission to do my job." But of course she *did;* he was her immediate superior. "What does Carlin think?"

"He and the commissioner are with me all the way. I . . . told them how I feel about you, and they couldn't argue with that."

"How *you* feel?" In spite of herself she was getting irritated. "What about the way *I* feel, Adam? You need me more than ever now. What am I supposed to do, sit here in a chastity belt and wait until the big strong knight is back from dragon killing?"

"Nooo," he drawled, giving her a one-sided grin. "A chastity belt is the last item on my mind."

227

She was not diverted. "Dammit, Adam, don't tease me. You know what I mean. I'm not a moron. I know how to take care of myself, after Chicago."

She flushed. She hadn't taken care of herself very well when she drank that coffee.

But he ignored that, picking up on the reference to Chicago. "If Chicago was so great," he asked her softly, "what are you doing in New York . . . with me?"

Eve wondered if he could have found out about Paul. The police seemed to have connections with other departments all over the country. Her expression gave her away.

"There was someone there, wasn't there, Eve?" Adam studied her. "A real loser, I'll bet. Otherwise he'd never have let you get away." His voice softened. "I know the symptoms of a lady who's been burned, Eve. And you had them all. You've got them now. You're talking like I have no place in your life. And that's what this is about. Your life . . . and mine."

The look he gave her melted some of her icy feelings, calmed her savage impatience. It was hard to fight him when he said those things and looked that way.

But she couldn't cave in at the snap of a finger.

"What about the others on the team?" she demanded in a more level tone. "Did they accept this, just like that?"

"I don't know firsthand. Carlin talked to them." Adam got up restlessly, began to put their dishes on the counter.

"You've got an idea about who did it," she hazarded. "Don't you?"

"Yes." He met her eyes.

"And I'm going to have to pull it out of you with tweezers. You've being very Scorpionic."

He didn't respond to her teasing prod. "You're not going to pull it out of me with anything, Eve. All I've got right now is suspicion without evidence."

That's all she had on Myers, but she still knew.

"All I need is for you to go off detecting on your own," he said flatly. "The gifted amateur can end up dead." She knew he was being purposely brutal to scare her off. But it wasn't going to work. Eve had a hard time, though, controlling her expression.

"What do you say I do this KP for you, lady?" He smiled at her; the sudden switch of topic was heavy handed, for him. "And after that . . . some television?"

"What do you say I join you?" she retorted. "There's nothing wrong with me now." Eve got up and began to take care of the dishes.

Adam grinned and grabbed her from behind, pulling her to him. "You're a corker. After a giant two-day vacation I can't hold you down."

For the first time she felt restless in his embrace.

"The only thing 'wrong' with you," he added, "is that you're stubborn as a rock."

"This isn't getting dishes done."

He kissed the back of her head and let her go. When they were watching television on the

couch, Eve sensed that neither of them really
knew what they were looking at. And there was
an unease, an awkwardness, between them.

He picked up her hand and held it on his palm;
she saw him looking at the ring. She felt a little
pang: she'd hardly looked at it herself since he
had put it on her finger. This man had pledged
himself to her, with all his heart. And she'd
barely referred to that since yesterday. All she'd
done this evening was nag him about the case.

That must have hurt him, but he was not the
kind of man who'd say so. The typical reticent,
proud, stoic Scorpion.

"Oh, Adam." She moved her hand in his and
squeezed his thumb. "I've been such a wretch.
Seeing the ring reminded me. When you gave it
to me, you gave me the only real happiness I've
ever had . . . and all I've done is—"

He stopped her with his mouth.

And then in a little while he was getting up,
turning off the videotape, holding out his hand to
her in invitation; his eyes gleamed with tenderness, with the prospect of their long delight.

It was the most perfect night they'd ever had
together, and they enjoyed a late and lazy morning. For hours at a time Eve was able to put everything else out of her mind.

Only in the afternoon on Sunday, when Adam
had to go out again, and Marnie arrived to replace him, did Eve recall her resentment of the
night before.

Nevertheless she busied herself around the

230

house, finished the last of her postponed work, and made an elaborate dinner for Adam.

He was enormously pleased with the attention, but during the rest of the peaceful evening she caught him studying her when he thought she wasn't looking. She surmised that he was waiting for her to bring up the subject of the case again, bracing himself for an argument.

But she didn't. She was resolved to go on with her private research, and she didn't want to give him the slightest hint of her intentions.

Adam Kane would stop her if he could.

Suddenly in the middle of the night she was wide awake, feverishly impatient for the morning. She slid out of Adam's arms and stared into the dark, planning the first steps she'd take tomorrow.

Adam was fast asleep; she listened to his rhythmic breathing.

Slipping out of bed she padded barefoot into the living room, turned on a light in her work area, and slid her desk-cabinet open. The Duluth chart and her notes were in a separate cubbyhole. She took them out eagerly and began to go over them again.

"Eve?"

Adam's query startled her. She hid Lilah Duluth's chart with another.

"What are you doing, darling?" He blinked in the light.

"Just looking over a chart. I have a client scheduled in the morning," she lied. She noticed that she hadn't put away her notes; they lay there

231

revealed, covered with references to "A.M." If he saw them, he'd know what she was up to, for certain.

Adam came into the room and sat down on the couch. "When did that happen, Eve? You didn't expect to be free tomorrow . . . not until I told you about the team's dismissal. And if you expected to talk me out of it—which you did—why would you schedule a private client?"

His accusing tone incensed her. "Why are you interrogating me?" she countered. "I'm not one of your felons."

Her inflection jarred him; he winced. And he began to look angry too. "Because I think you're up to something. And I'm trying to keep you from risking your neck in some idiotic enterprise."

"Idiotic? Is that what you think of me?" That hurt; she struggled to hold back the quick tears that had sprung to her eyes.

"Darling, I'm sorry." He got up and walked toward her. Hastily she covered the notes on Angela Myers. His sharp eyes caught her action.

"What's the big secret?" He had a half-smile on his lips. She could hear the relentless Scorpio curiosity in his question, see it gleaming in his eyes.

"No secret. Just a client's chart. It's always confidential."

"Come on, Eve. You know I have no interest in some innocuous 'client's chart,' " he mocked her. "You're hiding something a hell of a lot more

232

important, and I want to know what it is. It's about the Astro case. And the poisoning."

She was chilled by his perceptiveness. It was almost impossible to fool a Scorpion. His need to know seemed cold now, impersonal. That chilled her too.

Right now I hardly know him, she decided, stricken. *I've fallen in love with a man and committed myself to him without even knowing him.*

That was exactly what had happened with Paul.

The confusion and alienation she felt must have shown on her face, because she could see him draw back, turn cool, right before her eyes.

"Sorry. I won't press you anymore. I'm going to bed. I've got to be out of here very early."

He turned around and walked back through the archway into the hall.

Eve sat at her desk a moment. All of her new ideas were scattered; she couldn't think clearly anymore tonight.

And she also couldn't face going back to bed, not with the new distance between them. Miserably she put the papers away and slid the cabinet doors closed.

She turned on another reading light and, without much enthusiasm, found something to read.

Turning the pages listlessly, she read until she sensed that Adam had had time to fall asleep. Then, overcome with drowsiness, she turned out the light and stretched out on the couch.

CHAPTER NINE

"Don't let the sun rise on your anger."

Eve could hear her mother's voice as plainly as if she were in the room. She opened her eyes to a flood of daylight in the living room, that ancient advice ringing in her ears.

It was too late now. A whole night had passed without making it up with Adam. Maybe he was still there. She heard someone running water in the kitchen.

Eve got up and crept to the bedroom. It was empty, and the bed was awkwardly spread over, the way a man's impatient hand would do it. The sight of the bed, somehow, struck Eve to the heart: it was the action of a guest in a house without servants, and it made Eve feel desolate. She couldn't wait to go to him, to say she was sorry.

She rushed to the dresser, ran a brush through her hair, and hastily put on some lipstick, spraying her neck and hands with cologne. Retying her robe she went to the kitchen.

Marnie was looking out of the kitchen window,

waiting for water to boil. "Hello." When she greeted Eve she looked embarrassed.

What a mess. Adam had left, and Marnie had taken over, while Eve was still asleep on the couch. She flushed. How could he have done that? Leaving her without a good-bye, exposing her to this.

"I'm really making myself at home," Marnie said. "The inspector said you were still asleep, and sent me in here to make myself some coffee."

Eve realized then that Marnie hadn't seen her asleep on the couch, and was warm with relief. From the front door and the archway the back of the couch must have hidden her. "I want you to make yourself at home," she insisted, smiling. "Why shouldn't you? At least we'll have a change of scene today." *I'm practically babbling,* Eve thought. She was still confused and distressed, because he hadn't wakened her, hadn't kissed her good-bye. It was the first time that had happened. But she couldn't let Marnie see her feelings. They were too painful. And any discussion of a quarrel with Adam might lead her to admit what a juvenile she'd been.

"Let me get some clothes on," she said quickly, "and I'll join you. I have about a hundred errands."

"Sure." The coffee was done and Marnie was pouring two cupfuls.

Eve got dressed quickly and went back to the kitchen. "Okay," she said with phony cheerfulness, "here's how today shapes up." She gave Marnie a rundown. All the while she was wondering desperately how she could check up on Mrs. Duluth's registration without being overheard.

In spite of her depression about Adam she felt like a kid out of school when they went out into the cold, sunny morning. There was still a lot of snow on the roofs and the stoops and sills of the venerable houses; her street had never looked so beautiful or so inviting. Eve felt a pang when she remembered Adam's admiring comments on the house, the neighborhood; his saying that home was where she was.

But she dismissed the memory, concentrating on all the things she had to take care of. She treated Marnie to lunch at a cozy Italian restaurant on Montague Street. And took advantage of a phone booth to call the association. Eve said she was calling for Lilah Duluth; she was afraid there'd been "some mixup" in the reservation. Eve learned that all was in order, that the records showed Mrs. Duluth's fee was paid.

Eve hung up, satisfied. There was every reason now to expect that the house in Sea Gate would be empty Wednesday. Marnie had mentioned once that Myers and her mother lived alone.

When they went back to the apartment, Eve realized she hadn't put up a single Christmas decoration; the house seemed naked. But she wasn't feeling too festive after last night.

To get her mind off Adam, Eve did some busywork, phoning clients to advise them that their charts were ready. Nobody seemed in a tearing hurry to get them. The whole damned world, Eve decided gloomily, was preoccupied with the holiday.

As soon as she'd completed her last call, the phone rang.

Eve snatched it up. Maybe it was Adam.

"Eve! It's so good to hear your voice. How are you feeling?" She recognized Iris's soft intonation.

"Splendid," Eve lied. "It's good to hear *you.* Are you home?"

"You know, then." Relief. Iris hated bringing bad news.

"Yes. I know. How are you, Iris? Have you been talking to Clare and Betty?"

"Only Clare. Bill and Betty have gone to Florida for two weeks. Oh, Eve, it was awful, not being allowed to visit. When can I come over? There's so much to talk about."

Eve hesitated. She wanted to avoid Iris until after . . . Wednesday. Iris saw too much, intuited too much. And if she found out what Eve was planning to do, she might think it her obligation to tell Adam.

"Of course you can. But I'm up to my ears right now, and—"

"I understand. After all, you just got home today, didn't you? You are all right, aren't you, Eve?" Iris sounded so concerned that Eve hated having to deceive her.

"Yes. Honestly, I'm fine."

"Well, look here," Iris said quickly, "maybe we'll see each other Wednesday. I'm going to the conference. Are you?"

Oh, good Lord, of course Iris was going. Now Eve would have another lie to invent. "I might," she said vaguely. "It all depends on how much I have to do."

"Okay. If I don't see you there, I'll call you."

When they'd hung up, Eve thought, *This is getting more and more complicated. It'll look strange to a lot of people if I miss the conference.*

Or would it?

There couldn't be a more tempting target for the Astro Killer than all those astrologers gathered under one roof. And nothing could be more natural than Eve Darcy's wanting to avoid it. Likely DeLuise, the "other D," would do the same.

But that hasn't been my MO, Eve argued. Adam's bound to suspect something if I suddenly turn rational. Low as her morale was, Eve had to smile at that idea.

The "other D."

How had they missed Lila Duluth? Of course she wasn't young and probably not beautiful either. And she might well not be a member of the association. Eve had checked out only the general listing of astrologers.

Perhaps Myers's own mother was on her list. Eve wondered if Adam knew. He must. In any case the conference would be a sea of plainclothes, if not of blue, considering its nature.

The kitchen area was very still. Curious, Eve wandered in and discovered Marnie Osborne addressing a pile of Christmas cards. "A little late in the season." Marnie saw her and smiled.

Eve wandered out again, back into the living room. She was so restless she didn't feel like settling down to anything. Adam usually called by this hour. Maybe he wouldn't today; maybe he was still simmering over last night.

But he could have made the first move. Except that Scorpios were too proud—prouder than she was. Right now her pride was the last thing Eve valued.

Adam dialed Eve's number: before it could ring he saw the suspect come down the subway stairs. Hanging up he dodged behind a column, then lost himself among the straphangers, keeping an eagle eye on his prey.

He waited until the subject got on the train, then jumped on at the last possible second. Adam had a dozen men who could have done it better, but he couldn't assign a followed-up hunch to others. This one he'd have to handle himself.

Adam was still fuming over his stupidity last night—letting the whole night pass without making it up. But he hadn't had the heart to wake her this morning; when he'd kissed her she hadn't stirred. Then he'd called her three times without getting an answer. It was frustrating as hell for the prey to surface just when he was making his fourth try.

Sheer anxiety over Eve had made him snap at her. He should never have grilled her like that, but she looked so caught out about the guy in Chicago, Adam had had a lousy suspicion—that she hadn't gotten over the other man. Afterward, when she'd covered up those papers so fast, he'd gone nuts with jealousy, blurted out the first thing that occurred to him, that thing about her playing cop.

Now he reconsidered: maybe she did have some cockamamy plan to snoop on her own. The idea made him sweat—detecting without the tools: training, experience, muscle . . . or a piece.

Riders shoved off and on. The prey sat down. Hell. A seated rider was tough to make. Adam got into a more strategic position, smelling the cold, not unpleasant rankness of the river when the train rocketed through the tunnel. The suspect was reading a book now; when Adam saw its title, the hair prickled on the back of his neck. *Astrologers, the New Witch Doctors.*

There was no movement at the first stop on the other side. But before the second Adam saw the suspect put the book away, preparing to leave.

He smiled grimly. The perpetrator hadn't made the tail; an experienced felon would have, would not have made the giveaway movement.

Adam glanced out the grimy window as the train pulled into the station: not so many people waiting to get on—probably staying out late to do Christmas shopping—so it would be easy to keep up if he went out the other door. He strode in that direction, turned back quickly to be sure the suspect was still in his sights. When the doors opened, he was on the platform at once, and following. He had a feeling where the trail would lead. And he was right.

Christmas shopping, just like Thursday night. What a drag that was, he thought wryly, with all the heat and mobs in the stores. Christmas *looking,* more like, with this one. Why the hell people even went in a store without the intention of buying was something Adam Kane had never comprehended.

But this banana did just that. He was closer now, letting another person get ahead of him once when the perp seemed to glance back. The *perp.* Not the suspect. Good thing he wasn't in court or talking this up at Number One. He was being presumptive as hell; but he'd never had such a strong gut feeling. The problem was, the only clincher might have to be an actual move, the caught-in-the-act routine.

And that move mustn't be on Eve.

He turned cold again, despite the horrific body-heat of the jostling store, hoping the perp would stick to street level. Fortunately that's the way it turned out. A purchase was actually being made, he noted ironically. While it was, Adam glimpsed a handbag, farther along, that he would have liked to buy for Eve, but he couldn't take the chance. He'd come back, maybe, and hope it would still be there. It was a nice-looking thing, the size and type he'd seen her use; and it was exactly the color of her wonderful eyes—that beautiful, serene gray, like a pigeon's feathers, or a gray cat's fur.

Adam snapped to attention. It looked like the perp was through for the night, heading toward the exit. He went back to his shadowing routine, dismissing everything else for the moment from his mind.

This time the ride went on uninterrupted; home base was the destination now, apparently. This tail would take more care; there weren't that many people getting off at this stop. Adam acted accordingly. Now his extra layer of clothes, for the long stakeout, felt great; they'd almost burned him alive in the mobbed department store.

He longed for the shelter of his car, but he couldn't have chanced any transport but the train. And he couldn't tip a partner, either, by having another cop drive here to meet him.

The worst thing was the absence of a phone booth that was in sight of the residence. He watched the front door close.

Tonight was an important night, the first of Eve's alleged release from the hospital. The guard on her house had been beefed up; so had the one on DeLuise's on Staten Island. With the new MO, the change of date, the department was taking no chances. And of course Wednesday there was that blasted conference in Brooklyn.

They'd have that staked out like a UN affair. Adam was going to have to bring the matter up with Eve, and he hated to, especially after what had happened. If he knew her, she'd be planning to go. Just as well. He'd be there to keep an eye on her.

Sheltering the flame of his lighter Adam lit a cigarette. From his vantage point he'd be able to smoke, which was a bonus.

He decided to radio Marnie to check in; he could use the radio to have a word with Eve too. That was still uppermost in his mind. He wasn't going to go another night at odds with her. Adam signaled Osborne, got her instant "Yes, Inspector."

"All quiet on the waterfront?"

"Absolutely."

Adam heard music. "Can I speak to Eve?"

"Oh . . . she's in the shower. Shall I . . . ?"

"Hell, no. You'll be bunking there tonight, I'm on a stakeout."

"Ten-four."

Damned bad luck and rotten timing, he thought. A no-show after last night. She might think . . . anything. But he had no option.

Adam glanced at the house. Couple of hours, he figured, before lights-out. Then it would get interesting. The perp might come out, head for Staten Island . . . or Brooklyn Heights.

Suspect, Kane, not perp. He was going to do a lot of talking to himself tonight. One of the stakeout tricks was to occupy the mind with an unrelated thing while the eyes and reflexes kept on working. He couldn't imagine a better preoccupation than Eve.

He thumbed back through mental snapshots, agonizing, *I've got to make it right.* He already wanted to marry her—a world speed-record for someone like him.

Adam heard footsteps, killed his cigarette.

A thin old man, walking a dog. If he saw somebody Adam's size it would scare him witless.

244

He'd call a cop, for sure, and Adam's whole stakeout would go bang, tip off the prey. Adam held his breath until the dog-walker was gone.

He signaled Osborne one more time. "Marnie? Eve available?"

"One minute."

Adam kept his thumb on Listen, hearing Eve's voice, then Marnie's telling her how to work the radio.

"Hello." Her greeting was as cool as the night air.

"Eve," he said in a rush, "I called you five times today. Can you hear me?" There was nothing but crackling silence and background music.

"Yes." She sounded warmer now.

"I wish to hell I was there," he blurted. "I just wanted to tell you how sorry I am . . . about last night. I love you, Eve."

Before she could answer he heard those footsteps; they sounded like that damned dog-walker.

Adam didn't have time to say another word. He had to cut her off in midsentence.

Damn it to hell.

When the old man had gone past, Adam debated with himself about trying Eve again. He'd better; otherwise she might think he'd been mugged. Adam repressed a chuckle.

Thinking that he'd never, in all his life, experienced so many foul-ups, one after the other, Adam signaled Marnie one more time.

When Eve answered, there was a pause—she was waiting for Osborne to walk away, he conjectured—and then she said, "I love you, too, Inspector."

There wasn't much more to say, but it was plenty. Quite enough to keep going on, through a long and lonely night.

"Is this trip really necessary?" Marnie Osborne grimaced at the crowd gathered in the vestibule of the department store, waiting for it to open.

"Afraid so." Eve held out her pack of cigarettes to Marnie, who shook her head and dug out her own.

"I'm not too thrilled with crowds at this stage of the game," Marnie emphasized.

"It beats the conference," Eve returned in a low voice, watching Marnie watch the other people.

"It does and it doesn't." Marnie was still observing. "The conference is solid blue—with lots of other goodies to tempt Mr. Astro away from you."

Mrs. Astro, Eve countered in silence. She was beginning to doubt her own sanity. A sane woman would have turned her suspicions over to Adam and let him carry the ball. But he already knew her too well: if he found out she suspected Myers, he'd know she wouldn't let it alone. There were just too many arguments against letting Adam in on it. First of all he might not even take it seriously. As much as he disliked Myers, he still might balk at casting her as a murderer. But the main reason was that Adam would keep Eve

246

Darcy so locked up she couldn't get to the grocery store, much less Gravesend.

Right now she champed at the bit; the wait was maddening. The conference started at nine; Myers was at her desk even earlier. Eve wanted to get going. But this was the only way she could possibly lose Osborne; a Christmas-shopping mob was perfect.

"Here we go," a man said. The doors were opening, and the avid crowd began to surge forward. Finding the side doors locked many disgruntled people were waiting to take their place for the revolving doors.

Eve's impatience was rising to the pitch of fever. It would be far better to get away while they were still on the street floor, if she could manage. But from the look of things most of the people were heading for the escalators and elevators: the whole wretched bunch seemed to be going upstairs. That would leave the main floor a bit too sparsely peopled for Eve's getaway.

"Thank heavens," Marnie breathed. "We'll have some air down here after all."

Poor Marnie. If she only knew it, Eve was about as claustrophobic as she was.

"Where to?" Marnie inquired.

"You said you needed another present, didn't you . . . a scarf? Why don't you get it? I'll be at the counter right next to scarves."

"No *way*. I'll wait for you," Marnie insisted.

Eve's heart sank to the soles of her boots. "Okay." This was going to be very awkward. She'd planned to finesse it and tell Marnie she hadn't found what she wanted; this was no day to be burdened with packages, not where she was going.

So she went through the charade of looking over about three dozen handbags, pretending to find something wrong with each one.

Giving up she waited while Marnie quickly chose a gift scarf, waited some more until she could get waited on. Eve glanced at her watch. It was already ten-fifteen and she was feeling desperate. If Mrs. Duluth decided not to stay for the afternoon part of the conference, she was sunk. She might have very little time at all.

"Finally," Marnie sighed when she got her change.

"You're going to hate me," Eve said with mock reluctance, "but I've got to go to Toys."

"Toys! Oh, dear. It'll be a madhouse."

"I know. But I totally forgot to get a present for . . . my cousin's little girl," Eve invented swiftly.

"A little girl," Marnie repeated thoughtfully. "How about something pretty to wear? But I guess children's clothes will be as bad as toys right now."

"Every bit. Look, Marnie, I hate to drag you through that. Can't you trust me out of your sight for a while? Give yourself a break." Eve knew it was futile as soon as she'd said it.

"A break is just what I'd get if I did that. A break in *rank.* You know better than that, Eve. Let's go."

Marnie was studying Eve out of the corner of

her eye. Eve decided she'd better let up or Marnie would know she was plotting.

She felt Marnie take her elbow, follow right on her heels into the elevator, to the imminent peril of a tiny old lady trying to get out. Marnie said, *"So* sorry," but Eve saw people glaring at her.

The elevator spewed them all out like a cattle herd on the "kiddies'" floor. Marnie's scarf had slipped up over her nose and Eve's instep was smarting from an accidental kick from an energetic little boy.

"Oh, my *goodness."* Marnie expelled a relieved breath and took hold of Eve's arm again.

They plunged into the shrieking chaos of toyland, elbowing their way through mobs of harried mothers, dodging toddlers and baby strollers. Eve saw a sign that indicated EXIT.

Her heart pounded. There was a terrific crowd near the sign; maybe this was the moment.

An exhausted-looking woman pushing twins on wheels was heading their way. Automatically Marnie stood aside to let them pass, and a sudden surge pushed Eve in another direction. Marnie's back was to her now. Eve rushed through the curtain under EXIT, unbolted the stair door, and started running down. She made it for two flights before she encountered a startled boy carrying boxes. "You can't use the stairs, ma'am! Only store employees . . . MA'AM!" He shouted but Eve was already on two. She burst through the basement entrance to the subway, thrust a token in the turnstile, racing down the stairs. A train was waiting. Collapsing onto a seat Eve closed her eyes.

She'd made it, actually made it; outwitted one of the sharpest cops in the NYPD. Involuntarily she giggled. She opened her eyes. An elderly couple were eying her. Probably thinking she was a loony. And they might be right.

The Astro Killer's playground was trains and buses. And here she was, solo. What Adam would say she could only imagine.

The ride went on forever. Eve checked the names of stops, repeating them in a silent litany. She'd memorized them from a transit map: three more, two more. The trainman called out, "Last stop! Last stop!" in a hollow voice.

If she slipped up, it might be *her* last stop.

She was on her feet before the train braked, standing at the door, shoving at it with her hand. Only three other people got off, two of them the elderly couple. Eve thought she stood out like a sore thumb, despite the somber clothes chosen to attract minimum attention—a steel-gray hooded coat, black accessories. People in neighborhoods like this seemed to sense strangers.

On the surface she breathed the fresh, salty air from the ocean and the bay. Suddenly it seemed like the ends of the earth, and she felt so alone. Why in the name of heaven hadn't she confided in Adam?

She found Mermaid Court, a brief street at the end of the next block, and scanned the houses for 1223. A little old man with a genial face was approaching; he had a wirehaired terrier on a leash. "Morning," he greeted Eve.

"Good morning." Eve stifled an impulse to pet the friendly-looking dog, who wriggled at her. It wouldn't do to get into conversation: the old man seemed ready to. Eve hoped he'd take the dog for a good long walk. She had to get in that house before he came back this way.

But the dog had other ideas; it stopped to sniff at everything. Eve walked on briskly like someone with authentic business.

Before 1223 her breath shortened, her heart began to flutter. She'd expected some kind of Charles Addams structure. All it was was a small, weatherbeaten gray house, two stories high, in need of paint. On the front door was a neat sign, LILAH DULUTH, ASTROLOGER. Eve debated her next move.

Adjacent to the house was a vacant lot, which was a break. There was a near neighbor on the other side, but no lights shone. On a dark day like this one, that must indicate nobody was there.

Eve let out her held breath.

Out of the corner of her eye she saw the old man with the dog, coming back. He was bound to question why she was loitering there.

Fool, she chided herself. *You're a prospective client.*

And she strode up the weedy walk to the house, climbed the wobbly stairs, and rang the bell.

"Oh, miss!"

Eve turned. The old man was standing in front of the house gesturing to her.

"Yes?" She kept her voice from shaking, with a valiant effort.

"Nobody home. Miz Duluth went out with some ladies in a car a while ago. And her daughter goes to business."

Pretending disappointment Eve called out, "Well, thank you for letting me know. Did she say when she'd be back?"

"Won't be back all day." The little old man seemed proud of his encyclopedic knowledge. "Gone to a convention downtown."

Eve smiled her thanks and stepped down to the walk again.

"Don't mention it." The old man started off again with his dog. He didn't look back. Eve waited on the sidewalk until he disappeared, with excruciating slowness, around the corner. She fervently hoped no one else was going to come along.

The sky was darkening rapidly, and the wind from the water strengthened, blowing her hood back from her head.

The water.

She shivered, recalling the dark aspects of her progressed horoscope for December, the aspects of Saturn to her Scorpionic Mars—danger in, or near, the water.

But she had to get moving before another curious neighbor happened along.

She looked in both directions, then walked around the gray house to the back door, hoping the locks weren't that strong. This didn't look like a neighborhood that went in for tight security.

There was a big metal nail-file in her coat pocket. She slipped it out and went to work on the back door, glancing uneasily at the neighboring house. It still looked blessedly empty.

After a few moments she heard a tiny click. Triumphant, she turned the knob. The door opened.

Hardly daring to breathe Eve stepped into a murky kitchen, grateful that her boots had rubber soles and heels. When she moved, there was hardly any noise.

She stopped to listen. Aside from the whirring of the old refrigerator, the hiss of steam from pipes, and the faint moaning of the wind, all was silence.

The house felt utterly empty. And yet there was *something*. Something from below the kitchen.

Mice, maybe. She shuddered. Or the house settling. Old houses like this did; she'd noticed that on Sidney Place.

Nevertheless some impulse made her move more quietly. Leaving the kitchen she padded down a short, dingy hall toward the front room. There was nothing there of any consequence, that she could see; no desk, no papers.

Only a faded living-room suite, stiff and uninviting, a worn flowered carpet, and some old photographs. Feeling a rush of pity for Angela Myers and Lilah Duluth, Eve noticed a big, ugly television set, the only sign of luxury in the room. She examined the photos. Apparently Myers at various stages of growth, and several of a man and woman. Mr. and Mrs. Duluth. The woman pictured with the man was a twin of Angela Myers—small and thin with pinched features. The only difference was in the eyes. The eyes of Lilah Duluth blazed with intelligence and fierce feeling, even in the old photograph.

And the man, who must be Myers's father, was a huge, dashing fellow with a wide smile and merry eyes, an unlikely man for such a wife and daughter.

The dining room was just as innocuous, bare of meaning. Eve felt the significant rooms would be above the stairs.

The minute she stepped on the first step it made a sudden noise, startling as a gunshot. Eve's heart hammered so it took her breath; she felt weakness wash like cold water down her body.

But she steadied herself on the banister and slowly climbed upward. Evidently that was the only stair that made the noise. She found herself in another murky hall, contemplating three closed doors. Angela and her mother were the kind of women who would close doors when they went out, instead of leaving them casually open. It was symbolic of Virgo repression, Scorpionic reticence. But they probably had to preserve heat as well. The house was chilly, and the atmosphere was one of penury.

Once again Eve felt unwilling pity.

She opened the first door. It had to be Angela

254

Myers's room, prim, neat, and white. Everything polished and spare. On the shiny bureau in a silver frame was the photo of an extraordinarily handsome man in his twenties. He had an aura of lazy charm, with classic features, full, sensual lips. A very Libran look. Peter Myers, without doubt. And Angela still kept this old picture. It was set at an angle that let her see it from her prim, postered bed. Poor woman. Eve went out and closed the door.

What she had to find was Lilah Duluth's office. The next room was obviously her bedroom, splashy with flowered fabrics, bolder than Angela's, lacking its compulsive order. The royal impatience of someone with Scorpio ascending. There were several more photos of the merry-eyed man of the living room.

The third door opened on the prize: this was by far the cheeriest room in the house, where Lilah Duluth received her clients. The furniture was pale and contemporary, red upholstered. There was a home computer like Eve's own, shelves of astrological books. Rows and rows of neatly docketed tapes. Excited, Eve searched for the name of Angela Duluth or Angela Myers, finding neither one. There was no chart in the file cabinets.

Then, on the bottom drawer of the farthest cabinet, Eve saw the label FAMILY. Just as she'd suspected—most astrologers kept them separate. She pulled open the drawer, unable to resist the temptation of looking at the chart for "Howard"; from the birth year, apparently Mr. Duluth. Leo with Aries rising. An explosive combination with Lilah Duluth's astrology. And hardly the kind of father who would be tolerant of Angela.

Relevant as that was, it was not so relevant as the horoscope of Angela Myers. Eve replaced her father's folder and took hers from the drawer. The folder was fat and heavy: it also contained a tape.

That was odd: generally tapes were made for clients so they could play them over after they'd left with their charts. An astrologer didn't usually make a tape for family, just a chart. Not when the relative lived right in the house, and one could repeat information to the person at any time.

Eve put the tape aside for the moment and eagerly scanned the chart: Angela Myers was a triple Virgo, with aspects that emphasized the negative side of her sign, self-centeredness, carping, fear of sex.

Angela's Mercury was in Leo in close conjunction with Saturn; both planets fell in her twelfth house of constriction and inhibition. Such a configuration gave a spinsterish character to the personality, mixed up emotions toward the father.

There was also a close, adverse relationship between her Moon and Pluto. The Moon symbolized the mother; Pluto, death. This aspect was one of tension, stress, and violence. Eve scanned the rest, then eagerly put the tape on Mrs. Duluth's machine.

Something about Angela's Mercury-Saturn

and Moon-Pluto aspects haunted Eve; they were in the chart of some notorious person.

Eve didn't have to wonder long. The astrologer was speaking.

"My daughter, Angela Duluth Myers, was born with many of the aspects of Lizzie Borden."

Eve shuddered. That's who it had been.

"I have made this tape," the voice went on, with an eerie resemblance to Angela Myers's, "so that if anything should happen to me . . ." The thin voice shook and paused. "If anything should happen to me, she will be brought to justice. I cannot be responsible for the arrest of my only daughter. But in all conscience I am an old woman and may soon die of natural causes. And I cannot leave this world in peace without the knowledge that Angela will be protected from herself and others, that others will be safe from her."

Eve's legs were so weak she involuntarily sank to the floor; her entire body felt like ice.

"For years I have known that my daughter was not like other children. When her father deserted us both, she began to exhibit a hatred for the whole world. Only when she met her former husband, Peter Myers, did she ever show love to any creature. I warned my daughter not to marry the man: he shared the same unfortunate characteristics of my former husband, Angela's father. But my daughter would not listen. And as I predicted, the marriage ended in disaster.

"After Peter ran away, I feared that Angela was going mad. She talked of nothing but revenge against that worthless creature and his concubine. And then she began to show symptoms of hatred for me, her own mother, and for my art which has sustained us both for so many years.

"I am sure that Angela was the one who killed the young astrologers. I even offered my professional services to the police, hoping that if I were there, I would be able to watch my daughter, to prevent her from going on with her horrible vendetta.

"For I feel that each time she killed another young woman, she was killing Peter's mistress. And me."

Eve drew in a startled breath. This was precisely what she had theorized.

"Peter and his concubine are now far away, safe from Angela's violence. So is her father. But I, who live in the same house, live in constant fear of what she will do. This is the reason I have recorded this message, to be kept with her horoscope, which is further evidence of the terrible deformity of my child. I am confident that my child will never find this record of my betrayal; her hatred of me has increased to the point that she will not set foot in my office.

"I ask whoever finds this record, after I am dead, to help my daughter. Help her. Much of the guilt is also mine. I brought her into this cruel world, and she was formed of my own disappointment and malice. The guilt is also mine."

The tape ended there. Eve got up, trembling.

I must take this, and go, she thought coldly.

Such evidence might be totally inadmissible, and yet—

She wheeled about, terrified.

She had heard the turn of a knob, and now she saw the gradual opening of the door.

Angela Myers stood there, smiling horribly.

A shining kitchen knife was in her hand.

CHAPTER TEN

"Angela." Eve's throat was so tight with fear that the name emerged from her in a husky whisper. "You . . . you can't be here, you're . . ."

Eve could hardly think, saying the first thing that came into her mind. Foolishly the second followed: *She knows the noisy stair. She stepped over it so I wouldn't hear her.*

"I'm at *work*. Oh, yes." The woman's eyes looked blind with madness, almost as if she couldn't see Eve at all. The horrifying smile stretched her lips as she spoke. "You couldn't think of me in any other context, could you?"

The clarity of the woman's question was grotesque. She sounded so calm, standing there in her ugly robe, her feet in wool socks that deformed them so they looked like hooves . . . that had made her entrance soundless over the splintery boards of the hall.

All these impressions flashed to Eve in seconds as she spoke desperately to herself: *Keep her talking. Keep her talking.*

"No, not you, you . . . great greedy courtesan." The mad gaze flicked disapprovingly over Eve's clinging wool dress, exposed by her flung-back coat. "Carlin's and Hansen's courtesan . . . my father's mistress." Angela Myers took another step toward Eve, aiming the shiny knife at her breast.

Eve moved toward the window: if she had to, she'd open it, jump out. It would be better to jump from the low second story than to have the knife plunge into her heart.

Then the meaning of the last words reached her panic-scrambled consciousness: *my* father's *mistress.*

Eve gathered all her courage, forced herself to speak. "Angela, I never knew your father."

"Never knew him!" Angela Myers began to laugh, and the laughter was infinitely more terrible than her smile. It was a cackle, high and uncontrolled. "Why, he visits your lair every night!"

Eve's comprehension was immediate: the photo in the living room. The big, dashing-looking man . . . was Adam Kane, in Myers's twisted mind.

"I think there's some mistake." She gasped. "Some mistake, Angela," she repeated more evenly. "You're talking about Inspector Kane."

"Don't argue with me!" Myers shrieked, lunging toward Eve, whose terror was so whole now, she couldn't make a sound. She stood there like a statue.

Myers cackled again, letting the point of the knife rest against the soft wool of Eve's dress; if she made a sudden move, it would pierce her heart. She knew it. She could feel the tiny point of steel, already puncturing the fabric.

"Sit down and shut up! Sit down, I say."

With the knife blade still touching her, Eve sank gingerly down on the broad windowsill, with sudden hope. The curtains were drawn back: a passerby might see the maddened woman, leaning over another with the knife. Eve's mind was racing. There had to be some way out of this. Cautiously she let her hand move toward the tape machine.

"Don't touch that!" Myers screamed. With her free hand she swept the tape machine to the floor. "Just be quiet. You're going to listen to me before I kill you. And you're going to listen well. No one ever listens to me." The shrill voice was eerily quiet now. "I'm going to have my satisfaction . . . the satisfaction that I couldn't have with the others." Myers had that blind look again, as if she were gazing into some mysterious distance.

Eve took instant advantage: kicking out at Myers's legs she grabbed for the knife. The woman rocked backward, but her grasp of the knife had the strength of the insane; she did not let it go. Before Eve could get up, Myers leapt forward again. This time the point of the knife was at Eve's throat.

She could feel the clammy sweat now on her face and body. If she moved again she was going to die.

"I told you to be still." Myers's voice was pitched so low now that it sounded like a young boy's; this new sign of her utter unpredictability,

263

her capacity for dizzying change, was even more frightening. Eve sat so still, she hardly breathed.

"That's better." The demented smile was back on Myers's pinched lips. "You're all evil, you see. All of you young concubines." The same obsolete word her mother had used—Eve was amazed at the lucidity of her thoughts in the midst of this horror. She wasn't done yet: she could still think, maybe plan. She had to.

"All the young concubines you brought to that office," Myers spat at her. "To entice the men, to make trouble. You and the others . . . and the Queen." The wild, pale eyes were staring now into Eve's own; a scent of staleness, like moth-balls, wafted to Eve from the muddy skin and dingy robe.

"The Queen, my mother. Driving my father away to you . . . driving Peter into the arms of that little . . . Oh, I know you *all*. You think you can run everybody's lives with your spurious magic. Evil witches!" The last word came out in a hiss; Myers was almost babbling now. Moisture gathered at the corners of her grimly smiling mouth.

She had not relaxed her threatening position: the knife had lightly pierced Eve's skin, and she felt a warm trickle of blood. Now she could barely hear what the madwoman was saying. All she could think was, *I'm going to die. I'm going to die through my own stupidity.*

Myers raved on and on, and Eve's mind screamed, *I must not faint, I must not faint. I must stay awake and listen.*

The incoherent monologue drifted in and out of her frozen consciousness.

". . . too smart for Her Majesty! What ever gave her the idea I'd let her come to headquarters, spy on me? I 'confessed' to Carlin . . . tyrant, worthless Libra just like Peter, with his horrible Libran appetites . . . oh, yes, I 'admitted' to that roué . . . exploiting me all those years, no appreciation at all . . . I said the Queen Bee was too old to be employed on the case. Though it pained me to admit it. Pained me!" Myers started laughing hysterically.

"I loved it! Loved doing her down, at last. *Fool.* She actually thought I wouldn't listen to that filth on her machine. I listened to it many times. I've just been waiting . . . waiting and planning.

"She was supposed to be the D, you see . . . you overblown harlot. But then you, and Betty Dobson Rivers, came along. And I decided what fun it would be to kill two D's with one dose of poison. And the other two, besides."

Eve's agony was almost too great to endure: the creature was regaining her earlier lucidity. She was too alert now, too aware, to fall for any trick.

"Those two. Acting so innocent and pure . . . flaunting themselves before the men. And one of them a *Virgo!* Virgos must be stainless. We are the Maidens!"

Eve breathed shallowly, feeling the faintest hope. She was beginning to rave again, shaking all over, expressing even more total illogic—a deep belief in the discipline she most hated.

"Neat. So neat. You must admit that," Myers said conversationally, another chilling, sudden switch from her rabid tone of an instant before.

With the intention of appeasing her Eve started to nod. But she checked the gesture just in time: to do so would send the blade deeper into her throat.

Involuntarily Myers drew back the threatening steel, the barest fraction of an inch, looking vindicated.

"Yes. Even you must agree."

For the first time Eve risked speaking. She could just manage to make a sound; she was about to burst into tears of relief. "I do, I *do*, Angela."

"So orderly," Myers mumbled, the absent glaze returning to her eyes. Eve's desperate hopes returned. She gave Myers the travesty of a smile, although she could feel her numb mouth quaking. "Order, order. That's what the world needs. I chose them very carefully . . . and then, in alphabetical order, in the order of their signs, I rewarded them."

Rewarded them. Eve's stomach was sick and cold; she had to fight against a tendency to retch. "Yes. Yes, I understand," she whispered. "And of course an Aries had to be first," she added in encouragement. Anything, anything, to keep her going.

"How did you know that?" Myers shrieked, causing Eve to jump in her shock.

"I . . . guessed."

Myers glared at her with deep suspicion. Then

266

she began to shake her narrow head, over and over; her corded hands closed tighter around the handle of the glittering knife. "No . . . you . . . didn't. My father let you in. You've . . . been . . . spying . . . on me."

She drew back the knife with such suddenness that Eve was unprepared; she was going to plunge it in.

"NO!" Eve screamed. Butting into the frail body from a seated position, Eve knocked the knife out of Myers's hand and pushed her to the floor.

Darting for the knife she felt one of the corded hands grip her ankle: the woman's strength was incredible. Eve weighed at least fifteen pounds more than Angela Myers, was taller, stronger. But now, in the throes of her madness, Myers seemed to have taken on the furious power of a man; the fingers felt like metal clamps around Eve's booted ankle.

Knowing that part of her own apparent weakness was born of horror, Eve summoned up all the muscular force at her command, kicking at the hand as hard as she could.

Laughing maniacally Myers let her go at that very instant: losing her balance Eve tumbled to the floor. Now they were grappling for the weapon.

Before she could reach it, Angela Myers had the knife again, was straddling Eve, raising the knife to strike.

In the distance she could hear a siren. *Oh, God,* she prayed, *let them be coming to me.*

And with renewed fury she thrust her hands up, trying to take the knife, but Myers slashed at her with it, narrowly missing Eve's exposed wrist.

However, the aggressive thrust was a mistake: Eve caught the hand that brandished the weapon and squeezed with all her might. Still in the grip of her frenzy Myers was incredibly resistant. She would not let go.

The siren sounded nearer: it was not a fire, not an ambulance. It was a police siren, and now it sounded as if the car was on this block.

Eve made another frantic effort to shake the knife from Myers's grasp, but it was just as futile as it had been before. The eyes almost started from Myers's head: she knew they were coming for her now, and this would be her last chance.

Myers was turning her hand in Eve's, with that unabated, nightmarish strength, aiming it at Eve's chest.

They were coming. Too late. In her wild terror Eve was vaguely aware of the siren's dying wail, the breaking of wood from below, the thunder of heavy footsteps up the stairs.

Now the knife had sliced the breast of Eve's dress, and was sinking.

The door was flung open and she heard someone bellow, "Drop it, Angela!"

Adam.

It was Adam. Eve got a fleeting look at his blazing eyes, his terrified, enraged expression.

"Drop it!" He held his gun in both hands, aiming it at Myers's head.

Eve knew he couldn't fire, not then, not from

that angle: if Myers fell on her, the knife could be driven in.

Time stood on edge: her own life wobbled on its narrow surface.

"Kill me, Father!"

Transfixed, Eve looked at Adam, saw confusion mix with his fear for her.

"Kill me!" Myers squealed. "I'll take her with me!"

Something flared in Eve's numbed brain, an exploding light: Myers thought Adam was her father.

Eve signaled him with her eyes, willing him to understand the act to take.

His eyes lit.

He'd gotten it.

Adam lowered his gun and said quietly, "Now, Angie. Angie, give Father the knife."

Myers stiffened. Eve saw a puzzled look come into the feral eyes; the blade was drawing back.

It happened in seconds. Seconds were enough.

With a tremendous thrust Eve pushed at Myers, was rolling over, away from her, striking the desk with a painful thud, but that no longer mattered, because Adam was grabbing Myers's flailing arms, shouting at someone, "Get the knife! Call that medic!"

Everything then was out of sequence, a wonderful, marvelous chaos, and that didn't matter either. She was safe, and now Adam was kneeling beside her, gently urging her to turn over, murmuring to her, examining the cut on her neck.

The horrible screaming of Angela Myers was

fading away. Another man was leading her out of the room, half dragging, half carrying her; Eve caught the glint of handcuffs on her hands.

For an instant, while she and Adam were alone in the room, he stroked her head, stooped over to kiss her face, still murmuring inchoate words.

And soon someone else was there, a paramedic, and Adam moved aside, stood over her, as the paramedic cleansed her shallow wound, dabbed it with something pungent that tingled in her nostrils, placed a bandage.

When the man had gone, Adam knelt down again beside her. "Stay there a minute, sweetheart."

She raised her hand and touched his face. It was slick with the sweat of the terror he had felt for her.

"Oh, Adam, I'm sorry." She sat up, feeling shaky.

"Sorry?" Still kneeling he grabbed her arms. "Aside from making me sweat blood"—he grinned, but she could feel the aftermath of his relief in his quivering tendons—"you gave us exactly what we needed. We caught her in the act."

Eve got to her feet, straightening her clothes. "You must be furious at me. It was a stupid thing to do."

He was standing now, too, towering over her, and he had never looked so big or so protective. "Sure, I was for about thirty seconds. Furious with fear. Oh, Eve." He grabbed her in his arms. "When I busted in here, and saw you like that

. . ." Adam shook his head. "How are you feeling. Rocky?"

She nodded against his chest.

"What do you say I take you home, then? And as soon as we book her, I'll come right back to you."

"No. I want to go with you." She couldn't bear the thought of being separated from him right now. He had put her life back into her hands; he was all the security and strength there was in the whole wide world.

He hugged her. "Sure?"

"Absolutely."

"Okay, then, gutsy lady. Let's get going." The careful way he held on to her arm belied his casual tone. Preceding him down the stairs Eve considered how different the house was now. Only a poor, dismal house, no longer a cave of echoing, threatening shadows.

Outside she saw Hansen, standing beside a squad car. Right now she was even glad to see Hansen.

"Go get in my car, honey," Adam said, and walked toward the squad car.

She got in, watching Adam confer with Hansen, glimpsing Angela Myers in the backseat of the car between two uniformed policemen. All Eve could see was the back of Myers's head, her thin neck; her face was lowered.

Adam got in the car, waiting until the squad car drove off before he turned on the ignition and followed. At the end of the street he paused to let another car turn.

There were three women in it. One of them was Lilah Duluth. She was staring after the departing squad car, then turning her tortured gaze on Adam's car.

Eve's indrawn breath was audible.

"What is it?" Adam asked her quickly, driving off.

"That was Angela Myers's mother." Then she remembered. "Oh, Adam, the *tape!*"

"What tape?"

She scrambled in her pockets. The tape was in the right one. "Thank heavens." She sighed. "I've got it." And she told him the whole thing.

"Whew! That really wraps it, Eve. I couldn't get in that place without a warrant. And I didn't have enough yet to get one. Or to spring it on *Carlin.*"

"So you suspected her too. Of course you did, or you wouldn't have been there . . . at that very blessed moment." The weakness of recalled relief washed over her again. She put her hand on his knee and he covered the hand with his own for a second.

"What a moment." His voice shook. Then he went on, more evenly. "Yes, I began to suspect her as soon as Hansen let it drop that her mother was an astrologer. And I started to add up all the other things—her abnormal hostility toward you and your team, her generally neurotic behavior over all the years I've known her. She always seemed to hate younger, prettier women.

"This 'father' thing was a doozy. Now that I look back, it seems to me she always treated me

272

with more . . . respect than the other guys. Crazy, when she's nearly twenty years older."

"Crazy to normal people. Not to an obsessive. What else did you have?"

"Not much," he confessed. "Conjecture mainly. I staked out that house, a lot of nights. . . ."

"That's where you radioed from." Smiling, she moved closer to him.

"Yes. And followed her home on the train. That night I called you, she was reading *Astrologers, the New Witch Doctors.*" A grim smile played on his lips.

"That's just what she called us—the team—'evil witches,' " Eve murmured.

Adam's mouth tightened into an angry line. "The damned . . ." he swore mildy. Then, seeming eager to get off that particular topic, he went on, "I checked her neighborhood. She used to stop at a certain store on the way home, every weeknight. On the murder nights she didn't. The clerks remembered because they literally set the clock by her, they said."

"Textbook Virgo."

"Tell me. I even checked out her birth date; that's what my book said too. You're getting me hooked." He smiled a little. "But I still had no hard evidence. Until this morning. A witness showed up . . . didn't want to get 'involved' before. Made her picture. Even that, though, wouldn't have been enough."

They were already driving over the Brooklyn Bridge and Eve's heart lifted, as always, when she

273

saw the magnificent downtown skyline of Manhattan. It was Baghdad on the Hudson for her again; the threat was gone, the shadow of death had lifted.

"I'm not too crazy about the way we had to catch her, though." Adam was somber, still brooding.

"Neither am I. But it's over, Adam. It's over."

"Thank God. But it is and it isn't," he said teasingly, when they were pulling into the plaza of Number One. "What beats me is how you got in."

When Eve told him, he began to chuckle. "So a police inspector's going to be married to a burglar." He stopped the car.

"What's that you said, Inspector?"

"A burglar. You heard me."

"It was that other little detail I meant," she said, pretending impatience.

"Married, you mean." He wasn't laughing anymore, or even smiling. He looked supremely serious. "I should ask you, not tell you. You must know that's what I want. Do you? *Will* you?"

"Yes, Inspector Kane. I will." She smiled at him, enjoying his look of utter happiness, and came into his arms.

"There's one other little item," she said when she had breath enough to speak again.

"Name it."

"You're not going to bust Marnie, are you? Slipping out of her fingers was all my doing. I'm a full-grown woman—maybe with impaired judgment, at times—but an adult nevertheless. And the whole thing today was my fault."

"You are so sweet, lady." Adam kissed her again. "I wouldn't do it for the world. I feel too good to chew anybody out. Now, let's go. They're waiting for me."

When they walked into Number One, it was different too. Eve remembered how frightening the plaza had been after dark, when the Astro Killer was at large.

"You know," she said consideringly, "I can't help it. But in spite of everything I can't help feeling sorry for Angela Myers."

Adam glanced down at her, unsmiling, a little impatient. "You have a point. Insanity is quite a plea. But I save my sympathy for the victims."

She nodded, thinking of the three dead women.

"Especially the near victim," he added fervently, putting his arm around her. "The one who nearly got it twice. You know, I have a small prenuptial request too."

"And that is?"

"Let me be the cop in the family. Please." His words were light; his tone wasn't.

"I'll make a deal with you. First tell me how you knew where I was."

"Marnie and I were coconspirators. We spied on you. You remember that night we had our spat, and I asked you what the big secret was?"

She nodded.

"Well . . ." he flushed. "I thought those papers might have something to do with your past —your romantic past."

"Oh, *no,*" she assured him.

"I know that now. Anyway, that night I got a flash of the initials 'A.M.' Like a jerk, at the time, I thought those were a man's initials. But when Marnie told me you'd disappeared, the initials had a whole new significance. And I had an idea where you might have gone. I sent Marnie back to your house to nose around. She radioed me in my car that you already had a dossier on Myers. If I'd been driving fast before, after that I flew." He tightened his arm around her. "I found out Myers had the day off."

"Sheer Scorpionic intuition. Lucky for me." He let her go and they got into the elevator.

"Maybe. But that's your department."

"Come here," she said softly. He bent his ear to her lips and she whispered, so the others in the elevator couldn't hear, "And being the cop is your department. You've got your promise, Inspector."

He took her hand when they got out and walked toward the room where Angela Myers was being booked for the Astro murders.

Five days later, on the twenty-third of December, the first day of the month of Capricorn, Eve felt as if the murders had never happened.

She and Adam walked into the judge's chambers, where the wedding party was already waiting.

Everything was beautiful—the dark, gleaming wood, the crimson carpet, the gray-green urns of holly and poinsettia. There was even a miniature

Christmas tree, gleaming with multicolored globes.

At last, she reflected, on the very day the killer had been meant to strike, they were able to celebrate the festive season; she was about to be given the most exciting gift of her whole life.

Iris and Clare had seen to all this; Betty had wired the flowers from Florida. Eve blessed their unerring taste.

Her friends were beautiful in bright and joyous colors of the season. By prearrangement Iris was wearing a dress of crimson velvet; Clare was in vibrant blue-green.

Eve herself had found a wonderful dress in vivid golden-orange whose high neckline seemed designed for Adam's Venus pendant, and which ignited to new richness the honey topaz in her engagement ring.

Iris's "delicious Virgo" was now her fiancé. He and Clare's husband-to-be were wearing suits of light gray and dark brown.

Eve looked up at Adam. He had never looked so splendid to her, or so totally happy. His suit of charcoal-gray could not minimize the striking massiveness and power of his body. She had been touched to notice earlier that he'd chosen a dark-green tie printed with miniscule Venus and Mars signs in red.

His only attendant was Deputy Commissioner John Carlin, who was looking more elegant than ever in flawlessly cut navy blue. His gray eyes twinkled at Eve as he walked toward her. He was to act in a double role, giving the bride away. Carlin's chic wife had chosen a soft gold dress.

Eve was breathless with joy during the brief and simple rite. In a flash it was over, and they were all kissing and exclaiming; the men were wringing Adam's hand, and Clare and Iris were throwing the rice.

Adam had been mysterious about the reception, asking Eve if she'd "leave that to him." He'd seemed so eager to do it that she'd gladly consented. Now she had no idea of where they were going, and it gave her a jubilant sense of adventure; something, she reminded herself, that was all to the good for a "stolid" Taurus.

When they emerged from the judge's chambers into the bright December sunlight, a pair of the longest limousines she'd ever seen were parked at the curb.

"Mrs. Kane," Adam said tenderly, opening the door of one. The rest of the party got into the other limousine, and then they were driving away.

Adam gathered Eve into his arms and kissed her soundly.

"You haven't asked me where we're going," he teased her softly.

"I *know* where I'm going. With you. And that's all I care about."

He stared into her eyes, and she could see how much that had moved him. She marveled that she'd once thought his eyes looked like chips of anthracite. They were glowing now, and full of love. And the mischief of surprise.

She noticed the limousine was heading uptown and east.

"We're going to revisit the scene of the crime."

She recognized the neighborhood. They were stopping outside Chantelle. The scene of their first date for dinner.

"Will this do?" he asked her.

"Oh, Adam. It's perfect."

"I thought so too," he said to her in a low voice, as they started in. "Now I know this is where I fell in love with you."

She had no time to answer, because the door was opening with a flourish: Adam's friend Dave was bowing them in. A pretty blond woman dressed in Christmas green was standing next to him.

"I'd like to present my wife, Carol," Dave said to Eve.

"And mine." Adam beamed at Carol and Dave.

When she walked farther in, Eve gasped. The whole restaurant was a glitter of tiny star-shaped lights; it was like being inside the Milky Way. She was speechless for a second, but she knew that was Adam's greatest reward.

Finally she said, "I've never seen anything like it. Never. Oh, Adam . . . was this your idea? It's heavenly."

"I can't take the credit. It was Carol's."

"You're marvelous. Aquarius-marvelous. It's got to be," Eve rushed on. "It has that fantastic touch."

"Hang on to this woman, Adam." Dave

279

punched him on the shoulder. "She's a genius. That's what she is," he said to Eve. "The Leo's dream."

Eve had been so dazzled by the multitude of stars she hadn't seen anything else yet. Now she saw all the people at the small tables, the wedding party at the big one. When she saw them, they all stood up, applauding.

"Come on, bride." Adam led her to the honor table, and they sat down. When her excitement had abated enough for her to notice still other things, she saw the immense cake in the middle of the table. A tiny pair of gold-colored handcuffs joined the bride and groom figures on top of the cake.

"Look!" she said to Adam. They both burst out laughing.

There was a huge pile of presents around the cake. The whirlwind arrangements had left people no time to send them in the regular way.

The waiters were serving champagne, and then Carlin stood to toast them.

"I'm sure this lady didn't know what she was getting into, when she consented to work for the NYPD." He shot a look at Adam, who laughed with the others.

"I not only gave a bride away this morning," he continued, "but an invaluable detective. I hope someday she may come back." He exchanged a twinkly glance with Eve and raised his glass. "To the bride and groom . . . the ones who broke the Astro case."

There was another wild round of applause.

Eve and Adam got up to mingle with the guests. When they got to Marnie Osborne's table, she kissed Eve warmly and shook hands shyly with Adam. Leaning, she whispered into Eve's ear: "I don't know what you told the inspector, but he not only didn't bust me; he's talking about *upgrading* me!"

Eve giggled, thinking how wonderful Marnie looked in her bright blue dress. Out of the corner of her mouth Marnie said, "You've got to meet my Sagittarius. Isn't he gorgeous?"

Marnie introduced them. Eve liked his looks, genial and intelligent. "Throw your flowers my way, would you?"

Eve promised she would do just that, and they made their way back to their table.

When lunch was served, she noticed that each of the honor guest's desserts was garnished with the glyph of his sign—Adam's big letter *M* with the forked tail, her own circle surmounted by an arc.

"I detect a fine Piscean hand in this," Eve said affectionately to Iris.

"A finger, maybe." Iris moved over into the chair Carlin had temporarily vacated. "Oh, Eve, I'm so happy for you. I am too." She glanced at the big blond man talking to Clare's fiancé. "If it weren't for you, I'd never have met him."

Eve squeezed her small hand. "I'm glad. So glad." She had a feeling of unreality now about the whole case. So much had happened, so quickly, that her head was still spinning. It would be heavenly to be alone, and quiet, with Adam.

She turned and looked at him; she could read the same wish in his eyes.

Eve Kane lolled on giant pillows in front of the dying fire in the mountain cabin. Adam would be back soon with more wood . . . to bring more than one fire to life.

She stretched in lazy, deep content. Now they had their quiet and aloneness in full measure—the nicest aloneness of all, which was for two.

The last twenty-four hours had passed like a dream, and she still hadn't wakened. After their festivity of stars, they had made a swift and laughing getaway; but not before Eve had tossed her small bouquet of sunset roses into the hands of Marnie Osborne.

Eve moved in a mist of happiness, over city streets that had turned resilient as grassy earth below her feet, delivered to the spacious privacy of a compartment on the train to Montreal; they had agreed, the only way to travel. Adam quipped, "I want my hands on you, not on a steering wheel." And a plane would represent the haste and bustle they wanted to leave behind.

Spellbound in each other's arms they watched the snowy landscapes from their window; Adam buried his face in her hair, murmuring, "No beepers, no badges, no phones. Just Eve. . . ."

When they got to the Laurentians, he said, they would be even more blessedly alone. "Sure you want to stay in a cabin? It's not too late to change it to Montreal."

"I'm a farm girl, remember? From an endless prairie. It sounds just like my cup of tea."

In front of the fire now, Eve smiled to recall his uncertainty, his protests that a lady on her honeymoon should be "waited on."

But she'd quickly reassured him. "I don't want to *see* anyone but you."

And the last time they'd seen other creatures, apart from some curious and lovely deer, was when they'd stopped at the hostelry with its corduroy chesterfields, pine tables, and huge cozy fireplace.

Eve heard Adam stamp his feet on the porch of the cabin, ridding his boots of snow.

Cabin, she decided, was not the word for this chalet. They had everything. She'd brought along some Christmas tapes: golden waves of Handel's *Messiah* filled the room.

Eve watched him come in. For a city man he looked amazingly at home in the rough clothes, the heavy jacket. His skin was ruddy from the bracing cold, his eyes glittered. He took the axe from over his shoulder and leaned it against the wall by the door.

"Hello." She gave a languorous chuckle. "I think if we'd had enough wood, you'd have been devastated."

"I would." He grinned. Taking off his jacket and sweater he threw himself down beside her.

"Your lips are cold," she said.

"Warm them up," he murmured against her lips. She did. "Ummm." He opened his eyes.

"That's a sexy outfit, Mrs. Kane. Convenient too." He fiddled with the zipper. "My, my."

The firelight gleamed on her bare, vibrant skin, and then he was gently pulling the garment from her body. "You make me feel overdressed," he teased her.

"That will never do," she murmured, busy with his clothes. "There's only one way to be truly democratic."

Suddenly their laughing mood was gone; with a moan of excitement Adam was caressing her skin with his mouth, igniting her thrilled flesh, bringing her to a whole new abandon. She shuddered and cried out: her skin thrummed like the plucked strings of a metal instrument, resounding, resounding.

Through half-open lids she watched Adam rise and then descend to her, blot out the world with his dark, glowing eyes. And when their bodies were entwined, and he was closer than her very heart, she felt a greater joy, a fullness of the senses surmounting ecstasy, for this time they reached their happiness together; their bodies' meeting was a vow. They heard the glorious ascension of the mighty music.

Holding each other, with slackening breath, they gazed into one another's eyes by the orange glow of the sinking fire.

"Time to build it," Adam murmured drowsily.

She ran her hand over his sandy hair and down the austere planes of his beloved face. The tension and the grimness were gone; the skin was smooth, revitalized. And there was a depth in his eyes she had never seen before.

"Not yet, not yet." Her protest was a gentle whisper. "We'll keep each other warm, for a little while."

"An excellent suggestion." He pulled her body nearer, until all their skin was one long kiss.

Their desire was renewing, and this encounter was so excellent and sweet that her heart could barely contain its fullness.

In a moment Adam stirred, dressed himself, and went out to bring back some wood. Eve lay under the blanket she'd pulled from the couch and watched him build the fire.

Through half-shut eyes she marveled at his male beauty, the lines of his powerful legs as he knelt there on one knee, the play of his muscles under the soft flannel shirt.

"The phoenix." She realized she'd murmured it aloud.

His task over, Adam turned to her, smiling.

"The phoenix of the Scorpion." He sat down and gathered her in his arms again.

"Come here, papoose." He kissed the top of her head.

She laughed good-naturedly. Neither a Scorpio nor a Taurus could be high falutin for long, she decided.

"I was thinking," he began softly, "while I was out there playing Paul Bunyan"—one of the things she loved about him most was his self-mockery—"about what Carlin said. At our lunch among the stars."

Eve leaned back and looked up at his face. He could also surprise her, now and then, with this vein of unexpected poetry in him. She waited.

"He said he'd 'given away an invaluable detective.' You know, my darling, it was really you who cracked the case."

Now she *was* surprised. They'd tacitly agreed not to mention it again until they got back to New York.

"And I was thinking about your promise to let me be the cop. It isn't fair. We may be depriving the NYPD of some terrific counsel."

"Adam Kane, I don't believe I'm hearing this." She goggled at him, playing up her shock.

"You are, Mrs. Kane. I think you should be put on a retainer."

"Oh, Adam." She hugged him to her.

"Come on," he said briskly. "Get yourself dressed. It's Christmas Eve. And I want to see how you like your Christmas." He tugged at her hands, and the blanket fell away from her body. "Hurry up," he teased her. "You're distracting me."

She got into her velour jumpsuit and zipped it up. Standing they held each other. "I've had my Christmas, Inspector." She touched her wedding ring and his, their wedding presents to each other. Hers was ingeniously designed to follow the line of the horizontal rectangle of her topaz-and-emerald ring; she was always touching them, like a talisman. "In fact I've had it since the last of November," she declared, "when you first growled at me in Carlin's office."

286

"So have I. But here's another." He went to the small Christmas tree, with its red and gold, its blue and green and silver, globes, and picked up a square package from the pile of gifts already there.

Eve sat down and opened the package, removing two gold bangle bracelets with a chased design; they were attached to each other by a frail gold chain. "Handcuffs, Inspector. How could you?"

"No way." He slipped both the bracelets on her arm and clasped them.

"They're beautiful." She savored their antique gleam by the light of the fire.

Later, after they had toasted each other, and opened the rest of the presents, they relaxed again on the couch before the high and steady blaze.

They could see the bright, random stars from the window, glittering against the blackness of the night.

"Funny," Adam said in a meditative voice, "that people think of fate as 'doom,' when fate can be so happy."

The firelight glanced off his penetrating, night-black eyes when he turned his head to look at Eve.

"You taught me so much," he added softly. "Made me see that this was meant, decreed by some ancient order."

"I know." She caressed his face with her hand, as he kissed it. When those poor women died, she thought, their signs had been their doom. But all that was over and done with.

In the midst of death she and Adam had always been in life. From this day forward that was the way it would always be. And she would be silent now except to speak of joyous things.

"I know," she repeated, in her fullness of heart. "Our first sight of each other, Adam Kane, was like a sign from fate."

For all the rest of her days he would be the phoenix arising from its ashes.